Edwyn Gray

Devil Flotilla

Futura Publications Limited
A Futura Book

A Futura Book

First published in Great Britain by
Futura Publications Limited in 1979

ISBN 0 7088 1466 2

Printed in Great Britain by
Hazell Watson & Viney Ltd
Aylesbury, Bucks

Futura Publications Limited
110 Warner Road
Camberwell, London SE5

'You ask, what is our aim? I can answer that in one word: it is victory. Victory at all costs. Victory in spite of terror, however long and hard the road may be . . .'

Winston Churchill
House of Commons.
13th May 1940

CHAPTER ONE

1100 hours. 9th May 1940

Neidermeyer swore under his breath as the telephone jangled. Putting down his copy of the *Berliner Zeitung* he reached out to pick up the receiver and wondered whether it would be Ingrid or Ella on the other end of the line.

'*Oberleutnant* Neidermeyer speaking.'

The hoarse rasp in his ear was anything but feminine and Neidermeyer's expectant smile vanished abruptly as he recognized Koppenberg's voice. As *Kriegsmarine* liaison officer with *Fliegerkorps 7*, Neidermeyer spent most of his working day dealing with petty complaints between the two services. Co-operation, it seemed, was an unknown word in the *Luftwaffe* vocabulary and not once since he had taken up his duties at Elsbjorg on the second day of Exercise Weser[1] had he been given a single item of operational information which the Navy could use.

'*Fliegerkorps 7* here. One of our air patrol units reports an unidentified submarine in position 58° 30′ North, 10° 02′ East. If it's one of your damned U-boats you might remind its skipper to show the correct recognition signals.'

Neidermeyer ignored the jibe. 'I'll have to check with *BdU*,' he said stiffly. 'I'll call you back as quickly as possible.'

'Well get off your fat arse and do it. We've got two Dorniers circling the spot and if that sub shows itself again they'll sink it.'

'Why pick on a U-boat?' the *Oberleutnant* enquired sarcastically. 'Or is the *Luftwaffe* scared of British submarines because they fire back?' He slammed the receiver down quickly to cut off the inevitable retort, checked his list for

[1] The code name for the German invasion of Denmark and Norway which began on 9th April 1940.

the appropriate code number, and dialled the special direct line to the Operations Room at U-boat Headquarters.

'Unidentified submarine reported in Square 762,' he told the Duty Officer briefly. 'Do we have any boats in the vicinity?'

There was a short pause while Kruger checked the wall plot. 'None of our boys in that area,' he confirmed back to Neidermeyer. 'Nearest is *U-95* returning to Oslo – and he's at least one hundred miles to the north-east. Hang on a minute . . .'

There was another pause and Neidermeyer could hear the murmur of voices in the background. Then the phone was passed from the Duty Officer to someone else and Neidermeyer automatically stiffened as he recognized Rear Admiral Doenitz's clipped tones.

'Are you sure it's a submarine, *Oberleutnant*?'

'According to *Fliegerkorps 7* it is, sir. But ship recognition was never one of the *Luftwaffe*'s strong points.'

Doenitz knew what Neidermeyer meant. The German Air Force, while demanding complete control of all sea patrols and naval co-operation units, had done virtually nothing to help the *Kriegsmarine*. And it was a well known fact that Goering considered the *Luftwaffe* quite capable of obtaining command of the sea without assistance from the tin-pot Navy. Even the pilots of the catapult aircraft carried by Germany's pocket battleships and cruisers were *Luftwaffe* men and, despite the efforts of individual fliers to co-operate with their opposite numbers in the Navy, they received no support or encouragement from the *Reichsmarshal* or the Air Staff.

'Listen, Neidermeyer. This might be important.' Doenitz gave no indication why he thought so but the *Oberleutnant* accepted the statement without question. 'The information will be passed to OKM and OKW immediately, but, in the meantime, I want you to wangle a trip in one of the patrol aircraft to confirm the situation.'

Neidermeyer wondered what the hell the flap was all about. The Norwegian campaign was virtually completed and the whole of central and southern Norway was in Nazi hands. Only in the north, around Narvik, was there any fighting worthy of the name and from what he had heard recently even that was likely to be over soon. With no urgent military operations on hand it seemed foolish to make an issue about a lone British submarine. A flotilla of destroyers from Kiel would only take half a day to reach the area and if the enemy boat was still there they would soon make short work of it.

'I'll do my best, *Herr Admiral*,' Neidermeyer assured his Commander-in-Chief, 'But I can't see Putzig co-operating. He hates the Navy's guts.'

'Perhaps he does, *Oberleutnant*,' Doenitz said drily. 'Just tell him you are acting on my orders. And remind him that today is the 9th of May.'

Neidermeyer shrugged. The date meant nothing to him – except that Ella was now exactly a fortnight overdue and was beginning to get worried. A baby with a German father would not be a very welcome addition to any Danish family in the present situation and he had been checking his mail every morning for the pills his brother had promised to send him from Essen. There were times when it was useful to have a chemist in the family. Pushing Ella's problems from his mind he concentrated on more immediate matters.

'I will do what I can, *Herr Admiral*. *Leutnant* Heller will have to take over my liaison duties. I'll ring Putzig right away.'

The *Oberleutnant* put down the phone, glanced at Ella's photograph hanging on the wall, and swore at the silly bitch for not being more careful. He looked at the other picture. Ingrid's mouth smiled back at him from the frame and he decided to give her a call as soon as he got back. A sensible girl, Ingrid. She already had a husband tucked away somewhere so if anything went wrong her old man would think it was his. He made a mental note to stick to married women in future as he began dialling another number.

'*Oberleutnant* Neidermeyer speaking. Put me through to the Duty Officer.'

The piercing howl of a badly handled connection nearly deafened his right ear and he had little doubt that the *Luftwaffe* operator had done it deliberately. He waited impatiently as the Duty Officer took his time to answer.

'Koppenberg here.'

'Any further reports on that submarine? *BdU* says it's not one of our boats.'

There was a long pause at the other end of the line and Neidermeyer sensed an embarrassment in the silence that followed his question.

'Sorry – no further information.'

'Come off it, Hans. You mean you've lost track of it?' There was no answer and Neidermeyer knew his guess was right. 'Good God! Can't you silly bastards do anything right?'

'We've done a damned sight more than the Navy,' Koppenberg stung back. 'It wasn't the *Luftwaffe* that lost a flotilla of destroyers at Narvik. And we've sunk more enemy ships than the Navy. *And* covered the *Wermacht* land operations into the bargain!'

Neidermeyer decided they were getting nowhere. Arguments in the mess or over a drink at the bar did no harm to anyone. Interservice rivalries could be a good thing. But not when they were on duty. He ignored the challenge.

'Okay, Hans,' he said soothingly. 'I'll agree your lot have done better than the *Kriegsmarine* in this campaign. But this is serious. There seems to be something funny about that submarine. Doenitz says he's reporting the sighting direct to OKW. And that means it's *hot*. He wants me to be flown out over the area.'

'Not a chance, old boy. Most of our squadrons have been moved south into Holstein. Sorry I forgot to tell you about it, but it was a top secret operation and I assumed you'd been informed by your own people. We've got a couple of Dornier flying-boats patrolling the Skagerrak and that's about all.'

'What the hell's going on?'

'Search me,' Koppenberg shrugged. 'We're supposed to be in the front line so we'll naturally be the last to find out.'

Neidermeyer paused reflectively. Flipping open the notebook lying on top of his desk he glanced down at the daily log. An entry in *Leutnant* Heller's neat handwriting dated the previous evening triggered his memory.

'Panic over,' he told the *Luftwaffe* officer. 'I think I know what it's all about. There's a troop convoy moving down from Oslo to Kiel – left at midnight last night. I heard it's bringing the 19th Panzer Division back for training and regrouping. I suppose we don't need any armoured units in Norway now. They say it will all be over in a day or so.'

'No wonder they don't want an English submarine prowling around,' Koppenberg whistled. 'I suppose they'll turn the convoy back until we've cleared the area. A couple of day's delay won't matter much.'

Neidermeyer remembered the urgency in Doenitz's voice. He doubted if Koppenberg was right. 'The C-in-C was most insistent that I fly over the area. Can you put me through to Putzig? It's worth a try.'

'Okay. But it won't do you much good. You might just catch him. He's leaving with his HQ staff for Glückstadt after lunch. Hang on . . .' A series of clicks, a sharp whistle and a loud howl indicated that Koppenberg was putting him through and Neidermeyer waited.

'*Fliegerkorps 7* HQ. Major Zimmermann. Who is this please?'

Neidermeyer told him who was calling and asked to speak to Putzig. The Major's cold clipped tones offered little comfort.

'Quite impossible, *Herr Oberleutnant*. The *Herr General* is engaged. You should make your request through the usual channels – you know the regulations.'

Neidermeyer was tempted to tell him to stuff the regulations but he curbed his temper. There was something going on and somehow that enemy submarine was involved. 'I am acting on the direct orders of Rear-Admiral Doenitz,' he said stiffly. 'Will you please remind the *Herr General* that today is the 9th of May – he will understand.'

The *Oberleutnant* sounded confident and Zimmermann obeyed reluctantly. He was as ignorant about the importance of the 9th of May as Neidermeyer but, knocking on the door of Putzig's office, he went inside and delivered the message. There was little doubt that the General knew the significance of the date. He looked up sharply and reaching across the desk picked up the extension.

'Putzig here. What is this all about, *Oberleutnant?*'

'There's been a report of a submarine in the Skagerrak, *Herr General. BdU* asked that I be given an aircraft to report the situation for OKW.'

'Of course, of course. I will put it in hand at once. Find yourself a car and get across to the Luftwaffe base immediately. I will see that a plane is waiting for you.'

Neidermeyer put down the phone and frowned at the calendar on the wall opposite his desk. What the hell was so bloody important about tomorrow's date?

*

The conference had only been in progress a mere ten minutes but the protagonists had already taken up their traditionally hostile positions.

'I cannot allow you to over-ride my responsibility for naval matters, *Herr Feldmarschall*. Until that submarine is located and destroyed the convoy cannot be permitted to proceed. It has only two surface escorts and,' Raedar glanced significantly at von Erich, the *Luftwaffe* representative, 'no air cover whatsoever.'

'I would scarcely have thought a single enemy submarine beyond the capability of the entire Navy,' von Erich said sarcastically. 'But apparently I am wrong. The *Luftwaffe* would gladly dispose of this irritating little thorn but, unfortunately, all available aircraft have been concentrated for Operation Case Yellow.'

Keitel, head of OKW[1] rapped the table for silence with the urgency of an impatient medium at a seance. He was

[1] *Oberkommando der Wermacht*, the High Command of the Armed Forces.

sickened by the continual bickering between the Navy and the *Luftwaffe* and he resented the priorities Goering's influence had obtained for the Air Force.

'Childish arguments will get us nowhere, gentlemen,' he reprimanded the two men. 'May I remind you that *Case Yellow* commences at midnight. Army Group B will be spearheading the attack on Holland and the Panzer Division being transported in that convoy represents half of von Bock's armoured strength.'

'And remember also, gentlemen, we have only ten Panzer divisions committed to this operation,' Halder, the Chief of Staff, intervened. 'Two each with the 4th and 6th Armies, five with the 12th and one with the 18th. If the convoy fails to arrive on time it will reduce our total armoured strength by 10%.'

'Better, surely, for it to arrive a few days late than to leave it rusting on the bottom of the Skagerrak,' Raedar observed drily. He returned to his favourite hobby-horse. 'Because our scientific research programme has concentrated on the needs of the *Luftwaffe* the Navy has to fight submarines blindfolded. The British have perfected their Asdic. *We* have to manage with hydrophones that date back to the last war. I am quite willing to send my remaining destroyers to hunt the enemy but I must have air co-operation to find him.'

'Well, von Erich?' Keitel queried. 'Can you spare some aircraft to assist the Navy?'

'Absolutely impossible, *Herr Feldmarschall*. All machines are allocated to Case Yellow. The Heinkel and Dornier units will be bombing Rotterdam and other major Dutch towns and the transports are needed for parachute landings behind enemy lines. The Stukas, of course, will be giving tactical support to the army in the field and all available fighter squadrons will be required to provide air cover.'

'In that case,' Raedar said firmly, 'I shall order the convoy to return to Oslo until we have cleared the area.'

'And without that Panzer Division, Admiral, von Bock's Army Group will be minus half of its armour,' Halder reminded him. 'If it takes him four days instead of two to overrun the Dutch defences the entire offensive plan will be put in jeopardy. *Blitzkrieg* – the lightning strike – that is what it is all about, Admiral. Time and weight of armour at the enemy's weakest points are of the essence.'

Keitel sighed wearily. After months of planning, and with just twelve hours to elapse before the launch of the great assault, it seemed incredible that a single British submarine could upset the entire scheme. And yet – and he respected Raedar's judgement in such matters – that was the position. Why the devil did von Erich have to be so obstinate? There was only one way out of the impasse, he decided reluctantly.

'Very well, gentlemen,' he said slowly. 'You leave me with no alternative. I will convey your views to our *Führer*. It will be for him to decide.'

Keitel rose from his chair, bowed stiffly, and went out to the communications room where he had a direct telephone link to Hitler's headquarters. He was not looking forward to making the call. But duty demanded and it had to be done.

Keitel looked visibly shaken when he returned to the conference room. His normally grey face was flushed and his hands were trembling. The *Führer* had flown into one of his infamous rages and, even on the telephone, the torrent of verbal abuse was unnerving. The *Feldmarschall* sat down at the head of the table and waited to regain his composure. He turned to Raedar.

'The *Führer* forbids the convoy to be sent back. He says it is the responsibility of the Navy to get the transports to their destination in accordance with the timetable already set out in Case Yellow. He will listen to no excuses.' Keitel moved on to address von Erich. 'The *Führer* directs the *Luftwaffe* to lay on an air search of the Skagerrak. Patrols are to be maintained until the submarine has been located and destroyed. The success of Case Yellow depends entirely on the safe arrival of the 19th Panzer Division. The convoy must get through – *at all costs*!'

14

Neidermeyer clung to the struts of the cockpit canopy as Hochmann swung the big Dornier flying-boat into a tight banking turn towards the east. Far below, on the sparkling mirrored surface of the sea, a pair of destroyers were steaming hard for the centre of the Skagerrak. Just visible on the starboard horizon, two Heinkel 110 bombers droned monotonously towards the hunting area.

The *Oberleutnant* hated flying. And Hochmann, aware of his passenger's feelings, took a fiendish delight in throwing the aircraft about in the sky. The idea of acting as an unpaid chauffeur to the *Kriegsmarine* did not please him. And the fact that he had been withdrawn from a strike squadron of medium bombers which, in less than eight hours, would be pounding the defenceless city of Rotterdam to destruction only served to irritate him even further.

'Seen anything yet?' he taunted.

'No – and we're not likely to, either. British submarines are fitted with sky-search periscopes. If the enemy commander knows we're about he'll take care to remain well out of sight.'

Hochmann throttled back the tandem Junkers Jumo engines and leaned across to reach for his thermos. Holding the control column between his knees he carefully unscrewed the vacuum top.

'If that's the case,' he grumbled, 'why the hell are we flying air patrols? Can't the Navy do its own dirty work?'

'I don't want to be up here any more than you do,' Neidermeyer pointed out. The smell of the coffee in Hochmann's flask made him feel slightly sick. 'We're both here because the *Führer* ordered us to be here.' He shook his head and swallowed hard as the pilot offered him a mug of thick brown liquid.

'You haven't answered my other question,' Hochmann reminded him.

'The answer's simple enough. Our only means of locating a submerged submarine is by sound ranging – hydrophones. If the enemy knows there are surface ships around he only needs to lie on the bottom with his engines stopped and there'll be no sound for the detectors to pick up.'

'I still don't see the point of air patrols.'

'A submarine can only remain submerged for a limited period,' Neidermeyer explained patiently. 'Sooner or later it must come up for air, or a quick periscope observation. It's a waiting game. The surface hunters can also stop their engines. And then the enemy skipper doesn't know whether they're there or not unless he comes up to find out. The chances of spotting a periscope from the air are probably a hundred times better than from the bridge of a fast-moving destroyer. And *that's* why we're here.'

Hochmann swallowed his coffee and digested Neidermeyer's explanation with growing gloom. He glanced at his watch. Only seven more hours and Case Yellow would be put into operation. And here he was fooling about over an empty sea looking for a submarine which, in all probability, did not exist. Hardly a way to win honour and glory.

Neidermeyer ignored his companion and concentrated on the map. The convoy was only fifty miles to the north and there were now less than four hours of daylight left. If they could keep the enemy submerged until dusk there was a good chance the convoy would get through. Having marked their present position on the chart he glanced out of the cockpit window again. The destroyers had already disappeared over the north-west horizon and the two Heinkels were no longer visible. Alone and unsupported, everything now depended on the skill of Hochmann's team.

'Supposing it's a false alarm after all?' he asked, voicing the doubts he was beginning to accumulate.

'Then you've had a wasted journey and I've missed the biggest show since we bombed Warsaw,' Hochmann said unhelpfully. He glanced down at the instrument panel. 'We've only two hours' fuel left in the tanks. If nothing turns up by seven I'll have to head back for base. You and your bloody submarine,' he added with a sardonic snort.

Neidermeyer nettled. 'Don't forget, it was your people who said they'd seen it. If I hadn't passed the *Luftwaffe* report to Doenitz none of this would have happened.' He paused as he spotted something and, picking up his binoculars, he focused on the horizon. 'We've caught up with those two destroyers – about eight miles ahead and slightly to starboard. Looks as though they've stopped engines. I wonder if they've picked something up on their hydrophones?'

Hochmann slipped the thermos flask back into his pocket and grasped the control column with both hands. The Do-18 tilted on to its right wing tip as it swung towards the destroyers.

'Want to take a closer look?' he asked.

Neidermeyer was busy scanning the sea directly beneath the flying-boat. His eyes were aching and he was beginning to feel ravenously hungry. He had already decided they were engaged on a wild goose chase. The *Luftwaffe* patrol had probably spotted a couple of playful dolphins frisking on the surface and jumped to the wrong conclusion. Yet for some unaccountable reason he felt his eyes being drawn magnetically towards the patch of sunlit sea two miles to the east. It was a strange sensation and he tried to turn his eyes away. But something forced him to concentrate on that particular spot. Suddenly his hands tightened on the binoculars.

'Periscope 60° starboard – range four miles!'

Hochmann picked it up a few seconds later. Holding the big flying-boat in a tight right-hand turn he pushed the microphone of the intercom against his mouth.

'Batheim – fire two red flares and stand by to release the smoke float. Georg, I want you to get off a radio call. Most Immediate priority.' He looked down at the chart as Neidermeyer pointed to their position. 'Message reads: *Enemy submarine sighted 30 miles NNE of Hurtshalls light. Request all units concentrate.*'

Mendel read the signal back and began tapping the Dornier's identification call sign as Hochmann ran the engines up to full power and vectored the flying-boat towards the enemy. Neidermeyer leaned forward across the controls.

17

'You'll have to release the bombs on the first run,' he shouted above the roar of the motors. 'He'll go deep as soon as he spots us. And once he submerges we'll have to leave it to the destroyers – depthcharges are the only hope.'

Hochmann nodded, passed a quick warning to his crew, and reached for the bomb release lever on the left-hand side of his seat.

★

Lieutenant Nicholas Hamilton DSO, RN, turned over the page of his magazine and read the concluding paragraphs of the short story. He wondered how much longer the cat-and-mouse game could continue. *Rapier* had been submerged nearly twelve hours already and, for the last five, had been drifting gently with the current a hundred feet below the surface with engines stopped.

The unexpected appearance of the patrol aircraft just before dawn had been sheer bad luck and although Hamilton had taken *Rapier* beneath the surface with commendable promptness he felt sure the submarine had been spotted. A burst of maximum submerged speed and a sharp alteration of course was all he could do by way of evasive action and, for the first few hours, he thought he had got away with it. But the arrival of the destroyers and the increase in air activity quickly blunted his initial optimism and he had taken the submarine deep to escape the hunters on and above the surface.

Collis, *Rapier*'s First Lieutenant, stretched his arms and yawned. Lacking the experience of his skipper he hated the tedium and boredom of sitting it out and not knowing what was happening.

'There's not been a single HE report for two hours now, sir,' he reminded Hamilton. 'Do you think they've given up searching for us?'

'Your guess is as good as mine, Number One.' Hamilton shrugged as he put down the magazine. 'But if you want my candid opinion I'd say they've stopped engines as well and are lying on the surface waiting to pick up the first noise we make.' He got up out of the battered old wicker

18

chair he kept on hand in the control room. 'Sometimes I wish the Boche had Asdic equipment like us.'

Collis looked surprised by the remark. 'Well, I'm bloody glad they haven't,' he said fervently. 'We wouldn't stand a cat in hell's chance.'

'Don't be quite so dogmatic, Number One. When you're caught by an Asdic probe you can hear the echoes bouncing off the hull. You *know* the enemy has located you. And, equally, you also know when he's lost contact. But when they're using hydrophones you can't hear a damned thing. They might be up there right now listening for underwater noises – or they might have cleared off hours ago. And, unfortunately, there's only one foolproof way to find out the score.'

'So what do we do about it, sir.'

'There's only one thing we *can* do, Number One. We'll have to take a chance.'

'You mean try and creep out of the area at silent speed, sir?'

'No, I don't. I'm sure there's something big in the wind and I intend to find out what it is.' Hamilton picked the magazine up from the deck and put it tidily on the vacated chair. 'I'm going to periscope depth to take a look.'

'Curiosity killed the cat,' Collis observed drily.

'Agreed, Number One. But a cat has the advantage of nine lives.'

Collis considered that discretion would have been the better part of valour in the circumstances, but having served with Hamilton for a number of months he knew only too well that his commanding officer had no regard for danger once he scented a possible quarry.

'What do you expect to find, sir?' he asked, as Hamilton paused to check the depth gauges. 'The Germans have virtually conquered Norway. They'll need time to digest it before they think of attacking anywhere else.'

'Perhaps . . .' Hamilton looked down at the gyro repeater in front of the helmsman. 'My guess is an attack on Sweden. Hitler needs their iron ore and after his easy success in Norway it would be a tempting prize. Or perhaps they're preparing to send a couple of pocket-battleships into the Atlantic on a raiding cruise. Whatever it is, I'm certain they're planning *something* and as we're the only submarine in the Skagerrak it's up to us to find out what they're up to.'

Hamilton looked relaxed and confident – the picture of a man who has mastered his job and is in complete control of the situation. The ribbon of the DSO on his jacket was proof enough of his valour. And his exploits during the rescue of the British seamen from the prison ship *Nordsee*[1] had made him a national hero. To the men of *HMS Rapier*, however, the medals and the headlines were of little consequence. It was the two gold rings on Hamilton's sleeve that counted. They symbolized his professional competence. And *that* was what the crew trusted when the chips were down.

'Take her to periscope depth, Mister Collis. Stand by to surface when I give the word. But be ready to get the hell out of it if anything goes wrong.'

'Hands to diving stations. Stand by for blowing. Motors on! Group down – half ahead both.'

'Motor room, aye aye, sir.'

Having acknowledged the order, Tyson, the Chief ERA, turned to Mike Hubbard, the duty motorman. 'Switches on. Grouper down. Half ahead both.'

Rapier quivered gently as the power came on and Tyson cradled the telephone against his mouth. 'Motor room reporting, sir. Switches on. Motors on. Half ahead both.'

Collis moved to his diving station behind Venables, the 'outside' ERA and the man responsible for the controls of the blowing and venting panel, and carefully scanned the array of warning lights. *Rapier* was in a condition of neutral buoyancy and a touch of the hydroplanes would be sufficient to take her up through the water. Blowing the tanks to achieve positive buoyancy was only necessary if the skipper ordered the submarine to be surfaced.

[1] See *Fighting Submarine*.

'Coxswain – up 'planes!'

Harrison, *Rapier*'s second coxswain and in charge of the fore 'planes controlling the angle of the bows, moved the big diving wheel to the *rise* position. He was still a new boy as far as the rest of the crew was concerned and he knew that *Rapier*'s veterans would not fully accept him into their midst until he had proved himself in an emergency. It was not an easy seat to fill – especially when he was replacing an experienced and respected submariner like Bill Tropp. But Tropp had died with a German machine-gun bullet in his chest during the attack on *Nordsee* and the Admiralty, in its wisdom, had appointed Harrison as his replacement. Still, he consoled himself philosophically, we all have to start at some time.

Collis nodded approvingly as *Rapier*'s bows tilted upwards and, aware that the new Second Coxswain needed moral encouragement, Hamilton glanced across and murmured, 'Nicely handled, Harrison.'

'Fifty feet, sir . . . forty-five . . . forty . . .' Blood, the First Coxswain, reported from his station at the after hydroplanes control as he called off the decrease in the submarine's depth every five feet.

'Any HE, Baker?' Hamilton queried as the boat closed the surface.

'Nothing to report, sir. Quiet as a grave.'

Ernie Blood eased the aft 'planes back a fraction to compensate for a momentary loss of buoyancy caused by a layer of fresh water and grinned to himself. 'As long as it's not *our* grave you're talking about,' he said in a hoarse whisper, to no one in particular.

'Save it, Chief,' Hamilton warned quietly. 'Let's concentrate. We don't know what's waiting for us up there yet.'

'Thirty-five feet . . . thirty feet . . .' Blood swung the control wheel sharply as he steadied the stern at the correct depth.

'Midships fore 'planes,' Collis ordered. 'Trim level at thirty.'

'Fore 'planes midships, sir.'

'Aft 'planes level, sir.'

'Up periscope!'

Able Seaman Dorset pulled the lever of the telemotor gear and the column hissed smoothly up from its well in the centre of the control room. Reaching for the steering handles Hamilton thrust his face against the rubber cup of the eye-piece and waited for the lens to break surface. A sudden flurry of spray obscured the upper prism for a brief moment but it drained away quickly and as soon as two feet of the slender periscope column was protruding above the waves he ordered Dorset to shut off the telemotor power.

The setting sun was sinking slowly towards the western horizon in a fiery ball that dazzled the eyes and turned the sea the colour of blood. Hamilton swung quickly away before the glare blinded him and carried out a routine 360° sweep of the surface as rapidly as caution permitted. With only two feet of periscope protruding above the surface his horizon was barely three miles distant but it was sufficient to detect any immediate danger. Flicking the thumb switch of the upper lens into the sky-search position he began checking for patrol aircraft.

'Surface clear,' he called back to the attack team. 'Stand by to surface.'

'Stand by to close main vents. Stand by to blow,' Collis warned Venables and the wrecker – the submarine service's endearing nickname for the 'outside' ERA – leaned forward across his control panel in anticipation of the executive order.

The sky seemed innocently clear. There was less than 1/10th cloud cover and it was boldly blue to the east. Pink fingers edged into the azure as Hamilton swung back towards the dying sun and the shroud of blood-soaked clouds hanging low over the western horizon seemed strangely ominous. He paused for a moment before committing himself. He shrugged. It all seemed peaceful enough. And it would be damned bad joss – the Navy's own term for its particular brand of luck – if an enemy aircraft were lurking in the dazzling arc subtended by the setting sun.

'Surface!'

'Close main vents! Blow all tanks!'

The warning lights of the diving panel flickered from red to green as Venables moved the levers to close the vents. Then, grasping the valve cocks two at a time, he began the routine sequence for releasing the compressed air to blast the sea water from the ballast tanks.

'Belay blowing! Check! Check! Check!'

The sudden eruption of the smoke float warned Hamilton that, despite his caution, an enemy aircraft was hiding in the dazzling glare of the dying sun. His odds-on gamble had failed and *Rapier* was caught like an unwary rat in a trap.

'Dive, dive, *dive*! Down periscope!'

'Open vents. Stop blowing. Planes hard a-dive. Full ahead both.'

Long hours of tedious drill brought an instant, unthinking response from the crew. Their expressionless faces reflected no emotion, even though each man knew instinctively that *Rapier* had been ambushed. And as they went about their tasks with cool, unhurried efficiency their nerves cringed in expectation of the whining crash of the first bombs.

'Group up – maximum power!'

Hubbard thrust the rheostat forward and the loud hum of the 1300 HP electric motors rose to a shrill scream as they sucked current from the batteries like hungry leeches. Tyson watched the ammeter needles flick to maximum discharge and scribbled a rapid calculation on the note pad in front of him. He reached for the telephone.

'Motor room, sir. Only enough reserves for twenty minutes at full power.'

Hamilton acknowledged the report with his usual unruffled calm. *Rapier*'s long sojourn on the bottom had already drained her storage batteries by 75% and the cells had not been recharged for nearly thirty-six hours. As an experienced skipper, he had no intention of remaining on full power for a moment longer than necessary. But he needed the extra thrust of the propellors to push the submarine down quickly and he watched the needles of the depth-gauge impatiently.

'Flood Q[1]!'

Collis reached over the Outside ERA's shoulder and twisted the valve wheel to Q tank. There was a sudden roar of water and the inclinometer tilted sharply to reflect *Rapier*'s steeper diving angle. Hamilton stared up at the vaulted steel roof of the control room deckhead as he tried to picture the situation on the surface. There was nothing more he could do to save his boat – except pray.

★

Neidermeyer clung to a convenient strut as Hochmann pushed the heavy flying-boat into a full throttle dive that threatened to tear the wings clean off the fuselage. Staring down at the sea beneath, he wondered why the submarine was still on the surface. Surely the enemy skipper must have spotted the Dornier by now. It took him several seconds to realize that Hochmann had flown out of the sun. And for the first time in his service career he was forced to admit that the *Luftwaffe* was not quite as stupid as the Navy thought.

It was an age-old tactic to engage the enemy with the sun behind him so that he was silhouetted against the horizon. Von Spee had done precisely that when he destroyed Craddock's squadron at Coronel in 1914. But Neidermeyer had never anticipated an experienced pilot would do the opposite. Perhaps, he concluded, there was a little more to air fighting than he or anyone else in the *Kriegsmarine* had realized.

Columns of water suddenly fountained from the submarine as the vents swung open to release the compressed air and admit the sea into the ballast tanks and he saw the bows dip steeply into the angry white tumult of bubbling

[1] 'Q' tank was the quick-diving tank in the bows.

water. He gripped Hochmann's arm tightly in his excitement.

'Get him, Klaus! Quickly – the bastard's diving!'

Hochmann's hand closed over the bomb release. The Dornier was not designed as a bomber and both its weapons and its equipment were primitive. The bombs, mere 25-pounders, were slung from external racks under the wings and there were no sights or aiming devices. The pilot had to point the nose of his aircraft at the target, estimate the release point, breathe a quick prayer, and pull the lever. From then on it was a matter for God and the laws of ballistics.

The tip of the periscope vanished beneath the surface in a thin whisper of spray as the bombs dropped away and Hochmann circled to the left to watch their descent. They fell lazily and with maddening slowness. For the first few seconds he thought he would score a direct hit, but as the bombs tumbled down towards the now invisible submarine he realized his initial optimism was premature. He swore briefly as he saw them land fifty yards short and as the contact fuses detonated on striking the water they threw up a ragged circle of six uninspiring columns of dirty spray.

Neidermeyer said nothing. Despite his disappointment, he did not hold Hochmann to blame. He had done his best. And Neidermeyer asked no more of anyone – even the *Luftwaffe*. In any event, he consoled himself, the tiny bombs would have done about as much damage to the submarine as a pea-shooter firing at a Panzer tank.

As the Dornier climbed for height, the two destroyers raced towards the spluttering smoke-float. Their first depthcharges hurled enormous cascades of water fifty feet or more into the air and Neidermeyer sensed that the hydrophones had picked up the enemy scent before it had run cold. There was little doubt that the submarine would have to use its motors for a brief period to go deep and change course. And the destroyers had responded so rapidly that there was a good chance they had detected the submarine's engine noise before the enemy commander had shut off his motors and gone over to silent running routine.

The destroyers crossed and quartered the area with the purposeful air of hounds who had run their quarry to earth and Neidermeyer could see the deadly grey cylinders tumbling eagerly out of the discharge racks over the sterns of the two ships. Every thirty seconds an enormous fountain of water towered into the air as the depthcharges detonated fifty, perhaps a hundred feet down below the surface, where the hunted submarine was frantically striving to hide.

Neidermeyer did not envy the terrified men trapped inside her. They might be the enemy, but they were still human beings like himself. And to be snared inside an iron coffin in the fathomless depths of the sea with depthcharges exploding on all sides was not a situation he cared to find himself in. It was at times like this he thanked God he had not volunteered for the U-boat service, despite the attractions of extra pay and quicker promotion.

The grey surface of the Skagerrak heaved violently as another depthcharge exploded, but this time the rush of water seemed strangely muted, as if the kinetic energy had been expended elsewhere. The sea frothed angrily around the base of the collapsing column of water and two gigantic air bubbles rushed to the surface and burst. Neidermeyer gripped the strut excitedly.

'They got him with that one, Klaus! – They *must* have done.'

Hochmann, caught up in the excitement of the chase, pushed the Dornier into a steep dive in his eagerness to give his men a grandstand view of the submarine's final moments. The keel of the flying-boat kissed the wave-tops and then bounced upwards as he pulled back the stick and levelled off at zero feet. One of the destroyers was racing in for the kill and Hochmann stared out over the port side for a glimpse of the doomed submarine.

Another depthcharge exploded less than fifty yards away and the Do-18 bucked and swayed as he punched the aircraft straight through the cascading water thrown up by the violent eruption beneath the sea.

'There it is!'

The foaming waters belched angrily and the rust-stained bows of the submarine suddenly thrust above the surface, hung suspended for a brief moment, and then slid back stern first beneath the waves leaving a widening circle of oil scum to mark its final resting place.

In the breathtaking excitement of the moment Hochmann had forgotten the presence of the other destroyer. The flying-boat was still skimming the wave-tops as Neidermeyer's warning shout snapped him back to reality and he saw with sudden horror that they were heading straight at the squat grey bulk of the second boat. His hands clawed at the control column and the Dornier lifted sharply to clear the unexpected hazard. The throttles banged open and the Jumo engines screamed to maximum power as the aircraft fought for height.

There was a searing flash as the starboard wingtip snagged the radio aerials of the destroyer, followed by a screech of tortured metal as the float struck the ship's fore funnel. For an agonizing moment, the flying-boat hung poised like a dying vulture over the destroyer's charthouse and then, sliding drunkenly forward, it bounced off the bridge wing and splashed into the sea. Within thirty seconds it had vanished from sight and in those final horrific moments the child in Ella's womb had become an orphan even before it was born.

CHAPTER TWO

1850 hours. 9th May 1940

Hamilton's order to flood the quick-diving tank undoubtedly saved *Rapier* from serious damage and the submarine was safely down to twenty feet before the first bombs struck the water. Fused to explode on impact, they burst in a dramatic eruption of towering white spray which, to the uninitiated observer, spelled instant doom and destruction to their invisible victim. But, as Neidermeyer had appreciated, 90% of the blast energy had been dissipated uselessly above the surface and the effect on the submerged submarine was minimal.

Nevertheless, *Rapier* owed her escape to her skipper's instantaneous reaction. Had she been caught on the surface even Hochmann's tiny 25-pound bombs could have caused fatal damage to the pressure hull. And, as Hamilton realistically admitted, if the Do-18 had been equipped with heavier bombs fitted with delay fuses, the unexpected attack could have had disastrous consequences.

'If that's all the bloody Boche can do, I reckon we ain't got much to worry about,' Ernie Blood grinned. 'What do you say, mate?'

It had been Harrison's first experience of enemy attack and although he had performed his task at the bow hydroplane controls with outward calm and efficiency his stomach was still tightly knotted in fear. Relaxing slightly, he forced himself to grin. Blood was right. Perhaps it had not been so bad.

'Whatever you say, Chief,' he nodded.

'Concentrate on your job!' Collis snapped. 'And *you* ought to know better, Chief. Watch those gauges and remember we're still diving.'

Hamilton took no part in the reprimand. Collis was

quite capable of maintaining discipline. And right now he needed all his powers of concentration to work out the enemy's intentions and plan his own next move.

'HE approaching from starboard bow, sir.'

'Take her to one hundred feet, Number One.' Hamilton made his way over to Baker, the hydrophone operator. 'What do you make of the sounds?'

Leading Signaller Baker twisted the knobs and listened intently. 'Almost certainly destroyers, sir. Approaching at thirty knots. Range less than one mile.'

Hamilton nodded, touched Baker's shoulders reassuringly, and moved back to join Collis at the diving panel. Obviously the smoke float had been intended as a warning signal to a group of waiting destroyers and he cursed himself for failing to spot them. But, he reflected philosophically, it was too late for regrets. The battle was on. And now more than ever the life of every man aboard the submarine rested in his hands.

'Eighty feet, sir. Are we going to make a dash for it?' Collis asked.

Hamilton shook his head. 'We can't outrun destroyers, Number One. And they'd soon pick up our motor noises if we tried to get away. We'll have to sweat it out.'

'One hundred feet, sir,' Blood reported from the far side of the control room.

'Midships 'planes. Stop motors.'

The incessant whining hum of the motors faded into silence and a sharp hiss of compressed air echoed through the hull as Venables transferred water ballast to the compensating tanks to catch trim.

'Trimmed and level, sir.'

Hamilton nodded casually and stooped down to pull off his shoes. 'Silent routine,' he ordered. 'Stand by for depthcharges.'

The other men followed the skipper's example and an unpleasant smell of sweaty feet permeated the cramped confines of the control room – mingling the scent of matured cheese with the aroma of stale cabbage water and

29

diesel oil. It was one of the unpleasantnesses of life to which the veteran submariner became accustomed. But it was more than sufficient to turn the stomach of the inexperienced and Harrison felt his guts heave.

'We should be reasonably safe at this depth,' Hamilton told them confidently. 'But complete silence is essential. Settle yourselves down and don't talk. Grab some sleep if you can. We're likely to be submerged for several hours so we must conserve our oxygen reserves.'

Collis realized that the skipper's warning was a considerable understatement. *Rapier* had already been continuously submerged for more than twelve hours and her last attempt to surface had been too brief to permit the intake of air. The longest they could last out was another twelve hours and, even then, things would be uncomfortable for everyone towards the end. But his outward expression gave no hint of the doubts he was entertaining in his heart and, setting an example to the others, he sat down carefully on the steel plated deck, clasped his knees with his hands, and bent his head forward to doze.

The other men quickly followed suit, leaving only Hamilton and Chief Petty Officer Blood on the alert to watch the gauges and dials for signs of any untoward emergencies.

Throughout the length of the submarine, men settled down at their posts and resigned themselves to a long wait. Most of them had endured – and survived – depthcharge attacks in the past and while none welcomed the coming ordeal there was at least no novelty in it. *Rapier* was a stout Clyde-built ship and they had little fear of her succumbing to the enemy.

Floating gently at a hundred feet and suspended in the dark unreal world between the surface and the ocean bottom, *Rapier* resembled a giant whale peacefully sleeping, drifting gently in the current. She was moving at barely one knot but, as Hamilton quickly appreciated, the tidal flow was running in an easterly direction, carrying her even deeper into enemy waters with every passing minute. But until he could use the motors again he could do nothing to halt the situation.

Baker raised his arm and *Rapier*'s skipper padded quietly across the control room in his stockinged feet to join him at the hydrophones.

'HE still within one mile, sir,' Baker whispered. 'Seems to be circling around.'

'Have they reduced speed?'

'Yes, sir. I'd say they were running at fifteen knots, or thereabouts.'

Hamilton said nothing that might worry his men but he rubbed his chin thoughtfully. The enemy destroyer leader had obviously pin-pointed the submarine's diving position and the hunters were circling the spot searching for telltale noises with their sound detectors. It was only a matter of time before they launched a systematic depthcharge attack. Leaning over Baker's shoulder he lowered his voice so that no one would overhear the question.

'How many destroyers are there?'

Hamilton was totally reliant on the hydrophone operator's expertise. It was a mutual trust that every submariner understood. In a situation where even the most junior hand could make an error which could bring instant disaster to the entire crew rank was unimportant. They were a team – each man dependant on his shipmates doing their jobs efficiently. Rank was of consequence only as a means of preserving order from chaos. *Someone* had to give a clear command or the team would quickly disintegrate into an undisciplined mob.

And Baker, sitting at the hydrophones, was the only man in the submarine in direct contact with the enemy on the surface at that precise moment.

'The HE's a bit confusing,' Baker admitted. 'But I reckon there's four of them. Another couple have joined the first pair in the last few minutes.'

So the *Kriegsmarine* meant business, Hamilton said to himself. There was obviously something going on. After Germany's heavy losses at Narvik, Admiral Raedar would not spare four valuable destroyers to hunt a single submarine – unless that particular submarine was in a position to do untold damage to an important operation.

He was still considering the problem when the first depthcharges detonated in the distance and, almost casually, he glanced at his watch and scribbled his report in the rough log:

7.05 pm. Depthcharge attack. Explosions approx 500 yards to starboard. No damage.

CRUMP! CRUMP! CRUMP!

The next series of explosions, although still too far away to cause damage, was nevertheless closer and the more experienced members of the crew knew the worst was yet to come. The underwater shock waves rocked the submarine gently and the soothing motion calmed the nerves of the inexperienced sailors who did not know of, or could not even guess at the terrors that were to follow.

Hamilton entertained neither optimism nor pessimism. He was a fatalist by nature and he knew *Rapier* was helplessly trapped. Sooner or later the deadly deluge of depthcharges would close around them and, stressed beyond endurance by the tremendous pressures created by the explosions, the stout walls of the submarine would collapse like a crushed egg-shell. And then, suddenly, their bright, secure world would be swallowed by a wall of black roaring water and their part in the war would be over – for ever.

The air inside the submarine was already uncomfortably stale and the turgid atmosphere reeked of human sweat. Glancing up at the depth gauges, Hamilton wondered whether he dare take in more water ballast and sink *Rapier* to the seabed. If the charts were accurate, the maximum depth of water in this part of the Skagerrak was only about two hundred feet – even less if they were drifting towards the shoal areas – and Intelligence reports indicated that the hydrostatic valves of Germany's latest depthcharges were capable of detonating as deep as fifty fathoms. In which case there was little point in going deeper.

CRUMP! CRUMP! CRUMP! . . . CRUMP!

The first three explosions thrust the submarine sideways, but she quickly swung back on to an even keel as the shock waves rolled past. The fourth, however, was considerably closer and *Rapier* lurched violently to starboard as if struck by a giant fist. The lights flickered for a moment before returning to full power and the men in the control room exchanged anxious glances.

Hamilton seemed unconcerned. Taking a file down from the rack alongside the chart table he started studying the submarine's daily fuel consumption log. And, after a few minutes, he picked up a pencil and began jotting down various calculations. Collis wondered what the skipper was up to but decided on reflection that Hamilton was merely finding something to occupy his mind.

CRUMP! CRUMP!

Rapier rocked to port and staggered bodily in the water as the savage force of the exploding depthcharges struck her thin plated hull like a thunderclap. Inside the submarine, the men held on to the nearest support to keep their foothold on the slippery deck plating. Further aft, in the motor room, Chief ERA Tyson joined the Engineer-Lieutenant on the floor of the compartment as O'Brien lifted the gratings and examined the batteries for damage or contamination. Jones, the junior motor mechanic, hovered in the background looking slightly sick. Like Harrison, this was his first trip in an operational submarine and he felt his guts dissolve to water each time the thundering crash of the depthcharges shuddered through the hull.

CRUMP!

A vicious explosion threw *Rapier* on to her beam ends and there was a vivid blue flash from the main fuse panel as the ring circuit shorted out. An acrid smell of burning rubber drifted through the boat and the men began coughing in the darkness. The emergency lamps glimmered to life but the interior of the submarine had been suddenly transformed from a brightly lit and comforting piece of machinery into a dim shadowy maze of unidentifiable equipment that harboured fear and sapped confidence. Jones stared wide-eyed at the curving steel wall of the motor room bulkhead and shivered. An uncontrollable urge twisted his bowels. He stepped forward as the Chief ERA straightened up.

'Permission to use the heads,[1] Chief?'

'Denied, Jones,' *Rapier*'s Engineer Lieutenant snapped. 'If you use the heads the enemy hydrophones will pick up the sound of the valve being opened. I'm sorry, but if it's as urgent as all that you'll have to do it in your pants.'

The pained expression on the motorman's face made it obvious that he had carried out the Lieutenant's unsympathetic suggestion with instant, if involuntary, obedience. The Chief ERA quickly moved downwind with an alacrity learned from bitter experience.

'Can you isolate the fuses and get the ring main going again, Chief?' O'Brien asked Tyson.

'I can try, sir. Depends how bad it is.' The Chief ERA paused as Hamilton came through the bulkhead hatch.

'Main fuse blown?'

'It's the truth you're saying, sir,' O'Brien nodded. 'That last depthcharge shorted out the switch panel. Tyson here is just after taking a look at the little devil.'

'Good. Everything else secure?'

'Yes, sir. The Chief helped me check the battery cells and there's no water coming in. And young Dodds put out a small electrical fire that flared up when the fuses blew.'

Hamilton nodded. He seemed to be sniffing the air. He looked in the direction of the unhappy Jones. 'What the devil is that revolting stink, O'Brien?'

The Irishman grinned and made an obscene gesture. Hamilton turned away to hide his smile. Poor little sod, he thought.

'Carry on, Lieutenant. I'll be in the control room.' He paused for a moment before stepping through the oval opening of the bulkhead hatch. 'And you'd better let young Jones go and change his trousers. It's bad enough having

[1] The naval term for lavatory.

the shits – but it's even worse if you have to walk around in them as well.'

He was about to say something else when a deafening explosion reverberated through the submarine. There was a sudden hiss of compressed air as the pipes fractured and the men on diving watch hurried through the boat locating and isolating the broken sections. Hamilton's ears detected the soft gurgle of water and he felt the short hairs on the back of his neck stiffen. Leaving the sentence unspoken he hurried forward to the control room. Two more explosions jolted the submarine and he had to grab the steel pillars supporting the deckhead to keep his footing.

'Close all watertight doors! Send in damage control reports.' The heavy bulkhead doors sealed tight with a soft hiss as they were swung home and secured by a quick twist of the locking wheels. 'Bow compartment?'

'Bow One, sir. Water leaking through Number Three starboard tube and we have some sprung plates behind the spare torpedo rack. Making good damage.'

'Received and understood. Carry on Sub. Bow Two report please.'

'Tregarran, sir. Slight leak on starboard side. Nothing serious. Owen's sealing it off with putty.'

'Engine and motor rooms?'

'O'Brien here. All secure. No damage.'

'Stern compartment?'

'All secure, sir.'

Rapier rolled violently as another savage blast thundered on her port beam and in the confusion Hamilton heard three more depthcharges exploding in the distance. His optimism returned. If the Boche were dropping his ash cans *that* far away it meant he was not absolutely sure of the submarine's precise position. Despite the near misses, it was a random attack. And that meant they had a chance of survival. He walked across to the diving table where Collis was helping Venables shut off the air lines.

'We're losing trim, sir,' Collis reported anxiously. 'Can we put on the pumps?'

Hamilton looked up at the inclinometer. *Rapier* was clearly seriously down by the bows and he suspected that flooding in the fore torpedo compartment was making the submarine nose heavy.

'Can you get her level on the 'planes,' he asked Blood.

The coxswain's face was beaded with sweat as he strained at the big diving wheel. 'No chance, sir. I've been doing my best for the last couple of minutes. There must be too much water up for'ard.'

Hamilton lifted the telephone to the bow torpedo flat. 'What's the score, Sub?' He put the question with the calm detachment of an exercise drill. 'Are the leaks sealed off yet?'

Acting Sub-Lieutenant James Cargill, *Rapier*'s fourth hand and the officer responsible for the bow torpedo compartment, was yet another member of the submarine's crew on his first operational patrol. Shut inside the slowly flooding compartment and cut off from the rest of the boat by the massive steel watertight door as effectively as a nailed coffin lid, the fate of every man on board the submarine now rested on his cool appreciation of the situation.

'Hull leaks are sealed off, sir. But we're taking water in through the two lower starboard tubes. I think both the inner and outer doors have been strained.'

The presence of the water was, in itself, not a serious matter. Torpedo tubes were designed to be flooded when ready for firing and trim was normally restored by transferring ballast from the bow tanks into the bilges. But the noise made by the pumps would be swiftly detected by the listening hydrophones on the surface and Hamilton knew he did not dare take the risk. And, if Cargill was right, the sea was entering the submarine through the loading doors.

'How much water do you have in the compartment?'

'Six inches, sir. The TGM's closed off Number Five – but we can't stop the sea coming in through Number Six. The loading door seemed to have buckled.'

Hamilton did not like the idea, but he seemed to have

little alternative. He would have to evacuate the bow compartment and leave it to flood – *Rapier*'s designers had given the submarine sufficient reserve buoyancy to remain afloat with one compartment full of water – although it would mean writing off his main means of offence, the torpedo armament.

The submarine kicked with the slow agony of a dying bull in the arena as another depthcharge burst under the stern and cork packing sprinkled down from the overhead seams like a blizzard of soft brown snow that coated every flat surface with a layer of fine dust. More light bulbs shattered, but as *Rapier* was already on its emergency circuits it made no difference to the dim gloom inside the hull. Somewhere aft, he heard a man scream and he nodded to Collis. The First Lieutenant lifted the telephone to the motor room, spoke briefly to the Chief, and reminded him almost casually that there were morphine capsules in the first-aid box.

Hamilton waited until Collis had finished. He looked up at the inclinometer once more and made up his mind.

'Bow compartment. Abandon your station and shut for'ard watertight door. Repeat – abandon fore compartment and secure Number One door.'

'Bow compartment, aye aye, sir.'

Cargill sounded relieved. The cold black water was already lapping his knees and despite the TGM's valiant efforts to seal off the loading door of Number Six tube the sea was still forcing its way into the submarine through the narrow gap. But the men gave up the struggle with disappointed reluctance. Discipline stopped them from arguing, but it was plain from the expressions on their faces as they climbed through the narrow opening in the bulkhead that they felt they had let their mates down.

Hamilton waited until Grant, the petty officer in charge of the fore torpedo storage space, reported the watertight door as secure. The immediate danger had been averted. Perhaps he could afford to take a chance.

'I'm going aft, Mister Scott. Take over the Watch.

Transfer ballast from Seven and Eight tanks to level off the bows and then increase pressure in the fore compartment. It might slow down the rate of flooding.' He turned to Collis. 'Get along to the wardroom, Number One. I'll be with you in a couple of seconds.'

The click of the depthcharge's hydrostatic valve opening was clearly audible inside the submarine and, almost simultaneously, a tremendous explosion blasted the outer hull. *Rapier* heeled violently and Hamilton swore as he was hurled bodily sideways with bruising force against the unyielding steel plating of the starboard bulkhead. The emergency lighting circuit went out and scrambling to his feet in the darkness he felt like a blind man trapped in a pit of venomous cobras as escaping high-pressure air hissed sibilantly from a dozen fractured pipes. Yet, incredibly, there was no panic. Someone swore, invisibly. Another laughed. And as hand torches threw eerie yellow circles of light on the hull plating men searched out the leaks while their comrades reached up to spin valve wheels shut in an effort to close off the air lines.

Someone was holding a torch against the shattered glass of the inclinometer so that Blood could see the angle of the bows as he juggled the after hydroplanes to bring the submarine on to a level keel. Rivenham, always on hand in an emergency, directed his portable lamp at the pressure gauges as Venables, the 'outside ERA', began cautiously blowing the compensating tanks.

A silent miracle from the two electricians sweating over the smouldering remains of the secondary fuse panel restored the emergency lighting and Hamilton moved slowly round the control room advising, helping and encouraging the men as they fought to save the crippled boat. Three more depthcharges exploded astern, but those that heard them merely shrugged them off.

Having satisfied himself that there was nothing more he could do personally, Hamilton made his way back to the curtained privacy of *Rapier*'s wardroom, where Collis was waiting for him. A series of near misses rocked the submarine yet again and the young Lieutenant had to brace himself against the table to avoid being hurled to the deck. Magnified by the hollow accoustics of the hull, the noise of the explosions rumbled like thunder and it seemed impossible that the frail pressure hull could survive the savage onslaught for much longer.

'It isn't going to work, Number One,' Hamilton admitted quietly as he closed the curtain behind his back. 'What the hell do we do now?'

Collis was philosophical. He shrugged. 'Nothing we *can* do, sir, except sit it out. They've obviously picked up the sound of the pumps.'

Hamilton reached for the telephone to the control room. Scott answered it.

'This is the Captain. Belay the pumps. Revert to silent routine.'

Scott acknowledged the order and Hamilton heard him passing it on to the men. The throb of the pumps died away as he hung up the telephone and turned back to Collis. The sound of depthcharges continued to rumble in the distance and, for the moment at least, the enemy seemed to have lost contact. The insidiously steady drip of water from the strained hull plates, however, prevented any feelings of optimism.

'If we could only bluff the Boche into thinking we've had it,' he said, voicing his thoughts aloud.

'We could discharge oil from the bunkers and make them think we've been holed,' Collis suggested. 'The U-boats often made use of that dodge in the last war when things were getting too hot for them.'

Hamilton shook his head. 'That's the trouble, Number One. It's an old trick. Those destroyers know what they're doing. They'll never fall for it.'

Having thought of an idea Collis was reluctant to let go. 'Well, I suppose we could add a bit of realism by shooting bits of wood and equipment out of the torpedo tubes.'

'You can take it from me – it won't work this time. And in any case we can't clear the tubes without opening the

39

for'ard door and that's a risk I daren't take with the fore-ends partially flooded.' He paused. 'The only thing that would convince the Boche we're done for is a few dead bodies. And that's something we fortunately don't happen to have.' He stopped suddenly as a vague idea flickered through his mind. 'Have we got all our DSEA kits on board?' he asked sharply.

Collis nodded. He wondered what the hell was going on inside Hamilton's brain. It looked as if he had decided *Rapier* was doomed and was working out an escape plan. But it was not like the skipper to throw his hand in so early in the game.

'We may not have any *dead* bodies, Number One,' Hamilton said slowly. 'But perhaps a couple of live ones would be equally effective.'

'I don't follow you, sir.'

Hamilton felt his pulse quicken as the slender threads of the idea took substance. It seemed a crazy scheme and yet, somehow, it held a germ of hope. It would certainly call for a degree of self-sacrifice never before demanded from any officer or man of the Royal Navy in its thousand years of fighting history. And yet it *could* be the million-to-one chance of saving his boat from destruction.

'Let's suppose we tried your idea, Number One, and released some of our bunker fuel. It might work but the odds are against it. However, if we developed it a stage further, I reckon I could call their bluff. All I'd need is a couple of volunteers who won't mind spending the rest of the war in a German prison camp. Now, listen carefully, and see if you can spot any snags . . .'

Another series of explosions rocked the trapped submarine and Collis reached up to grab an overhead pipe. Clinging on like a subway passenger strap-hanging in the rush-hour he did as he was told and listened.

'The next time we have a near miss,' Hamilton continued calmly as if he was discussing the next day's exercises in Stokes Bay, 'I'm going to blow the tanks and take *Rapier* to the surface. I shall stay there just long enough to make sure the Boche get a good view of us and then I'll flood up and go for the bottom before the destroyers can get close enough to ram. At the same time we'll discharge a couple of tons of fuel oil to make it look like we're holed. Then, when we're safely on the bottom, I'm going to send up two volunteers in DSEA kits to make it look good. They'll be picked up and, if they tell a good tale, the German attack commander will believe that we're crippled helplessly on the bottom. He'd be a fool if he didn't swallow the story because no one in their right minds would voluntarily give themselves up and be taken prisoner unless the submarine was doomed.'

The sheer audacity of Hamilton's plan took Collis's breath away. There seemed no reason why, given a modicum of luck, it couldn't work. And yet the utter ruthlessness of the mind capable of creating such a scheme frightened him a little.

'Can you spot any flaws?' Hamilton asked.

'No – other than the fact that you've got to find a couple of men willing to volunteer to spend the rest of the war in a prison camp. It's not exactly a health farm, from what I've heard.'

'I don't expect any difficulties in that direction,' Hamilton said easily. 'Men have volunteered to die for their comrades on many occasions – I'm offering them a chance to *live*. In fact, to be brutally honest, they probably stand a better chance of survival than the rest of us.' As if to confirm Hamilton's gloomy prognostication, two more explosions vibrated through the hull and, for a moment, the emergency lighting went dead although, mercifully, it glimmered back to life a few seconds later. 'You go aft to the engine and motor rooms and explain what I'm planning to do. And bring back a couple of volunteers. We can't spare any men from either the control room or the for'ard sections.'

Collis nodded, pushed through the curtains of the wardroom, and started towards the stern. He hoped

Hamilton's faith in *Rapier*'s crew was not misplaced. It was a hell of a thing to ask of any man.

Alistair Scott, Coxswain Blood and the other members of the attack team gathered in the control room accepted Hamilton's plan without a murmur. They had resigned themselves to a slow death trapped on the bottom in the crippled submarine and the skipper's macabre scheme at least offered a faint chance of survival. None of them felt optimistic about it. But anything was better than nothing when Death was knocking at the door. And having quietly absorbed the details, each man set about preparing for his part in the gigantic gamble.

Collis returned to the control room a few minutes later, accompanied by Leading Stoker Parker and Petty Officer Ernest Burke.

'I had eight volunteers, sir,' he told Hamilton. 'I picked these two. They've both been through the escape course at Blockhouse and neither of them have any dependants.'

Hamilton looked sharply at the bearded Petty Officer. 'What's all this nonsense, Burke?' he snapped. 'You're a married man.'

'I *was*, sir,' Burke corrected his commander politely. 'But my old woman upped and left me at Christmas. Gone off with some bloody sergeant in the Marines. And she ain't likely to be coming back.'

'I don't recall seeing any note of this in your pay-book. You're still claiming your allotment.'

Burke rubbed his nose and drew himself rigidly to attention. Despite the continual thud of depthcharges on all sides he felt as if he was up on a fizzer. It was as bad as being on Captain's Report in one of the big battle-wagons. And he had had a few of those in his time. All it needed was a Master-at-Arms hollering in his left ear: *Right turn, prisoner halt, off cap, name and number!* He swayed on his feet to maintain his balance as another underwater explosion rocked the submarine.

'Sorry, sir. I meant to give you a chitty but what with the rush I clean forgot about it. No harm intended, sir.'

42

Hamilton repressed a smile. Burke was a good Petty Officer. And it wasn't the first time he had had wife trouble.

'Very well, Burke. I'll accept you as a volunteer. Once you're in a POW camp you won't have much chance of reporting your domestic circumstances to the Admiralty. Looks like you'll be killing two birds with one stone.' He turned to Parker, the Leading Stoker. He was barely nineteen years old and his face was thin and pale. 'How about you, Parker? Any dependants?'

'No, sir. Parents are both dead – that's why I was sent to *Ganges*.[1] I reckon I've got less to lose than anyone else on board.'

Hamilton glanced over the stoker's shoulder and saw Collis nod his head in approval.

'Right – then that's settled,' he told the two men. 'You've both been through the escape tank at Blockhouse. But don't imagine that means you know the lot. You only come up fifteen feet in that – and believe me it's a hell of a difference surfacing from a hundred feet.[2] I take it you are familiar with the drill?'

'Yes, sir,' Burke said, speaking up for both of them. 'And I've been reading up the reports of the *Thetis* escape. I reckon I can soon teach young Parker what he has to do.'

'Good. Now remember what we're trying to achieve. You've got to convince the Germans that *Rapier* has had it. There might be more survivors but you doubt it. I know I can rely on your imagination, Burke.' The Petty Officer wondered whether the skipper was being sarcastic, but decided the remark was intended seriously. 'And don't think you're going to get the VC for this. I don't want any heroics. I just want an efficient, straight-forward job. If the rest of us manage to get out of this caper in one piece I'll put a word in for you with the Admiralty. But don't expect recognition. Another skipper might want to use a

[1] The Royal Navy's Boy's Training Establishment at Harwich.
[2] The 100 foot instructional tower at Fort Blockhouse was not built until 1954.

43

similar bluff one day and the Boche would soon smell a rat if you were the only two men decorated.' He paused, looked each man straight in the eyes, and held out his hand. 'Good luck, the two of you. Carry on, Number One.'

Collis led his two charges to the watertight door at the rear of the control room, ducked through the shoulder-width hatch opening, and made his way towards the aft escape hatch behind the engine and motor rooms. Although he did not personally relish the thought of sitting out the war in a prison camp he could not help feeling slightly envious. At least Burke and Parker had a 50% chance of survival. And that was considerably more than the rest of them had.

Seven minutes later a violent explosion close under the starboard bow of the trapped submarine provided Hamilton with the trigger he needed to put the gigantic game of blindman's bluff into operation. He did not underestimate his opponent's intelligence and he knew the plan would only work if the enemy was totally deceived. And to achieve such deceit the German commander must be convinced that a well-placed depthcharge had forced *Rapier* to the surface, out of control.

'Blow all tanks! Up-helm 'planes!'

The men inside the submarine swallowed their fear and waited tensely as *Rapier* shot to the surface. If the skipper's idea misfired, the grinding crash of a destroyer's razor sharp bows cutting into the hull would be the end of their hopes – and the end of everything. Those who could pray did so. Those who could not merely stared silently at the grim, grey walls of their underwater prison and waited.

The escape chamber was situated astern of the motor room and for'ard of the steering compartment and stokers' mess space. It was a square steel box of forbidding countenance that resembled in many ways a medieval instrument of torture hiding in the shadows of an ancient dungeon. The crew, in fact, often referred to it jokingly as the Iron Maiden.

A small circular hatch, just large enough for a man to

squeeze through, was set into the front. Three external control wheels, one operating the flood valve which admitted water into the chamber, the patent clip securing the exit door in the roof, and the entry hatch release mechanism, were grouped to one side of the box, while a further valve for draining off the water if anything went wrong during the escape routine was situated inside the cramped claustrophobic compartment. There was no form of lighting and the men shut inside the chamber had to follow out the escape drill by feel and from memory with only the aid of small hand torches.

Burke looked at the chamber and shrugged as he lifted his DSEA kit down from the ready-use locker. Pushing his head through the halter strap he adjusted the oxygen bag and filter and comfortably on his chest and buckled the harness tightly into place. Then he slipped the goggles on and, leaving them pushed up on his forehead in the style of a pre-1914 Grand Prix racing driver, helped Parker struggle awkwardly into the second outfit.

'The air inside the boat is getting pretty foul, lad,' he told him quietly, 'and that means you're going to feel mighty sick when you start breathing the oxygen. So take your first couple of breaths before the water level rises too high and you can be sick without messing up the equipment. Got that?'

'Thanks, Mr Burke. I'll try to remember.'

'Good lad,' the Petty Officer nodded encouragingly. 'And don't forget to open the exhaust cock on the breathing apparatus as you start going up. If you don't,' he added dispassionately, 'your lungs will probably burst.'

Burke sounded more confident than he felt. Escaping from a hundred feet was a hazardous undertaking. The men trapped inside the ill-fated *Thetis* only had to rise twenty-five feet to the surface and yet at least four of them had died in the attempt. On the other hand, over half of *Poseidon*'s crew had survived an ascent of a hundred and twenty-five feet almost ten years earlier, in 1931, so it was not impossible.

Opening the entry hatch, he squeezed his muscular frame into the empty tank and flashed his hand torch across the bare steel walls to familiarize himself with the details and to get his bearings as the submarine angled towards the surface in a flurry of hissing air and frothing water.

'Twenty feet – stand by.' Hamilton's disembodied voice crackled through the intercom loudspeaker set high on the bulkhead, behind the escape chamber. 'Stop blowing!'

An uncanny silence shrouded the submarine as it hung poised on the surface. If Hamilton's trim calculations were correct only the bows would be showing above the waves but, despite the encouragement of the inclinometer, no one could be sure. And every man held his breath in readiness for the shriek of torn metal as one of the destroyers rammed the boat. Hamilton counted off exactly five seconds.

'Open main vents. Hard a-dive!'

'Flood Q – 'planes to maximum diving helm. Flood all tanks!'

Rapier slipped quickly beneath the water stern first, levelled off on to an even keel, and then plunged her bows towards the bottom of the Skagerrak. Taking his cue from the skipper's executive order, Collis nodded to the two men inside their cold black cavern of steel.

'Here we go, chaps. Good luck.' He turned to Hodgeson, the Able Seaman responsible for the escape chamber. 'Shut the hatch, Hodgeson. Start flooding.'

The seaman closed the circular hatch and spun down the six butterfly nuts to hold it secure against the pressure of the sea when the inlet valve was opened.

'Hatch shut and clipped, sir. Flooding up . . . *now*.'

Collis peered through the glass inspection window. It was pitch black inside but, pointing his torch through the glass, he could just make out the shadowy forms of the two men. The water was rising rapidly and was already level with their waists and, as Burke saw the officer's face pressed against the circular window, he raised a thumb to signal that all was well.

Further for'ard, in the dim gloom of the control room, Hamilton kept a wary eye on the depth gauges as *Rapier* sank slowly to the bottom. The air was getting uncomfortably stale and the increased carbon dioxide was making every breath a laboured effort. He was conscious, too, of a growing lethargy and a vague nagging headache.

'Stand by Port Five and Starboard Eight fuel bunkers. Start discharging.'

The stokers wound the valve wheels into the 'open' position and reached upwards to switch on the pumps. With reduced electrical power they responded sluggishly but the men were too exhausted to use the alternative manual pumping system. Even the physical effort of moving the pump levers brought a film of sweat to their faces and they gasped the tainted air into their aching lungs like a team of broken-winded nags straining up a steep hill.

'Green Eight, discharging, sir.'

'Red, Five, pumps on, sir.'

A black cloud of turgid oil streamed from the valves and to the underwater observer *Rapier* resembled an enormous grey-green cuttlefish throwing off a smoke screen to escape one of its many predators. In the circumstances, it was an apt analogy.

'Level off at one hundred, Cox'n. Silent routine.'

'Stop flooding. Switches off. Stop motors. Trim level at a hundred feet.'

Hamilton reached for the phone. 'How's it going, Number One?' he asked, as Collis acknowledged.

'Nearly ready, sir. The chamber's almost flooded up. No snags so far.'

Petty Officer Burke fastened the clip over his nostrils and pushed the breathing tube into his mouth as the water level in the chamber reached its cold black fingers around his neck. The freshness of the air quickly revived his waning strength and the initial wave of nausea soon passed. He glanced across at Parker and saw the young stoker vomit violently. Reaching out he put a reassuring hand on the lad's shoulder.

Parker wiped his mouth with the back of his hand, retched again, swallowed the sour taste of bile gathering in his throat, and jammed the tube into his mouth for another attempt. A searing pain stabbed his ears but, remembering the escape drill at Fort Blockhouse, he swallowed a couple of times to equalize the pressure and the discomfort eased. Now that the sickness had gone away he, like the experienced Burke, felt better and, reaching upwards, he found the hatch wheel above their heads, wound it down, and began pushing.

The Petty Officer joined him and together they strained to thrust it open. Within seconds they were both gasping for breath and when a final concerted heave failed to move it Burke signalled for him to wait until the chamber was fully flooded. Once the pressure of water inside the narrow steel box was equal to the pressure of the sea outside, the counter-weighted hatch cover would open with minimum effort.

It was a nerve-wracking interval, but as the water finally closed over their heads they renewed their attack. This time it opened easily and Burke pushed Parker upwards towards the circular hole in the roof of the chamber. The young stoker floundered towards it and, as he floated past the Petty Officer's face, Burke's experienced eye saw the exhaust valve of his breathing gear was still closed. He had just sufficient time to push it open and then Parker had vanished from sight through the opened hatch on his way to the surface.

Burke seemed in no hurry to follow. With the disciplined caution of a veteran submariner he checked that everything inside the chamber was in order, waited until Parker had had time to float clear of the jumping wires, and then allowed himself to rise slowly upwards. The reserves of oxygen in the chest pack were already nearly exhausted and he could hear an ominous bubbling rattle in the flexible tube each time he drew a breath. Gliding out through the hatch opening he kicked his feet and stared upwards through the dark green water.

A hundred feet was a hell of a long way to go. He only hoped that his oxygen supply would last out until he reached the surface.

CHAPTER THREE

1850 hours. 9th May 1940

Korvettenkapitan Schneider ducked instinctively as the flying-boat tangled its starboard wing-float in the destroyer's aerials and cartwheeled over the exposed bridge in a shower of crackling blue sparks before dropping over the side and vanishing beneath the black surface of the sea in a flurry of white spray. Even the *Korvettenkapitan*'s customary phlegmatic calm was momentarily shaken by the unexpectedness of the impact but, quickly recovering his composure, he straightened up and turned to assess the damage.

Despite the violence of the disaster, casualties were surprisingly light. Krasker, the starboard lookout, hung limply over the bridge coaming and two ratings trapped against the fore funnel had been killed instantly. More horrifically, Baden, the destroyer's coxswain, had been neatly decapitated by the leading-edge of the Dornier's port wing and his body was sprawled in a bloody heap against the binnacle, leaving the ship's wheel spinning wildly out of control. But, as Schneider reminded himself, men were expendable.

'Take over the helm, Spielmann!' he yelled to the surviving seaman on duty at the voicepipes. 'Full ahead both. Steer for the enemy! Stand by to ram!'

The rust streaked bows of the submarine were still poking forlornly above the surface some five hundred yards off the destroyer's port bow and with the enemy at his mercy *Korvettenkapitan* Schneider was concerned only with the kill. The crashed flying-boat could go to hell – it might teach the *Luftwaffe* a lesson in air-sea co-operation – and, despite the casualties, the material damage to his own boat was fortunately minimal. The ruptured fuel tanks of the aircraft had spilled petrol in all directions and flames were already licking hungrily upwards from the base of the charthouse. Ohlson, the First Officer, could attend to that. As Flotilla Commander, and operating under the direct orders of Grand Admiral Raedar, Schneider had more important matters to attend to.

The other three destroyers were too far away for immediate support and it was up to the *Heinrich Ullmann* to finish off the submarine with her deadly razor-sharp bows. The *Korvettenkapitan* crouched forward over the bridge screen and stared at the bows of the submarine sticking out of the water through his binoculars, as the destroyer swung towards its helpless victim. *Heinrich Ullmann*, one of the only German warships to escape from the holocaust at Narvik and with the scars of battle still proudly visible on her grey-painted upperworks, was about to take her revenge on the British navy.

'Casualties cleared, sir. All systems functioning. Damage control party have put out the fire in the charthouse.'

Schneider nodded. He had scarcely absorbed a single word of Ohlson's report. The submarine was now barely four hundred yards away and they were closing fast.

'Give me more speed!' he shouted down the voicepipe.

A fierce tongue of flame leapt from the funnels as the engineers squirted additional oil into the hungry boilers. But, already moving at two knots more than her designed speed, *Ullmann* failed to respond.

'One point to starboard, helmsman,' he rapped sharply to Spielmann. 'Steer to ram her just abaft the conning tower.'

'One point a'starboard, sir,' Spielmann repeated un-emotionally. Recalled to service in September 1939 after ten years on pension, he was a veteran of the Kaiser war and he had seen it all before. It was no good the skipper getting excited. It would not be the first time an enemy submarine had slipped through his fingers. And it probably would not be the last.

'Do we drop life-rafts for the flying-boat crew, sir?' Ohlson enquired anxiously. Unlike the *Korvettenkapitan*, he was a Merchant Marine officer called to the colours as a reservist. Saving survivors from the sea seemed more important than killing the enemy.

Schneider shook his head angrily. 'Don't waste time on the *Luftwaffe*, *Oberleutnant*. They wouldn't rescue you if the situation was reversed. And,' he added callously, 'they're probably dead anyway. You'd do better checking the for'ard gun crews – the stupid bastards seem to think they're enjoying a football match. Get them into action!' He turned to Fischer, his Yeoman of Signals, as Ohlson hurried down the companionway to the forward guns. 'Call up *Z-14* and *Z-27*. Tell them to circle me at five hundred metres range. If the enemy dives they're to drop depth-charges at thirty second intervals. Then call *Oberleutnant* Arne and tell him to bring *Z-19* astern and support my attack.'

Fischer lifted his lamp, directed it over the starboard side at the nearest of the two destroyers, and began flashing the message. A few moments later, a winking light on *Z-14*'s bridge acknowledged and the destroyer began circling obediently.

Heinrich Ullmann dug her bows into a wave crest, lifted steeply, and hurled a wall of green swirling water back over her fo'c'sle. Schneider felt the cold spray on his face as he stared ahead. Only three hundred yards to go – and the bows of the crippled submarine were still sticking out of the sea like a black rock exposed by the falling tide. He lifted the telephone to the stern.

'Put the charges on shallow setting, Kuntz. And stand by to fire as soon as I give the word.'

Two hundred yards!

A few well chosen words from Ohlson had brought the gun crew hurrying back to their battle stations from their grandstand position in the bows. The for'ard five-inch quick-firer swung on the target, recoiled smoothly, and spat a tongue of yellow flame from its muzzle as the *Oberleutnant* gave the order to open fire. But the ill-aimed shell exploded harmlessly fifty metres to the left of the submarine and Schneider cursed the gunlayer's incompetence. Then suddenly, while he was watching it through his binoculars, the submarine slid quietly back beneath the surface and vanished from sight. The *Korvettenkapitan* wondered whether she had taken her final plunge to the bottom or whether her skipper was making a last desperate effort to escape. It might be a case of kicking a man when he was down – and Schneider smiled grimly at the unintentional pun – but he could not afford to take chances.

'Stand by, depthcharges . . . *Fire!*'

He timed the command carefully and at the exact moment the destroyer passed over the spot where *Rapier* had disappeared four grey canisters catapulted from the stern throwers, climbed briefly into the air, and fell with a sullen splash into the sea. With the hydrostatic valves on their shallowest setting they detonated almost immediately they had sunk beneath the surface and the *Heinrich Ullmann* jolted with the shock of the underwater explosions. Petty Officer Kuntz clung to the rail as the destroyer's stern lifted and fell back again. He was prepared to swear that the deck plating had flexed with the savage strength of the blast wave and he wondered briefly what effect the explosions were having on the crippled submarine struggling for survival in the cold black depths. Dragging himself upright, he yelled at his crew to reload the mortars, grabbed the lanyard of the discharge cartridge, and waited for the executive order from the bridge.

Z-19 was following close astern and as *Oberleutnant* Arne crossed the foaming circle of water left by the flotilla leader's first salvo of depthcharges he added his own lethal contribution to the angry cauldron.

'Hard about!'

Spielmann spun the wheel and *Ullmann* heeled sharply to starboard with dense columns of smoke and glittering sparks billowing from her funnels. At that moment she looked the very epitome of a destroyer in action – lean, fast, and aggressively pugnacious. Only the battle ensigns streaming from her truck and the long lines of ironclads she was protecting were missing. In the hard realities of war at sea in 1940 her enemy was invisible and the romance of battle had gone. But her purpose remained the same — to run down and utterly destroy her enemy.

'We've got him, sir!' Ohlson yelled excitedly. 'Can you see the oil — the depthcharges must have ruptured the fuel tanks.'

The *Korvettenkapitan* raised his binoculars and scanned the thick black sludge polluting the sea in an ever widening circle. He paused for a moment as the destroyer hurtled towards the slick.

'It's probably a trick, sir,' Spielmann warned. The *Oberbootsmann* had spent most of 1915 hunting British submarines operating in the Baltic. There was little he did not know about underwater warfare. 'If an enemy sub wants to give us the slip, the skipper often pumps off surplus oil fuel to make it look as if his boat's been holed. If there's no wreckage I'd say it was a bluff.'

'Half ahead both.' Schneider felt the destroyer suddenly slow and heard a sharp squawk of annoyance from *Z-19*'s siren as *Oberleutnant* Arne had to reverse engines to avoid running his flotilla leader down. He ignored the protest but made a mental note to reprimand the destroyer's skipper for insubordination when they returned to base. He turned to Ohlson, who had rejoined him on the bridge. 'What do *you* think, Number One?'

Ohlson examined the oil slick silently. As a professional seaman and not a career naval officer he could not help feeling a pang of pity for the unknown men struggling for their lives inside the crippled submarine somewhere in the black depths beneath the surface. They might be the enemy but he bore them no personal ill-will. And it was only by chance that he wasn't serving in an *unterseeboot* himself.

'I reckon we should give them a chance, sir. After all, they can't get away.'

Schneider nodded his agreement. Despite his hard

exterior he was blessed with an imagination and he shared Ohlson's compassion. But he *had* to make sure.

He lifted the bridge telephone. 'Kramer? I've reduced speed to fifteen knots. Switch on your set and let me know if you can hear anything.'

If the submarine was finished, the sensitive mechanical ears of the hydrophones were quite capable of hearing the sounds of the hull breaking up even two hundred feet down. And if the enemy was trying to creep away on his motors the apparatus would be able to detect the whispering hum of the electrical power units. Schneider leaned over the bridge and stared down at the spreading circle of oil while he waited. In his own mind he was certain he had made a kill but, as Spielmann had pointed out, it could be a ruse. The Royal Navy's submarine commanders were notorious for their cunning. The telephone buzzed at his elbow and he lifted the receiver.

'No engine noises detected, sir,' Kramer reported.

'Any other sounds?'

'No, sir. No HE whatsoever. It all seems quiet as a tomb.'

Schneider thought it was an appropriate simile. 'Carry on, Kramer. And report to me immediately you hear anything.' He turned to Ohlson. 'The hydrophones are not picking anything up. I must make a report to Kiel shortly. What do I tell them?'

Ohlson looked down at the oil again and shrugged. 'Personally speaking, sir, I'd say we'd sunk it. But I must admit I have a considerable respect for the Bo's'n's opinions. He's been through this sort of situation dozens of times. And if he has any doubts, I think I must have some as well.'

The telephone buzzed again before Schneider could reply. He put the instrument to his ear.

'I'm picking up faint water sounds, sir,' Kramer reported hesitantly. 'A sort of gurgle . . .'

Schneider frowned. 'You're the expert on hydrophone

effects, Kramer,' he snapped impatiently. 'What do you think it means?'

'I'm not sure, sir. It could be the noise of the bilge pumps in *Z-19* – or it could be the sound of water flooding into the submarine's hull.'

'Look, sir! Over there!'

Schneider cradled the phone against his shoulder and stared over the starboard side as Ohlson shouted and pointed excitedly. An enormous bubble of air swelled upwards in the centre of the oil slick like the black domed head of an ancient sea monster emerging from the depths. It expanded rapidly and then suddenly burst.

Perhaps that was what Kramer had heard on his hydrophones, Schneider decided. The hull of the submarine had broken up and the pressure of the sea flooding into the compartments had forced the trapped air out under pressure to create the giant bubble they had just witnessed. It all followed in a logical sequence of events. There seemed no other possible explanation. He picked up his binoculars and searched the oil slick carefully as if to confirm his conclusions.

The black scum heaved and he focused on the new disturbance. A series of smaller bubbles forced their way to the surface and, suddenly, a weird goggled head covered in oil broke through the reeking sludge.

'Stop engines! Away Number Two cutter. Survivor sighted two hundred yards off starboard bow.'

Heinrich Ullmann lost speed and from his vantage point on the bridge wing the *Korvettenkapitan* watched the starboard sea-boat swing out smartly and drop down into the water.

'There's another one, sir. About ten metres to the left – he looks in a bad way.'

The destroyer's crew crowded the rails as news of the first survivors swept the messdecks. Now that victory seemed secure they could afford to be magnanimous and even Schneider felt a pang of pity for the two miserable submariners struggling in the filthy black muck. The cutter reached the first man, hauled him out of the water, and then turned towards the second.

Parker was barely alive. He had taken longer to reach the surface than Burke, even though he had been the first out of the escape chamber, and his oxygen supply was exhausted. A searing pain hammered inside his skull and his lungs felt as if they were on fire. Unaware of the dangers, he ripped the breathing tube from his mouth and tore off his goggles as his head broke surface. And, almost immediately, he retched violently as the oil fumes hit him.

The lop of the surface swell threw the acrid oil scum into his face, burning his unshielded eyes and blinding him. Striking out in sudden panic he struggled wildly in the clinging black muck until, exhausted by his efforts, he momentarily lost consciousness and slipped under the water. His eyes were still clogged with oil when he emerged a few seconds later and he choked as he swallowed a mouthful of sludge. Suddenly a strong hand grasped his neck and an arm passed under his back as one of the German sailors lifted him clear of the water and scooped him into the boat. Someone bent forward with a wad of cotton wool and wiped the oil from his eyes and mouth – a kindliness he promptly rewarded by being sick over the man's knees.

Korvettenkapitan Schneider was waiting amidships as the cutter came alongside and he watched anxiously as willing hands gently lifted the two English sailors up to the deck. He took one look at Parker and ordered him below to the sick bay before turning his attention to Burke.

'Are you all right?' he asked.

The Stoker Petty Officer grinned. 'Yes, sir. Thank you, sir. Young Parker didn't carry out his drill – I suppose he didn't realize we'd come to the surface in the middle of that oil slick.' He nodded appreciatively as one of the German sailors handed him a mug of Schnapps. The spirit burned his throat as it went down but the warmth soothed his belly and he felt surprisingly little the worse for his experience.

'Are you fit enough to answer a few questions?' Schneider asked.

Burke thought quickly. This was the moment to make his story sound true. But he had to play it carefully if the bluff was to succeed.

'I reckon so, sir. But can you tell me something first? Did you pick up the other lads?'

Schneider frowned. 'We rescued your comrade – is that what you mean?'

'No, sir. I know about him. A couple more of our chaps came up with the First Officer about five minutes before we escaped. Are they okay?'

The *Korvettenkapitan* turned to Ohlson. 'Did you see any other survivors, Number One?'

Ohlson shook his head. 'No. sir – only these two.'

'You'd best double the lookouts, *Oberleutnant*. I doubt if they're still alive but there is always the possibility of more men coming up.'

Ohlson saluted and hurried back to the bridge. Burke suppressed his grin of triumph. The mask of black oil coating his face made it impossible to read his expression.

'I don't think there'll be any more, sir,' he told Schneider as he played his trump card with the innocence of a veteran poker player. 'The for'ard escape hatch was jammed and something went wrong with the flooding valve in the second chamber just as we were ready to leave.' The Petty Officer knew that German U-boats had no similar means of escape and he was relying on the *Korvettenkapitan*'s ignorance of the DSEA apparatus. 'Only five of us got clear. The rest are trapped. But she was flooding so fast I doubt if they'll last long any way.' He stopped abruptly as if realizing he may have given away too much information to the enemy.

'The submarine is finished?' Schneider asked.

Burke contrived to look guilty. He averted his eyes from the destroyer captain's face.

'Couldn't rightly say, sir,' he said woodenly. 'My name

58

is Charles Burke. Rank, Stoker Petty Officer. Service Number 737 6377.'

'What was the name of your submarine?'

'Sorry, sir. Not permitted to say. Name, rank and number only.' Burke wondered whether the propaganda stories about German brutality towards prisoners were true. If they were he only hoped he could stick to his story under interrogation. Thank God young Parker was in such a bad way. They would not be able to question him for several hours. And by that time it would be too late.

Schneider did not seem annoyed by the reply. In fact he smiled. 'I understand, Petty Officer. You have nothing to fear – not all Germans behave like the Gestapo, whatever you may have heard. The *Kriegsmarine* respects the rules of the Geneva Convention.' He paused to decide his next line of questioning. 'I am not asking you to betray any secrets. But my orders are to destroy that submarine. If your boat is crippled and sinking I have no wish to add to the agony of your trapped shipmates by a further depth-charge attack. Is she finished?'

Burke nodded his head reluctantly. 'She won't come up again, sir. And I'd swear to that. We were flooded back as far as the control room. And when I got out, the sea water was already seeping into the battery compartment . . .' He left the rest of the sentence unfinished and Schneider nodded understandingly.

'Chlorine gas,' he said simply.

'That's right, sir. Which is why young Parker is so bad. He got a couple of whiffs before we entered the escape chamber. Lucky he's still alive, I reckon.'

'Thank you, Petty Officer.' The *Korvettenkapitan* paused, took a small cigar from his pocket, and lit it. He thought carefully for a few moments before taking his decision. 'In view of what you have told me, I will not renew the attack. Your comrades will be allowed to die in peace.' He gave a curt bow. 'Now if you will excuse me. One of my men will take you below and get you cleaned up. We shall be back in Kiel within twelve hours.'

Burke hoped he was not overplaying his hand. 'Aren't you going to wait to see if any more survivors come up?' he asked.

Schneider shook his head regretfully. 'You said yourself that no one is likely to get out. And we are too low on fuel to hang about. It is disturbing to know your shipmates are dead – but at least they had the honour of dying for their country. They can do no more than that.' He turned away before the British prisoner could see the emotion in his eyes and made his way to the bridge.

'Signal the rest of the Division to abandon the attack,' he told Fischer. 'Steer 0-9-0, helmsman. Full ahead both. Hands to secure from Battle Stations.' He glanced across at Ohlson who was still staring moodily at the oil slick as it passed astern. 'Tell the pilot to give me a course for Kiel, *Oberleutnant*. And tell him I want to cross the bar on the morning tide.'

Moving to the fore section of the bridge he watched the other destroyers wheel obediently into line astern and then, as if reluctant to abandon the area, he searched the patch of oil darkened water with his binoculars in a last effort to spot survivors. He shrugged at the futility of his hopes and picked up the telephone.

'Wireless room? Send the following signal to Kapitan Miskin, Flotilla 6 HQ, Kiel. And repeat it to OKM and OKW. Message reads: *Most Immediate. Enemy submarine destroyed. Returning with two prisoners. Oslo route now clear.*'

Grossadmiral Raeder had difficulty in concealing the look of triumph on his face as *Kommodore* Villem entered the conference room and handed him the signal slip. He waited impatiently for Keitel to finish speaking and then rose to his feet.

'I have just received a message from my Flotilla Commander at Kiel, gentlemen. The enemy submarine has been located and destroyed by the *Kriegsmarine*.' He paused and glanced across at von Erich, the *Luftwaffe*'s senior representative. 'I understand the Navy's success was obtained without the assistance of the *Luftwaffe*. But,' he added complacently, 'I need hardly say this does not unduly surprise me.'

Halder, the Chief of Staff, put his pen down on the table with a heartfelt sigh of relief. 'My congratulations, *Herr Grossadmiral*. The convoy is no doubt now safely on its way. Von Bock will have the additional armoured units he needs.'

'But not *when* he needs them, *Herr General*,' von Erich retorted sourly. He had a sneaking suspicion that Raeder was taking undue credit for the Navy's success and the thought rankled. He paused as a smartly uniformed *Luftwaffe* staff officer came into the room, raised his arm in a Nazi salute, and handed him a piece of buff coloured paper. He took it, slipped on his reading glasses, and scanned it quickly. 'This is a signal from *Reichsmarshal* Goering, gentlemen,' he explained importantly. 'It seems that the enemy submarine was actually located by *Luftwaffe* aircraft.' He took off his glasses and threw a crushing glance in Raeder's direction. 'I will not comment on the Navy's customary attempt to steal all the glory. I only wish to point out that, because of the *Grossadmiral*'s excessive caution, the convoy will have been delayed unnecessarily and the tanks will not reach von Bock's Army Group until it is too late.'

All eyes turned on Raeder. His normally grey face flushed pinkly as he fought back his anger, but he had difficulty in concealing the tremor of fury in his voice as he stood up to speak.

'On the contrary, *Herr Fliegergeneral*. When my Staff checked the charts at OKM it was decided that the *Kriegsmarine* would have ample time to dispose of the enemy submarine before the convoy reached the critical danger zone. The Convoy Commodore was accordingly instructed to maintain speed and course. The Panzer Division will therefore arrive at Eljsford at precisely 4 am as planned. You may rest assured that Operation Case Yellow will have its full armoured strength available.'

Von Erich snorted but said nothing. Raeder may have outpointed him on this occasion but there was plenty of time to settle scores at a later date. And at least he had the satisfaction of knowing the *Luftwaffe* would be playing the leading role in the assault on France and the Low Countries. The *Führer*'s memory was notoriously short. He would soon forget the matter of the convoy. But he would take a long time to forget the destruction Goering intended to wreak on Rotterdam.

Feldmarschall Keitel nodded as he listened to Raedar's assurance. He was relieved that von Erich seemed content to accept the situation. With only a few hours left before Hitler unleashed his *blitzkrieg* against the West, he had more than enough problems to handle without the complication of a personality clash between the Navy and the Air Force. He glanced sharply at the faces of the men sitting around the table, picked up his silver pencil, and brought the conference back to its main task.

'May we proceed, gentlemen? I think you may take it that von Bock will have the 19th Panzers available by zero plus twelve, Halder. Will that be satisfactory?' He paused and waited for the Chief of Staff's nod of agreement. 'Very well. We must now move on to consider Item 54(a) – the railway concentrations which von Rundstedt has brought to our attention. We have very little time left and I want the amended routes confirmed back to *A Gruppe* HQ by midnight . . .'

Hamilton opened his eyes and looked at the luminous face of his wristwatch. His head was pounding and it seemed strangely difficult to draw an adequate amount of air into his lungs.

Rapier was still operating under emergency lighting conditions and, in the dim glow of the low-power lamps, the men sitting at their diving stations resembled a line of shadowy anonymous corpses. The air, already stale after nearly twenty hours of battened hatches, was tainted with the smell of scorched rubber and smouldering insulation from the burned out main fuse panel. And although the fire had been quickly extinguished the combustion had consumed a substantial amount of the submarine's precious oxygen reserves.

Hamilton had no idea how long he had been unconscious. As far as he could estimate, only thirty minutes had elapsed since *Rapier*'s final plunge to the bottom. And apart from the initial salvo of depthcharges, when the submarine began submerging the enemy had left them in peace. He tried to recall the details of his escape plan but, starved of oxygen, his bemused brain refused to function. Without fully comprehending what was going on he concluded that the world had suddenly moved into slow motion. He remained sitting on the deck of the control room while he tried to digest this fascinating prospect.

Staring down at his watch again, he struggled to work out the time. The hour hand was pointing to the figure eleven. He managed that part of the exercise without too much trouble. But it took several moments to distinguish the minute and second hands. The effort of concentration brought a film of perspiration to his forehead. He decided it was 10.37 pm.

'It's 10.37, Number One,' he told Collis and, to emphasise the importance of the discovery, he pointed to the watch. Having stated the obvious, he relapsed into a morose silence, as if unable to follow the thought process to its logical conclusion.

Collis nodded. He was, if anything, in an even worse condition than the skipper. The energy expended in supervising the DSEA escape had drained his last reserves of stamina and he had literally collapsed on the floor of the control room after reporting completion of the operation.

Hamilton tried to clear his fuddled brain and think clearly again.

'Pull yourself together, Number One,' he said unsympathetically. 'Don't you realize it's over three hours since Burke and Parker went into the chamber? That means we've been submerged for more than twenty hours.'

63

Collis digested the information. Any attempt to think constructively only made his headache worse and he felt too exhausted to move.

'Things aren't so bad then, sir,' he said finally. 'We should be able to stay down for about thirty hours without any trouble.'

'In normal conditions perhaps, Number One. But that electrical fire burned off a hell of a lot of oxygen before we put it out. If we don't do something pdq, we've had it.'

Collis wondered vaguely what fire Hamilton was talking about. He could detect a faint aroma of burned rubber in the atmosphere, but its significance made no impression on his wandering mind. He was totally unaware that he had been semi-conscious and comotose for the past two hours. He could not understand the urgency but, inspired by the skipper's example, he made a determined effort to rouse himself and, gingerly grasping one of the vertical pipes running up the bulkhead, he dragged himself to his feet. His head swam with the physical exertion and he would have fallen but for Hamilton's timely helping hand.

Conditions inside the submarine were worsening with every passing minute and Hamilton was forced to bend forward from the waist in an effort to draw an adequate amount of air into his lungs.

'What's the damage situation, sir?' Collis asked as he forced his sluggish brain to concentrate.

'We're flooded for'ard and I'm only holding the water at bay by increased air pressure in the bow compartment. We can't use the pumps. The circuits have blown and the hand pumps make too much noise. Apart from that,' he grinned with forced confidence, 'we've managed to caulk most of the leaks and O'Brien says he's cleared the water from the battery well.'

Collis smiled weakly. 'What with, sir? A bucket?'

'Yes – and a sponge.' The First Lieutenant's attempt at a joke was a reassuring sign. If they were to get *Rapier* out of this mess, Collis's help was vital.

'What about the instruments?'

'The master gyro's gone wild. And most of the gauges are smashed. O'Brien reckons the motors are still working, and the blowing gear. But he's not so sure about the diesel units. We've lost telemotor power for the search periscope and the attack 'scope is unserviceable. Apart from that,' Hamilton added cheerfully, 'we seem to be okay. At least the pressure hull is intact.'

Collis steadied himself against the bulkhead, drew the foetid air into his aching lungs, and wiped the sweat from his face with the back of his hand.

'So what's next on the agenda, sir?'

'We've got to get *Rapier* back to the surface, Number One. If we delay much longer there'll be nobody left with enough strength to operate the blowing and venting gear. Do you feel up to it?'

Collis nodded. He knew he was lying, but he could not let the skipper down. 'There's just one thing, sir,' he said slowly. 'What happens if the Boche are still waiting for us?'

Hamilton paused, glanced around the control room to ensure no one could overhear the answer, and lowered his voice.

'If that proves to be the case, Number One, I'm afraid we have no option. We surrender.'

Collis said nothing for a few moments. He understood what the decision had cost Hamilton and he admired him for making it. A fool would have brazened it out and prepared to fight. But *Rapier* was in no condition to do battle. The skipper had done more than his best. Now his duty lay in saving his men.

Hamilton picked up the telephone and pressed the button to the engine room. There was a long pause but finally the receiver was lifted and he could hear O'Brien coughing.

'Are you alright, Chief?' he demanded sharply.

'Now don't you be after worrying about us, sir. We're doing fine . . .' He broke off as another paroxysm of coughing racked his lungs. 'Just a wee whiff of the old

65

chlorine, sir. We seem to have got sea water in the cells again. Tyson and Lane are sorting it out.'

For a moment, even Hamilton's iron resolve wavered. The men were in a bad enough state already, without the added threat of chlorine gas. But the new danger only served to make it even more imperative for *Rapier* to be brought to the surface without delay.

'We're surfacing in a few minutes, Chief,' he told O'Brien. 'I want you to lay out the demolition charges. But don't set the fuses unless I give the word.'

'Understood, sir. I'll stand by the kingstons with Tyson, just to be on the safe side. But it'll be seeming a bit strange going to heaven downwards.'

'Let's hope they let you in,' Hamilton said drily. He wondered how the Irishman could still find a spark of humour in their present desperate situation. 'Good luck.'

He replaced the telephone, leaned against the bulkhead for a few moments to get his breath, and then moved to the periscope. Dorset was waiting by the controls with his head drooped forward on his chest. His breathing was shallow and he was obviously trying to conserve oxygen and, at the same time, preserve his strength. With the telemotors out of action the periscope would have to be raised manually – and that entailed physical effort. But Dorset had no intention of failing the skipper.

'Stand by to surface.'

'Hands to diving stations – stand by to surface.'

The normal unhurried routine of a well-trained crew responding to the executive order was missing. As Hamilton watched the exhausted men moving to their positions it seemed more like a slow motion ballet sequence from an old film. The fact that they could move at all was nothing short of a miracle and he felt a lump in his throat as he saw some of the older men literally dragging themselves to their diving stations.

'Close main vents. Put on the blow when you're ready, Mister Collis. Up-helm 'planes. Level at thirty feet.'

Hamilton picked up the telephone to the motor room. 'Half ahead both, Chief.'

Rapier responded sluggishly and the customary smooth operation of the surfacing drill was shattered by the agonisingly slow reactions of the men at the controls. Blowing valves opened out of sequence and compressed air screamed uselessly from fractured pipes until skilled hands could locate the leaks and bring the by-pass valves into use. The submarine rolled to starboard as the port ballast tanks emptied and her bows tilted upwards despite the efforts of the two coxswains to maintain trim. But the fact that she was rising at all in the circumstances was something of a minor miracle and Hamilton waited grimly as she lurched towards the surface like an inebriated whale.

By good fortune the depth-gauges were still functioning, although Blood was sweating with concentration as he tried to interpret the swinging red needle. In normal conditions he would have called off the readings automatically without bothering to think. But now his oxygen-starved brain was fuddled and slow to react. Staring up at the big round dial as if he had never seen a depth-gauge before his forehead creased into a frown as he struggled to make sense of the figures. And the needle had already reached the fifty feet calibration by the time he had collected his thoughts sufficiently to report, 'Sixty feet, sir.'

It was a similar story throughout the boat. Men collapsed over valve wheels and control levers, exhausted by the sheer physical effort required to move them and others took their places until they, too, fell to the deck gasping for air. The younger ratings coped better with the conditions than the veterans but it was the hard core of experienced Petty Officers who shouldered the main burden and, urging themselves on by sheer grit and determination, kept the submarine moving upwards.

'Forty feet, sir.'

Hamilton glanced at the depth-gauge and saw the needle already wavering on the thirty feet mark.

'Stop blowing; 'planes amidships – trim level. Up periscope!'

Harrison levelled off the for'ard 'planes to bring the bows down while Blood juggled the stern 'planes with the delicate care of a motorist steering on ice, as he tried to compensate for the loss of trim resulting from the half-open vents on the starboard side. Across the control room, Dorset was sweating blood over the manually operated mechanism of the periscope. The heavy bronze column rose from its well in the deck with agonizing slowness and Hamilton could hear the Leading Seaman gasping for breath. Stepping forward he pulled down the guide handles, grasped them firmly, and pushed his face into the rubber cup of the eyepiece. He offered a silent prayer that the optical prisms were still intact and waited while the tip of the column thrust above the wave-tops.

It was pitch dark on the surface and the glittering vault of the stars swayed gently against the rim of the black horizon. The periscope's questing eye swept through a complete circle as Hamilton surveyed the empty sea.

'Surface clear.'

Thumbing the lens into its sky-search position he checked the sparkling backcloth of stars for the tell-tale shadow of a patrolling aircraft.

'All clear! Down periscope. Surface!'

Taking his binoculars from the hook above the chart table, Hamilton made his way to the steel ladder leading to the conning-tower hatch. He paused at the barograph, but the delicate instrument had been shattered by the exploding depthcharges and its needle swung uselessly like a broken pendulum. Without the barograph he had no idea of the pressure inside the submarine, but experience told him it had obviously built up to a dangerous level and it was as well to take precautions.

'Hang on to my legs, Dorset. Once the upper lid is opened the pressure inside the boat will force the air out like a Force-8 gale. And I don't want to find myself being shot out of the hatch like a jack-in-the-box.' He started up the ladder and paused after removing the clips of the lower hatch. 'The fresh air will make everyone feel sick,' he warned the men in the control room. 'I don't care how ill you are – I can't control Nature. But it must not be allowed to interfere with your duties. As far as I know, the surface is clear. But the enemy might be hiding somewhere in the darkness waiting to attack us as soon as we appear. So no matter how ill you may feel, remember that the life of every man aboard this boat depends on your instant obedience to orders.' It sounded callous, but the men understood what the skipper meant. 'If I sound the diving klaxon, all hands are to abandon ship immediately. We're in no condition to submerge again and whether we like it or not there is no alternative. The engine-room staff have been ordered to lay out demolition charges so the rest of you must get out as quickly as you can.'

Dorset's muscular arms clasped the skipper's legs as he slid the bolts off the hatch and unfastened the clips. The pent-up pressure inside the submarine was like that of a volcano poised to erupt and its sudden release tore the hatch-cover from Hamilton's hands. It flew back with a metallic clatter that sent frightening echoes bouncing round the empty steel vault of the conning-tower compartment. He just had time to grasp the sides of the hatch as a roaring blast of foetid air funnelled past his body. The smell was indescribable and he retched violently. But, ignoring his personal discomfort, he dragged himself out of the narrow hatchway on to the bridge.

'Start the fans, Number One. Bridge party topsides at the double!'

As the fresh salt air ventilated the control room the majority of the men were sick on the spot and the sour smell of vomit marred the clean taste of the sea breeze for which they had waited so long. But it did not deter them. And despite the unpleasantness of their physical reactions they drew the oxygen deep into their starved lungs with thankful relish.

CHAPTER FOUR

0125 hours. 10th May 1940

A spume of phosphorescent spray whispered back from *Rapier*'s bows as she gathered speed and steered westwards towards the open wastes of the North Sea. It had taken more than two hours of unrelenting slog to make good the damage to the diesel engines and plug the leaks in the hull. But the fresh air had given the crew a new lease of life and the ragged cheer that echoed through the submarine when O'Brien finally persuaded the engines to fire again testified to the soundness of their morale.

Despite the men's enthusiasm, however, Hamilton had few illusions about their chances. *Rapier*'s radio remained out of action and the flooded bow torpedo compartment had been evacuated and sealed off from the rest of the boat. In addition, the temporary ring main which the electrical artificers had jury-rigged through the submarine was unlikely to stand up to the strains placed upon it and they had lost over 25% of their amperage reserves when Tyson had had to disconnect and isolate the battery cells contaminated by sea water.

Rapier was a submarine in name only and, as Hamilton reminded himself soberly, they were all living on borrowed time. He did not dare to dive. Once the leaking hull submerged they would never return to the surface again. And he had no weapons with which to fight. Their survival so far was due only to his own stubborn determination to live, backed by the courage and resource of his men.

But if *Rapier* was to make it safely back to base they needed something else. Luck. And Hamilton knew they had already overdrawn their account with the notoriously fickle goddess of fortune.

He suppressed a yawn, rubbed the sleep from his eyes,

and leaned over the edge of the bridge as he stared ahead into the darkness. The soft throb of the diesel engines rumbled comfortingly behind his back and the exhaust smoke drifted lazily astern where it hung suspended like a black canopy, sheltering the bubbling white wake that marked the submarine's passage through the water.

'Objects to starboard, sir!'

Hamilton bent over the voicepipe. 'Stop engines. Mister Collis to the bridge please.' Closing the lid of the speaking tube he joined Rivenham on the starboard side. 'What bearing?' he asked the lookout.

'Almost ninety degrees off the bow, sir. About three miles distant. Looks like a ship.'

Hamilton put the binoculars to his eyes, swung towards the rough bearing Rivenham had given him, and searched into the night. The horizon seemed completely empty at first but, as his eyes adjusted to the darkness, he was able to detect a vague black shape moving slowly in the distance. He watched carefully for a few seconds and saw the shadow resolve itself into two separate and distinct objects, both moving towards the submarine, each with a whisper of spray curving from its bows. He lowered his glasses as Collis joined him.

'We've got a couple of ships approaching at about ten knots, Number One. Do we have any contact on Asdic or hydrophones?'

'Sorry, sir. All our detection gear is still u/s. And so's the blasted radio.' The First Officer scanned the northern horizon with his own binoculars. 'Do you think our destroyer friends are coming back to finish us off?'

'No. The shapes are too indistinct to be certain, but they're standing too high in the water for destroyers. They look more like freighters.'

'Enemy?'

'Probably,' Hamilton confirmed laconically. 'They're steering south. I'd say it was a German convoy coming down from Norway in ballast.'

The ships were nearer by now and Rivenham, who had

been keeping them under close observation with his high-powered Ross lenses, broke into the whispered conversation.

'I can just pick out a couple of small ships on the wings, sir. Seem like armed trawlers. And I've got three distinct merchant ships in sight now.'

'Nothing else?'

'No, sir.'

Hamilton opened the cover of his voicepipe. 'Half ahead both. Steer 2-3-0.'

Rapier swung slightly south of her previous course and, glancing up at the sky, Collis reasoned that the skipper was moving into the dark shadow of the moon.

'We'll have to open up the bow compartment, sir,' he warned Hamilton.

'Why?'

'We've sealed off the torpedo flat, sir. We'll have to open up if we're going to attack.'

'No chance, Number One. I've no intention of tangling with the enemy with a crippled boat.'

'But supposing it's a troop convoy, sir,' Collis protested.

'Then they're going to be lucky, Number One,' Hamilton said decisively. 'And use some commonsense. They'd have a stronger escort than a couple of armed trawlers if they were troop transports. In any case, Hitler's not likely to pull his soldiers out of Norway at this stage of the campaign. Don't forget we're still holding Narvik.'

It was so totally unlike the skipper to refuse battle that Collis wondered whether the unbearable stresses of the previous twenty-four hours had finally broken Hamilton's nerve. Not that he could be blamed. After eight months of continuous operations – many of them in minus zero conditions north of the Arctic Circle – battle fatigue and sheer physical exhaustion were bound to take their toll. Even so, he decided it was worth making one last effort.

'I reckon we could make a surface attack, sir,' he urged. 'That way we can avoid the risk of diving. And we could easily outrun the trawlers if they spot us. The U-boats have been using a similar tactic against our Atlantic convoys – and getting away with it.'

'We are not engaging the enemy, Mister Collis,' Hamilton said firmly. 'And that's final.' He could appreciate his First Lieutenant's eagerness but, relieved of the heavy responsibilities that rested on the shoulders of a Commanding Officer, it was easy to think more of the glory than the harsh realities of a given situation. 'Get below and tell the Pilot to give me a course for Harwich. And make it crystal clear to Murray that he *must* get that radio working.'

Collis examined the skipper's face carefully in the dim glow of the binnacle light. Hamilton's expression reflected the strain he was under. His face looked grey and haggard and his mouth was set in a grim straight line. The First Lieutenant felt sure that the CO's hands were trembling as he grasped the bridge rail and stared ahead over the bows, but the iron bonds of discipline stopped him from speaking his mind and, with a shrug, Collis turned towards the hatch. He was just thrusting his legs down into the circular hole when a vivid red glare lit up the northern horizon. And, as he paused, he heard a low rumble drift across the black waters.

Heaving himself out of the hatchway he hurried back to the starboard side of the bridge to join the other men straining their eyes through the darkness in the direction of the mysterious convoy.

One of the merchant ships was lying stopped in the water with a ball of fire hanging over her stern as angry flames took hold of her poop. And as Collis reached the bridge wing the ship shuddered under a violent internal explosion that rolled like a clap of thunder beneath the night sky. A second explosion followed moments later. And, tilting sharply on to its beam ends, the stricken ship turned turtle. The hiss of red hot steel quenched by the cold sea was clearly audible to the men on the submarine and, for a few seconds, they stood transfixed in stunned silence.

'Christ All bloody Mighty!'

Hamilton ignored Rivenham's incredulous blasphemy. 'Must have run into a floating mine, Number One,' he observed dispassionately to Collis. 'Can't be a submarine attack – we're the only boat in the Skagerrak. Even the Norwegians have abandoned this area.'

But, even while they watched, the developing drama on the northern horizon gave the lie to his words. The third freighter, lying slightly astern of the main group, heaved violently as another torpedo struck home and, almost immediately, began settling by the bows. She blew off steam and a ghastly shriek wailed across the sea as her siren jammed. She was obviously sinking fast and the watchers on *Rapier*'s bridge saw her boats being lowered in a frantic effort to escape before she vanished beneath the surface, like her erstwhile companion.

'I've never seen a mine blow up *two* ships,' Collis said quietly. 'If that's not a submarine attack, then I'm a Dutchman.' He looked hopefully at Hamilton. 'I reckon we ought to give our friend a hand, sir. There's only one ship left. It seems a pity to let it go.'

Hamilton moved away from the side of the bridge and leaned over the magnetic compass to check *Rapier*'s westward course. Then he put his mouth to the voicepipe and ordered: 'Full head both.'

Collis looked at the skipper incredulously. What the hell were they running away for? Even if *Rapier* was unable to make a torpedo attack, her mere presence in the vicinity would serve to confuse the convoy escorts. And a skilful piece of coat-tailing could give the unknown submarine a chance to close and finish off the last remaining transport. Hamilton seemed to read his First Officer's thoughts.

'I'm sorry, Number One, but we keep out of trouble. We don't know the identity of the submarine making the attack. For all we know it could even be a U-boat making a rather expensive mistake. *Or* it could be one of our own convoys. Without radio communication we have no way of knowing what the true situation is. Now get below and carry on.'

Another ear-splitting explosion thundered across the sea and Collis saw the third and last transport list sharply to port as a torpedo struck her amidships in the boiler room. The possibility that it might be a friendly convoy had not occurred to him before. But, rather than deterring him, the thought only increased his inclination to turn north and investigate. One glance at the skipper, however, was enough to warn him that his hopes would be in vain. Hamilton was once again staring straight ahead over the bows ignoring the holocaust taking place on the starboard horizon. He seemed intent on one thing only – getting the hell out of it before *Rapier* became involved in the slaughter.

Collis had never served with a coward before. And it was an experience he had no desire to repeat.

*

Captain Reginald Crockett-Jones· listened to Hamilton's report without comment or apparent interest. As a veteran member of the Royal Navy's submarine branch – his first appointment had been back in the halcyon pre-war days of 1913 – there was little he did not know about the art of underwater warfare. And he had a formidable reputation for not suffering fools gladly. In his time he had served under Max Horton in the Baltic and with Martin Nasmith in the Dardanelles. He had commanded one of the notorious steam driven K-class submarines in 1919 and escaped from a sunken submarine in the Irish Sea. The row of campaign and medal ribbons on his chest testified to his experience and courage but, unfortunately, he was a remote and self-opinionated man who believed in keeping people at a distance.

He was short in stature, but squarely built and his pepper-and-salt beard bristled intimidatingly as *Rapier*'s skipper completed his verbal account of the ill-fated patrol. The unventilated office was hot and stuffy, but the Captain's dislike of fresh air kept the windows firmly closed.

A pregnant silence followed, but Crockett-Jones gave no indication of what was going through his mind and his stubby fingers drummed the top of the desk as he digested the contents of the report.

Hamilton had not slept for seventy-two hours and the strain of keeping *Rapier* afloat over the last three days and nights had drained every last reserve of energy from his body. The heat inside the cramped office did nothing to help and he felt his eye-lids beginning to droop.

'Better sit down before you fall down, Lieutenant,' Crockett-Jones barked at him unceremoniously.

Hamilton obeyed thankfully. He wondered what the Captain's reaction was going to be. He was under no illusion that it would be favourable or even appreciative. Crockett-Jones's reputation for petty snobbery was well-known in the Service and Hamilton knew he was starting off with a severe disadvantage as an upperyard man.[1]

'I suppose you did the best you could in the circumstances, Lieutenant,' he said finally.

Thanks for nothing, Hamilton thought to himself. What the hell does the old bastard want – blood?

'Thank you, sir.'

'A pity you made no attack on the convoy,' Crockett-Jones continued disparagingly. The fact that *Rapier*'s torpedo compartment had been evacuated and that, without a radio, Hamilton had no means of identifying the mysterious group of ships, was conveniently overlooked. 'It was sheer luck the Dutchman attacked as you were leaving the scene.' The Captain somehow contrived to make it sound as if Hamilton had been running away. 'But of course I suppose you couldn't be expected to know the enemy ships were carrying a complete Panzer division.'

Hamilton's sleepiness fell away as he digested what Crockett-Jones was saying.

'I beg your pardon, sir. I must have misheard you. I thought you said a *Dutch* submarine carried out the attack.'

'Quite so, Lieutenant. A Dutch submarine.' The Captain

[1] The Royal Navy term for an officer promoted from the Lower Deck.

saw the bewilderment in Hamilton's eyes and his customary asperity softened as he permitted himself the rare luxury of a smile. He always took pleasure from being the bearer of bad tidings. 'But you've been out of radio contact for the last four days so you don't know what's been happening.' He leaned forward with obvious relish. 'Things were pretty bad when you left. But you can take my word for it, they're a bloody sight worse now.'

Hamilton wondered what he had been missing. If a Dutch submarine had torpedoed the convoy it meant that Holland was now in the war – and, thank God, on Britain's side. But surely that was good news. So why the devil was old Toffee[1] so pessimistic.

'I suppose I'd better fill you in with the details,' the Captain continued. 'Hitler launched a *blitzkrieg* attack on Belgium and Holland the same night *Rapier* was depth-charged. That's why the Dutchman acted against the convoy. Apparently he'd been watching the destroyers attacking your boat but, like a good little neutral, he did nothing about it. When he received the War Signal from the HQ of the *Koninklijke Marine* at The Hague, just after midnight, he guessed – wrongly as it turns out – that you'd been patrolling the area for an enemy convoy. So he waits around and it turns up. Then bang, bang, bang. And it's gone.'

Crockett-Jones's enthusiasm made it only too obvious that he admired the Dutch submarine commander's initiative and thought Hamilton should have been equally enterprising. But, for the moment, the Lieutenant was not particularly worried what Toffee thought. The events of the past few days were too shattering to digest immediately and he was still puzzled by a number of things.

'But how did you hear about *Rapier*, sir?'

'From the Dutchman, of course. The Netherlands Government surrendered at 11 am this morning. All their naval forces capable of moving were already in England, or

[1] Crockett-Jones's nickname at Dartmouth Naval Academy had been Toffee-nose; for obvious reasons.

on their way.' He stood up and walked across to the tightly latched window and beckoned Hamilton to join him. Together they looked down on the grey, murky waters of Parkstone Quay. 'There's his boat, the *Swaardvis*, tied up to Number Six mooring pontoon. She came in yesterday on the afternoon tide. Her Commanding Officer told us about the attack.'

Crockett-Jones turned away from the window and sat down behind his desk again. He waited until Hamilton was seated before continuing.

'When *Swaardvis* arrived in Harwich, her skipper, van Drebbel, reported that he'd seen survivors from a British submarine coming to the surface in DSEA kits and he naturally assumed the unfortunate boat had been sunk by depthcharges. We checked Flotilla records and found *Rapier* was the only unit operating in the Skagerrak, so when you failed to transmit your routine radio call on two successive nights, we inevitably came to the same conclusion. Added to which, Berlin Radio put out a report of a British submarine being sunk by German escort forces north-east of Denmark.' Crockett-Jones paused for a moment, stared up at the wall chart in silence, and then looked down at his hands. 'The Admiralty issued an official communiqué last night.'

Hamilton's stomach turned over as he thought of the wives and families of his men. And, with something of a shock, he realized that his own parents would have heard the dread news as well.

'Have the next of kin been informed, sir?' he asked.

Crockett-Jones shook his head. 'I don't think so. There's been such a flap these last few days I doubt if the Admiralty is handling any routine paperwork at the moment. They've more important things to do.'

Routine paperwork!

That was all it meant to the top brass, Hamilton thought bitterly. No consideration for the grieving relatives who received the fateful telegram with its terse and unsympathetic: *Missing believed killed in action*, nor remorse for the unnecessary suffering caused by jumping the gun.

'Don't you think we should advise the Admiralty at once, sir. The issue of the telegrams should be stopped at all costs, assuming we're not too late anyway.'

Crockett-Jones dismissed the idea with a curt shake of his head. 'Later, Lieutenant, later. We've too much on our plate at the moment to worry about a few erroneous casualty telegrams. First things first.'

Hamilton flushed with anger and the sudden rush of blood restored a little of the colour to the grey exhaustion of his drawn face. 'I agree, sir. First things first. If you won't do it give me the telephone and I'll do it myself.'

'You will do nothing of the sort, Lieutenant,' the Captain snapped. 'And kindly remember you are addressing a senior officer. *I* give the orders around here.'

Hamilton allowed himself a cynical smile.

'And perhaps you will remember, sir, that according to the Admiralty I am officially dead,' he said quietly and with studied politeness. 'In the circumstances, I can hardly be given an order – *or*, for that matter, disobey it.'

Crockett-Jones looked up sharply. Temper blazed into his eyes as he confronted the young submarine officer across the width of the desk. But he realized he was beaten. And despite his arrogant egotism he was wise enough to acknowledge the fact. A tactical withdrawal in the face of the enemy's superior fire-power was the commonsense thing to do. He was beginning to realize the reason for Hamilton's reputation and he hid his retreat behind the smokescreen of a forced laugh.

'Very well, Lieutenant. This time you win.' His eyes hardened. 'But next time you will find it more difficult. Grenson warned me you were a problem when I took over this Command. And I'm beginning to see what he meant.'

Picking up the telephone he gave a number and extension to the Wren operator on the switchboard and, as he waited for the connection, he put his hand over the mouthpiece. 'You might be dead, Hamilton. But they haven't buried

79

you yet. Help yourself to a cigarette and then we'll discuss your funeral.'

Hamilton was still seething inside, but he acknowledged the gesture of conciliation with a thin smile and took the cigarette. He was beginning to realize the advantages of being dead. It was certainly the first time a junior submarine commander had ever got the better of Crockett-Jones. Lighting the cigarette, he waited while the Captain passed his message to the appropriate Admiralty clerk, and he noticed a thoughtful look on Crockett-Jones's face as he replaced the receiver.

'Whatever might have happened to the crew, Hamilton,' the Captain said slowly, 'I think *Rapier* will have to remain sunk. If your little ruse fooled the Dutchman it's quite certain the Germans fell for it as well. And it would be a pity to give the secret away. We might be able to use it again on another occasion.'

'I agree, sir. But there's still that communiqué. Even though the telegrams will be cancelled, the men's families are certain to have heard about *Rapier*'s loss on the wireless – and if there's no word of survivors they'll assume the worst. It isn't fair on either them or my men, sir.'

Crockett-Jones rooted through the untidy pile of papers on his desk. 'Fortunately, I don't think it's as bad as that, Lieutenant,' he grunted as he searched for the file he wanted. 'Ah, yes . . . here we are.' He opened the folder and took out the slip of a Telex message. 'We've been a bit cagey about submarine losses recently,' he explained. He put on his reading glasses. 'This is the actual text of the communiqué: *The Admiralty regrets to announce that one of our submarines is overdue and must be presumed lost. The next of kin are being informed.*' He put the slip back in the file and took off his glasses. 'So, you see, the Germans have been told just enough to confirm that they sank the submarine they attacked. But, and thank God in the circumstances, we haven't revealed its name.'

Hamilton nodded. He felt a little easier about the situation. 'So presumably no one will connect *Rapier* with the communiqué, providing the casualty telegrams are not despatched. But I can't see the point of maintaining a lie.'

'There are two reasons, Lieutenant. Firstly, as I indicated earlier, your idea of sending a couple of survivors up through the escape hatch obviously worked. It convinced the Germans and our communiqué has confirmed their assumption. We might want to use the scheme again, so we won't want to give the game away if we can help it. Sooner or later the enemy will discover the truth. But that could take them a long time and I intend to exploit the bluff in the meantime.'

'And what's the second reason, sir?'

Crockett-Jones shrugged. 'Frankly, Lieutenant Hamilton, I don't know. But I'm damned sure there's some way we can make use of a submarine that, officially, has been sunk. You'll have to leave that one to me.'

Hamilton could see the Captain's point. But he had little doubt that news of *Rapier*'s survival would soon be common knowledge. The Royal Navy's submarine branch was a small, close-knit organization and it would not take long for the truth to leak out.

'*Rapier* has suffered serious hull damage, sir,' he reminded the Captain. 'It will be several weeks before she's operational again.'

'Don't you believe it,' Crockett-Jones snorted. 'Hitler's invasion of Holland and Belgium has done wonders for the morale of the British worker. Our dockyard mateys would work through twenty-four hours non-stop if we let 'em. As it is, we have to practically drag them away from the job and send them home for a good night's sleep. And then they spend most of that on ARP duties or fire-watching. Take my word for it, they'll have your old tub operational again within seventy-two hours. And if they don't, they'll have me to reckon with!'

Hamilton stifled a yawn and tried to fight off the drowsiness that was threatening to envelope him. So much had happened since he had left Harwich on that last fateful patrol. And he found it difficult to grasp the enormity of the disaster that had befallen the Allies.

'Are things really *that* serious, sir?'

'Officially – no. The BEF is making an organized withdrawal – "shortening its lines of communications" and all that bloody rubbish. But the Service chiefs and the civil servants at the top who know about such things reckon the French will crack. If they do, England will be wide open to invasion.' It was obvious from the expression on Crockett-Jones's face that he relished the prospect of some real fighting at last. 'The Dutch capitulated this morning and the Belgians won't hold out much longer. They tell me no one has ever seen anything like Hitler's *blitzkrieg* tactics before. We just can't stand up to them.'

'But what about the Maginot Line? I thought it was impregnable.'

'And so it might be – to a frontal assault. But the Boche have got more sense. They swept around the side of it and outflanked the defences. I've been receiving reports from Whitehall all through the day. It's sheer bloody chaos. The Panzers have broken through the line of the French 1st Army, their 9th Army is in a state of complete disintegration, and the 7th has retreated on Antwerp leaving the BEF exposed to a flank attack. Thank God I'm in the Navy and not the poor bloody army. They must be going through hell.'

'Surely there is something we can do?' Hamilton asked. The scope and magnitude of the disaster left him feeling stunned and, in his present exhausted state, he found it difficult to understand the sheer speed of the collapse.

'What do you suggest? We can't send our big ships in to give gun support. The *Luftwaffe* would blast them out of the water within twenty-four hours. And in any case they're fully committed to some damn fool scheme to hold northern Norway.[1]

Hamilton rubbed his hands across his face in an effort to

[1] Crockett-Jones was referring to Operation Hammer and the dispositions made by the Home Fleet following its abandonment.

82

clear away the sleepiness. He felt sure the Captain was exaggerating. But, completely absorbed by his own little corner of the war since September 1939, he was, like many officers involved in day-to-day combat operations, out of touch with world events. Unable to accept the brutal truth of Crockett-Jones's comments he felt appalled and ashamed at his senior officer's apparent defeatism.

'It can't be as bad as you say, sir,' he protested. 'And if it *is*, then I'd like permission to do something about it.'

Crockett-Jones smiled wearily. 'Don't worry, Lieutenant. You'll be doing *something* about it very shortly. In fact we *all* will. We won't have the option. I know what's going through your mind but, take my word for it, we're in the most dangerous spot we've been in since Napoleon threatened to invade us – and it was the Navy who got us out of that particular little problem too. There is no army in Europe, least of all our own, capable of standing up to Hitler's Panzer divisions. And once Goering lets his *Luftwaffe* loose on England I don't give much for our chances. But we'll win. Somehow we'll win. I'm not going to let that damned Austrian corporal get the better of us – even if I have to go down to the beaches and fight the Boche with my own bare hands.'

The thrust of the Captain's jaw and the belligerence of his bristling beard showed he meant what he said. And Hamilton suddenly realized that Crockett-Jones was not being defeatist. He was merely speaking the plain, unvarnished truth.

Seemingly unaware of the impression he had made on the young submarine skipper, Crockett-Jones changed the subject abruptly. He had had his say. Now it was time for business.

'I'm building up a scratch flotilla from the various allied submarines that have escaped to join us,' he told Hamilton. 'We've got a Polish boat, the *Bielik*, just down from Scapa and the 7th Flotilla. Been working with us since September last year. Top-notch skipper and damned fine crew. And a couple of small Norwegian boats joined us after their

Government surrendered. They're not large enough for long-range work, but they'll be useful in the Narrow Seas. And, of course, there's *Swaardvis*, the Dutchman who arrived yesterday. They're a good bunch and they've got good reason to hate the Boche.'

Crockett-Jones paused to light his pipe. He puffed hard to get it going and a wreath of blue smoke curled lazily over his head as it searched for a way out of the tiny airtight office. He threw the spent match into his ashtray.

'I suppose we ought to count *Gladiateur* as well,' he added, as if reluctant to do so.

'Isn't that the French boat that joined us a few months ago on an exchange basis, sir?' Hamilton queried. He could recall the arrival of the French submarine and he could still remember the bad impression made by her skipper, Gaston Bourdon, on his first night in the wardroom. He wondered how the Frenchman would fit in, but decided that, as it was not his problem, there was no point in worrying about it.

'That's the one,' the Captain nodded. 'Queer sort of a cuss. I don't think he likes us very much.'

'Nor anyone else, from what I've heard. Still, I believe he's a good skipper and that's what matters.'

'So we've got one Polish, two Norwegian, a Dutch, and a French submarine. A bit of a mystery flotilla, what?' Crockett-Jones chuckled over some private joke. 'And who better to lead them than the skipper of a boat that's officially been sunk by the enemy.'

'You can't be serious, sir,' Hamilton protested, as he realized what the Captain was getting at.

'I most certainly am, Lieutenant. I want a group of commanders who are prepared to do things which I dare not order an officer of the Royal Navy to do. This little bunch fit the situation to a "t". And you're just the man to command them.'

'But I'm an officer of the Royal Navy too, sir,' Hamilton pointed out. Toffee was notorious for his piratical views on the sanctity of International Law. And God knows where his wilder flights of fancy might lead when he got the bit firmly between his teeth.

'You might well be, Lieutenant. But there is one small point you seem to have overlooked.' Crockett-Jones chuckled deep inside his beard at the thought of turning the tables on *Rapier*'s commander. 'You're *dead*. And that, no doubt you will agree, makes all the difference.'

*

The wardroom of *Bielik* measured no more than twelve feet by seven feet, but its snug brightness made it an ideal meeting place for the exiled skippers now gathered in Harwich to join Crockett-Jones's new flotilla. Despite its cramped confines and grey steel walls, it looked comfortable and homely. And the other submarine commanders found Sosnkowski's Polish charm plus his apparently inexhaustible supply of Russian vodka a combination difficult to resist.

It was van Drebbel's first acquaintance with the formidable little Pole and he was suitably impressed. Sosnkowski looked the perfect image of a story-book pirate captain. Short in stature, but with the powerfully squat physique of a Japanese *sumo* wrestler, he wore a black eye-patch over one eye and sported an aggressively pointed beard. The Dutchman felt almost disappointed that he was not carrying a parrot on his shoulder, but decided, reluctantly, that perhaps it was too much to expect. Parrots and submarines hardly made an ideal combination, although he could remember reading of a German U-boat skipper in World War 1 who had taken a camel across the Mediterranean in his submerged submarine.

'Ah, the Flying Dutchman!' Sosnkowski greeted him as he entered the wardroom. 'Most appropriate. We all sail the seas without a home port to which we can return. Perhaps,' he shrugged sadly, 'we are all Dutchmen.' He unscrewed the top from a fresh bottle of vodka and filled one of the empty glasses. He handed it to van Drebbel with a formal bow. 'Your health, my friend.'

The clear fiery liquor burned the Dutchman's throat as

he responded to the toast and Sosnkowski laughed as van Drebbel spluttered for breath.

'Drink up, Dutchman. Tonight we must be merry. Tomorrow we die.' He drained his glass with a flourish and added inconsequentially, 'An old English proverb, you know.'

Erik Nansen nodded solemnly. At twenty-two he was the youngest of the submarine commanders present, but the serious expression on his face made him look almost the oldest.

'It is true what the *Kapitan* says,' he agreed dolefully. 'Our countries are dead. We should die too.'

'You can die when you like, Erik,' his companion grinned cheerfully. 'But I refuse to enter Valhalla until I have sampled the pleasures of Sosnkowski's girlfriend.' He raised his glass in a mock toast to the photograph hanging on the bulkhead. 'Blitzen titzen!'

Van Drebbel had not noticed the picture before. And as he glanced up at the bulkhead he immediately regretted having done so. His Calvinistic upbringing brought a flush of embarrassment to his cheeks as he found himself staring at the girl's naked breasts.

'I suppose it keeps the men amused,' he observed coldly.

'You mean it keeps Stanislaus amused, Dutchman,' Nils Laugen smirked. 'Not to mention myself.' He stared up at the picture wistfully. 'You know, my friends, one day I am going to visit Paris and . . .'

'You have everything wrong,' Sosnkowski protested. 'I only have the picture for a joke. It is the gallant Captain Bourdon who would not be amused if he could see all of you staring at his sister.'

'You do not expect me to believe that she is his *sister*,' van Drebbel said primly. 'No gentleman would allow his sister to pose for such a picture. And never would he display it.' He shook his head disapprovingly and salved his wounded decency with a large gulp of vodka.

Sosnkowski shrugged. 'I am telling you what Bourdon tells me. His sister is a star at the Lido in Paris. And the only photographs he has shows her . . . how do I put it? *Deshabillée?*'

'But why have *you* got it?' van Drebbel enquired. Despite the puritan blood pulsing in his veins he found his eyes irresistably drawn to the two thrusting breasts and the pert nipples.

'It's a long story, Dutchman. Our friend from Norway stole it from Bourdon's cabin. And I fought him for it.'

'And you damn well won,' Laugen added ruefully. He could still feel the bruises. Sosnkowski was like a wild bull when roused.

The Polish skipper clapped his arm around the Norwegian's shoulders and squeezed him in a playful bear hug. Reaching for the vodka he refilled his comrade's glass. 'It was a good fight. And, telling the truth, you enjoyed it.' His solitary eye twinkled merrily. 'And remember, I allow you to look at it for free.'

'Where *is* Captain Bourdon?' van Drebbel asked suddenly. 'I thought all the flotilla was meeting here tonight.'

'Probably sitting in his cabin, trying to work out a scheme for getting his sister out of the clutches of the Germans,' Sosnkowski grinned. 'He is absolutely convinced that Hitler will be in Paris within a fortnight. And he wants to get her away before the Boche get their hands on her.'

'Perhaps it is a good thing he is not here,' Laugen said. 'Bourdon is too full of his own importance. He certainly won't approve of our new flotilla commander.'

Sosnkowski looked up quickly. 'What is this, my friend. I have heard nothing. A new flotilla commander?'

'That's what they told me at HQ. A Lieutenant Hamilton, the skipper of *HMS Rapier*.'

The Pole whistled in surprise. 'Bourdon definitely won't like that. Aside from the fact that he hates the English almost as much as the Germans, it will upset his dignity to take orders from an officer junior in rank to himself. I hope I am there to see it happen.'

'But you are also senior to a Lieutenant, Stanislaus,' Nansen pointed out.

'Perhaps I am, my nordic friend,' Sosnkowski agreed sadly. 'But the Polish Navy no longer exists. And what is the use of rank when you have no country to serve. I am quite content to serve under *any* officer of the Royal Navy – even a midshipman – if I'm told to.' He turned to van Drebbel. 'I see you also have three rings on your sleeve. What do *you* say, Dutchman?'

Van Drebbel paused before answering. Although it was now nearly a week ago, the savage depthcharge attack on the English submarine was still vividly fresh in his memory. And even now he found it difficult to believe that anyone could have survived.

'Lieutenant Hamilton was in command of the submarine I reported as being sunk in the Skagerrak,' he said slowly. 'I would feel honoured to serve under a man who had proved himself to be a braver and better seaman than myself. Believe me, gentlemen, Lieutenant Hamilton is such a man.'

Sosnkowski opened a fresh bottle of vodka. He did not like being solemn. Life was too short for melancholy. Walking around the narrow wardroom he quickly refilled the empty glasses of his guests.

'My friends – let us drink a toast to this Lieutenant Hamilton. We are all going to hell anyway. And even if the Devil himself was sent to command our flotilla it would make no difference.' He drained his glass in a single gulp and put it back on the table with a grin. 'Now let's find the Frenchman and tell him the news.'

CHAPTER FIVE

1420 hours. Tuesday 28th May 1940

Capitaine de Corvette Gaston Bourdon had decided views on the conduct of the war and on the part he was destined to play in it. He also had equally strong opinions on the Royal Navy and its place in history.

One of his ancestors had been killed on the poop of the *Duguay-Trouin* at Trafalgar and another taken prisoner at Aboukir Bay. On his mother's side of the family, the Spanish branch, three other relatives had been killed by the English during the struggle for sea supremacy in the eighteenth century. Not that the British were always the enemy. His father had served in the Dardanelles in 1915 and had gone down with the battleship *Bouvet* in Eren Keui Bay, after she had run into an uncharted Turkish minefield. Every Frenchman aboard the mighty ironclad had been lost and, in Bourdon's opinion, the British Navy had looked on and done nothing to help the survivors.[1]

And now, to add insult to injury, he had been placed under the orders of a British officer. And worse – an officer junior in rank to himself. The insult rankled and he fumed in silent fury as *Gladiateur* threaded its way through the tortuous shallows of the Goodwin Sands on its way south to the Dover Straits. Standing alone and isolated on the port wing of the conning-tower bridge, he stared morosely at the eastern horizon.

Hamilton sensibly remained on the starboard side of the bridge with *Gladiateur*'s First Officer Henri Ailette. It had been Crockett-Jones's idea that he should take a trip in the French submarine. It was certainly not his own. Sosnk-

---

[1] In fact *Bouvet* sank too quickly to be given assistance and within minutes of the disaster to the French ship the British *Inflexible* and *Irresistable* also ran foul of the same minefield.

owski or van Drebbel would have been far more congenial company than Bourdon, but the Captain had insisted more forcibly than usual and Hamilton knew it was useless to argue.

He knew, moreover, that Crockett-Jones's selection of *Gladiateur* was no accident. The war situation in Europe was deteriorating with alarming speed and the French army was literally disintegrating under the powerful onslaught of Hitler's Panzer divisions. The German war machine was thrusting headlong towards the coast and there were already grave doubts whether the BEF could be extricated from the trap.

But, over-riding the military disasters, there was growing concern over France's will to fight on against such over-whelming odds. Certain French politicians – Pierre Laval, for example, and others like him – were known to sympathize with Hitler's Germany and a systematic campaign by Nazi collaborators was busy sapping morale.

If France were to fall, the allegiance of the French Fleet would become a matter of paramount importance and Hitler could on no account be allowed to gain control of the powerful warships now flying the French tricolour. And, if Mussolini decided to enter the war in support of his Axis partner, Britain would face an impossible task in the Mediterranean without the assistance of her Ally's navy. Yet, as the War Cabinet and other senior officers well knew, Admiral Darlan, C-in-C of the French Navy, was unreliable. And although he could probably be trusted not to surrender the Fleet to Germany on his own initiative, it was known that he would carry out whatever orders his Government gave him. And with sinister figures like Laval lurking in the political background, anything might happen.

The idea of acting the part of a spy aboard an ostensibly friendly ship was totally abhorrent to Hamilton's sense of fair play. But Crockett-Jones had spelled out the Government's dilemma with typical bluntness and, like it or not, he accepted there was no viable alternative. It was absolutely vital for Britain to find out what the ordinary matelots thought about continuing the war and how the officers were likely to react in the event of a French collapse. Until French morale could be accurately assessed, it was impossible to make contingency plans for the future.

Hamilton appreciated the reasons, but he found it difficult to see how the catastrophic military situation could be retrieved in the face of Hitler's successful *blitzkrieg* tactics. Even the war maps no longer made sense. And, having swept aside the shattered remains of General Blanchard's 1st Army, Rundstedt's victorious Panzer Divisions were now striking *northwards* in a devastating pincer movement that threatened to destroy what was left of France's once famous army. And news had come only that morning of the Belgian Government's capitulation.

Fighting a bitter rearguard action against overwhelmingly superior forces, the BEF was retreating westwards towards the Channel coast – their escape route to the south already blocked by enemy armoured units which had reached and occupied Abbeville on the night of the twentieth of May. The possibility of evacuation by sea was now being discussed at War Cabinet level, although professional military and naval opinion was pessimistic about the chances of success in the face of the *Luftwaffe*'s command of the skies above the beaches. And, in private, Service chiefs were preparing themselves for the possibility of losing over 300,000 men.

The Navy, as usual, was doing everything it could to assist and light forces had already moved close inshore to add the weight of naval fire power to the army's dwindling reserves of artillery. But the support bombardment was claiming a heavy price and losses were mounting on an alarming scale. To guard against a counter attack by enemy surface forces and U-boats, the Admiralty had decided to send all available submarines to cover the seaward flank of the bombardment units and Hamilton's newly constituted flotilla had received instructions shortly after breakfast.

The two Norwegians, van Drebbel in *Swaardvis*, and

Sosnkowski, had all left Parkstone Quay on the morning tide but, inevitably, Bourdon had protested against the order. In accordance with previously agreed arrangements, he argued for his release from the flotilla so that he could proceed to the Mediterranean. And, when Crockett-Jones pointed out sarcastically that, for the moment at least, there was no fighting in the southern part of France, Bourdon had flown into a rage and despatched a signal to his Commander-in-Chief for instructions. It was at this point that the Captain had sent him somewhat unceremoniously to sea pending Admiral Darlan's reply and ordered Hamilton to go with him.

The Frenchman was still smarting under the insult to his honour. He felt no more than a prisoner on his own ship, with Hamilton cast in the role of his jailor. And no amount of persuasion on the part of the British lieutenant could persuade him otherwise.

'Is he always like this?' Hamilton asked Ailette, as *Gladiateur* steered past the East Goodwin light-vessel and altered course to the south-east.

The First Officer shrugged. 'He has much on his mind,' he explained in defence of his skipper. 'Like all of us, he is worried about his family. It is only natural.'

'I can understand that,' Hamilton agreed. 'But we aren't going to beat the Boche by sitting around moping. There's not much we can do in submarines at a time like this. But at least we can try.' He glanced across at the dapper uniformed figure hunched morosely over the rails on the port side of the bridge. 'Why should it be any different for him than it is for others?'

'I do not know,' Ailette admitted. 'But I know he is worried about his sister – you may have seen her picture in *Bielik*'s wardroom.'

'Sosnkowski left on patrol before I had a chance to pay him a visit,' Hamilton told his companion. 'Why? You make it sound as if I missed something.'

'Only the finest pair of tits in Europe, my friend,' the Frenchman grinned. 'She is one of the stars of the Lido.

And with the Germans almost at the gates of Paris, I'm not surprised that he is worried.'

'I suppose I would be too.' Hamilton felt suddenly very curious about the photograph. 'But surely she's old enough to look after herself. I've heard of brotherly love but this seems to be taking things a bit too far. Are you sure she isn't really his . . .'

'They are quite definitely brother and sister,' Ailette confirmed hastily. 'Twins in fact. I understand their parents are dead and Bourdon took it upon himself to bring her up.'

'And you're trying to tell me he's more concerned for her safety than he is with the command of his own submarine.' Hamilton sounded understandably incredu- lous. It seemed that Bourdon was taking his fraternal responsibilities a little too seriously.

'Well, that's the way it is, my friend. He spends the whole of his time working out schemes to get his sister out of France before the Boche arrives. The rest of the war seems to take second place.'

The arrival of a runner from the wireless room put an end to the whispered conversation and Hamilton watched carefully as the seaman handed a slip of paper to *Gladiateur*'s skipper. Bourdon read it quickly, stared out to seaward in silence for a few moments as if considering a problem, and then moved to check the magnetic compass. He bent over the voicepipe to the control room.

'Alter course to 0-4-4, helmsman. Stand by to submerge in five minutes.' He looked up from the voicepipe. 'All hands clear the bridge for diving.'

'You've got the wrong course, Captain,' Hamilton pointed out politely. 'We'll be running too far south to reach the bombardment squadron before nightfall. And we certainly don't need to submerge until we're through the Oost Dyke. We've been promised maximum air cover until we're twenty miles from the Belgian coast.'

Bourdon restrained his anger with difficulty and, as the

93

other men cleared the bridge in obedience to his order, he confronted Hamilton across the top of the binnacle.

'You may be in command of the flotilla, Lieutenant,' he said sharply and with undue emphasis on Hamilton's rank. 'But please remember *I* am in command of this boat and, accordingly, I have complete authority to do as I wish.'

'The hell you do!'

'Quite so, Lieutenant. As you say – the hell I *do*.' The Frenchman's ability to twist the inflexion and change the meaning of the phrase demonstrated his almost perfect command of the English language. 'If you disagree with my orders, you are at liberty to have me courtmartialled. But only when we return to Harwich. Until then *I* give the orders and *you* will obey them. Understood?'

Hamilton remained completely cool, despite the provocation of the challenge. He knew that Bourdon was right and even though this, in itself, would not have normally deterred him, he was curious to know what the Frenchman was up to. Give the bastard enough rope, he thought, and he will hang himself.

'I appreciate the situation,' he said coldly. 'But if by changing course you are disregarding flotilla orders without a good and adequate reason, you may be quite sure I will deal with the matter on our return.'

Bourdon smiled. It was not a smile of triumph. It was more the smile of a man who had surmounted one difficult obstacle, but who knew there were more lying ahead. 'Thank you, Lieutenant Hamilton. I can assure you I have a very good reason. If you will wait in my cabin I will try to explain matters more clearly once we have submerged. Now if you will please go below . . .'

Bourdon's cabin was little more than a steel sided cupboard into which was squeezed a small desk, an armchair, a folding table, and a bunk. The bulkheads were covered by a maze of conduits carrying the electrical circuits and the main high-pressure air line ran down the centre of the deckhead. Small hand-wheels controlling the emergency by-pass valves projected in odd and unexpected places while, set in a panel over the desk, a duplicate set of instruments mirrored the more important gauges in the control room. It was much like Hamilton's own tiny cabin in *Rapier* and he glanced around it without much interest until his eyes chanced on a small framed photograph on the desk.

He recognized Bourdon immediately and decided that, judging by the background, it had been taken at Nice. On the right of the picture, and sitting beside him on the stone promenade wall, was a young woman. He wondered whether this was the sister he had heard so much about. If so, Hamilton concluded sourly, she seemed a far cry from the legendary beauty Ailette had spoken of so admiringly. It was, admittedly, a rather poor amateur snapshot. Perhaps it did not do her justice. He put the picture back on the desk and turned sharply as he heard the door open.

'I see you are admiring my sister, Lieutenant,' Bourdon said as he entered the cabin. 'That is the trouble,' he shrugged complacently. 'Like all men you find Antoinette irresistible.'

Hamilton flushed. The girl was not unattractive but he would have hardly described her as irresistible. However, he decided it politic to lie.

'She's certainly very beautiful, Bourdon. I'm not surprised you are worried about her.'

The Frenchman took a bottle of cognac down from a locker above the desk, found two glasses, and poured a generous tot of brandy into each. He pushed one across to Hamilton and motioned him to sit on the bunk.

'Of course, as you have probably heard, it is unusual to see a photograph of my sister with her clothes on.' He looked down at his cognac in obvious embarrassment. 'She is on the stage – one of the stars at the Lido in Paris,' he explained. 'Sometimes I wish she had chosen a more conventional profession. But she has a good body and she earns ten times as much money as I do. So how can I object?'

Hamilton tried not to look as if he was imagining the laughing dark-haired girl in the photograph without her clothes on. And he grinned to disguise his sudden interest.

'I am sure you do your best to look after her,' he said lamely. He was beginning to wish he had seen the picture Sosnkowski had pinned to the wall in *Bielik*'s wardroom. 'But I think you are worrying too much. I'm sure she is old enough to look after herself.'

'Perhaps so, Lieutenant. But there are many things you do not know – that nobody but Antoinette and myself know.'

'Such as?'

'I am convinced that Paris will fall to the Germans within a month. And, after Paris, France herself.'

Hamilton made a mental note of the French officer's defeatist attitude. Crockett-Jones had been right. Bourdon would have to be watched. He wondered what the French-man would do if his Government surrendered to Hitler. And, more immediately, what the hell had all this to do with the submarine's unscheduled alteration of course. He said nothing, but waited for *Gladiateur*'s captain to continue.

'You may consider that the fall of Paris would create no new problems. Militarily speaking, that may be true. But there is the personal side. I am sure you will agree that no man would wish to see his sister living in a city occupied by the Boche. I appreciate that many other Frenchmen will find themselves in a similar situation. But, in Anto-inette's case, the matter is more immediate.'

'I can understand your concern,' Hamilton said placat-ingly. 'But surely we ought to be concentrating our minds on defeating Hitler – not on tamely accepting the certainty of his victory. And I for one certainly do not accept that Germany has won the war, by a long chalk.'

Bourdon spread his hands. 'The ultimate defeat of France is inevitable. We are losing thousands of men every day the battle continues. The sooner we can negotiate an honourable peace the better. And that is why I must get my sister away from the country without delay.'

'For God's sake!' Hamilton snapped impatiently. Bourdon's defeatism was irritating in the extreme. If the rest of his compatriots shared his attitude it was little wonder that France was tottering on the brink of abject surrender. 'Your sister will be no more at risk than any other attractive French woman. Try to look at the situation objectively. Why should she be specially selected by the Germans?'

'Because Herman Goering wants her.'

'Good God, man! What next?' Hamilton had tried to hide his disbelief, but the Frenchman's statement was so far-fetched he gave up the attempt and allowed his incredulity to show. 'Who the devil put that damned-fool idea in your head?'

'I know it is difficult to believe, Lieutenant,' Bourdon said seriously. 'But, nevertheless, it is a fact. Goering paid several visits to Paris, incognito, in 1938, and he also visited her when she worked at the Taussig Palatz in Berlin last year. He has written to her and telephoned her many times begging her to go to Germany. But always she has refused. Once the Germans occupy Paris, any further refusal will be impossible. And would *you* like to see your sister as one of Goering's mistresses?'

Hamilton shook his head. He was beginning to understand the reason for Bourdon's obsessive fixation about his sister's escape. Even so, the whole thing seemed too ridiculous.

'Have you any proof?' he asked.

Bourdon fumbled for his wallet, slipped his fingers inside one of the pockets, and pulled out a folded letter and a photograph. Hamilton stared down at the picture. It was impossible not to recognize *Reichsmarshal* Goering – the fat jowls, the small, pig-like eyes, and the unctious smile that made him look like a chubby, overfed gnome. He glanced at the letter and saw the official crest at the top. *Meine lieber Antoinette* . . . He read no more.

'So what's the plan?' he asked Bourdon as he handed

him back the letter and the photograph. 'I will do everything possible to back you up.'

'Thank you, my friend. I will not forget to repay you.' *Gladiateur*'s skipper paused to sip his cognac. 'You will already have realized that I received a radio message a few minutes before I ordered the alteration in course. It was from an old naval colleague in Ostend. You will appreciate I prefer not to give his name.' Hamilton nodded and Bourdon continued. 'My sister arrived there safely this morning, but apparently all civilian traffic across the Channel has been suspended indefinitely. Calais and Boulogne are already cut off, so my friend will drive her to Nieuport, where he has arranged to hire a small motor launch. The signal I received gave me the rendezvous position and the time – 2300 hours tonight. It is against orders, I know, but will you give me your support?'

Hamilton thought quickly. He had little doubt that Crockett-Jones would take a less sympathetic view of the affair. But he had a feeling that, at some time in the future, it could be very useful to have Bourdon under an obligation. When the final crunch came and loyalties were divided, such a committment might just tip the scales. It was a cynical attitude to take, but Hamilton was fast learning that honour in times of war was an outdated concept – if you wanted to win. If rescuing Gaston's sister would ensure his loyalty to the Allied cause in the event of a French surrender, he considered that breaking flotilla orders was a very small price to pay.

'Very well,' he nodded. 'But the entire operation must be concluded by dawn. I cannot risk a submarine being exposed on the surface. And, of course, our orders to join the bombardment squadron must be obeyed once your sister is safely aboard.'

'But of course.' Having won his point, Bourdon was happy to accept any requirements Hamilton might make. He opened the drawer of his desk, drew out a large-scale chart of the Flanders coast and began to study it.

*

Gladiateur rolled gently in the off-shore swell as Bourdon shut off the motors and allowed the submarine to drift with the flood tide. Scudding clouds obscured the stars and the darkness of the sea merged imperceptibly into the black shadow of the low-lying Flanders coast. All navigation lights had been extinguished and the Frenchman had conned the submarine into position with all the ancient skills of a Napoleonic master mariner. Using the starboard bow hydroplane as a makeshift platform, the leadsman heaved his line, pulled it taut and called back the depth of water under the keel in a monotonous litany.

'*Mètres . . . dix. Mètres . . . huit.*'

Hamilton appreciated the superb seamanship involved as *Gladiateur* edged cautiously through the treacherous shoals of the Nieuwpoort Bank and, despite his personal dislike of the Frenchman, he had to admit that Bourdon knew how to handle his boat.

A slither of gravel under the keel-plates, so quiet it was audible only to trained and experienced ears, pin-pointed the rendezvous and in obedience to the skipper's order, a seaman on the foredeck threw out a light holding-anchor to prevent the submarine drifting with the tide. Bourdon glanced at his watch.

'Only three minutes to wait, Lieutenant,' he observed with a complacent smile.

Hamilton did not believe in handing out bouquets. He grunted, picked up his glasses, and searched along the coastline. He could just distinguish the shaded lights of a troop convoy moving out of the darkened town towards the battle line and a continuous flicker of red flame on the eastern horizon indicated how close the enemy had approached. It would only be a matter of hours before every French and Belgian harbour was sealed off by von Rundstedt's armour. And he speculated idly how Britain would extricate the BEF from the mess the French had landed them in. Even if Lord Gort succeeded in getting his troops safely to the sea before Hitler's Panzer divisions cut them off, it would be an impossible task to evacuate an entire army and its equipment under fire. He wondered why the hell the French did not counter-attack in an effort to relieve the pressure on Gort's rapidly narrowing escape route.

A soft burble of exhaust suddenly caught his attention and he swung his binoculars towards the stern. A small motor cruiser, looking distinctly unwarlike in its shining white enamel, was approaching from the direction of the shore and as the pilot glimpsed the submarine in the darkness he switched on a small searchlight.

'Turn that bloody light out!' Hamilton yelled angrily.

The Frenchman clearly did not understand English. The silver beam remained on and it danced like a fire-fly on the black water before focusing on *Gladiateur*'s conning-tower. Ailette, sensing the same danger as Hamilton, swore loudly in French, but the man in the wheelhouse of the launch seemed totally oblivious of the consternation he was causing. The boat continued to close the stern with its glaring spot-light still shining with blinding intensity.

Hamilton ducked behind the bridge screen. Either the man was a fool - or they had walked into a trap. And why the devil did Bourdon not *do* something? The submarine must be clearly visible both from the shore and from the sky and, half grounded on the sandbank, there was no chance of diving out of trouble if an enemy aircraft appeared unexpectedly. Hamilton had the familiar sinking feeling in his stomach that inevitably presaged danger and, like a cat, his senses pricked alert for the first warning signs. He cursed himself for allowing Bourdon to carry out his crazy plan. Next time, he promised himself, if there *was* a next time, he would not be so easily persuaded.

Bourdon was leaning over the side of the bridge, shouting a stream of excited instructions to the man in the motor launch. And, to judge by his growing impatience, it was obvious that the other man was making a mess of coming alongside the submarine. Hamilton decided he had waited long enough and he made his way across the bridge to join *Gladiateur*'s skipper.

'Tell that fool to switch off that bloody searchlight before he gets us all killed,' he told Bourdon crisply.

'There is no danger,' Bourdon reassured him. 'Phillipe is not an experienced boat handler and he needs the light to see where he is going.' He stopped while he yelled another string of instructions to the bewildered man in the launch and then turned back to Hamilton. 'He cannot come alongside the beam because of the ballast tanks. We will have to embark Antoinette over the stern – but he seems to be having trouble with the tide.'

'Why the hell don't you tell her to bloody well swim,' Hamilton said unsympathetically. 'We'll be caught with our pants down if the *Luftwaffe* shows up.'

Bourdon ignored the warning. Hoisting himself up on to the narrow rim of the bridge screen and grabbing hold of a periscope stay for support, he edged his way cautiously aft. His instructions seemed to confuse Phillipe even further and the launch suddenly shot backwards as he threw the engine into reverse. The searchlight swung towards the stern of the submarine and, as if eager to throw more light on the problem, he switched on the boat's red and green navigation lamps.

Hamilton fumed with impatience as he watched the clumsy handling by the boat's helmsman. And, snatching an unexpected opportunity to enjoy their skipper's discomfort, three members of the submarine's crew gathered over the edge of the bridge screen, making rude comments to each other in hoarse whispers.

But Hamilton was not interested in their coarse insults and lavatory wit. His ears had detected the whisper of another sound and he strained to identify it. It was difficult to isolate from Bourdon's shouts and the sharp crackle of the cabin-cruiser's outboard motor but, by an effort of concentration, he was able to distinguish the insistent throb of aircraft engines in the distance. He listened intently, like a terrier waiting for the rustle of a rabbit in the long grass. This time there was no mistaking the rhythmic rumble of a Ju 88's twin Jumo engines.

'Enemy aircraft approaching!' he shouted to Bourdon. But the Frenchman seemed too intent on his own immediate problems to concern himself with any other form of danger. 'For God's sake, man! Tell him to kill that light!'

Ailette recognized the sharp urgency in Hamilton's warning and with commendable speed he hurried to the voicepipe to order the submarine's gun crew on deck. Then, after instructing the bow number to cut the anchor line, he made his way back to join the British Lieutenant. He, too, could hear the dull roar of the approaching aircraft by now and he glanced anxiously at the sky.

'What the hell do we do?' Significantly he directed his question at Hamilton rather than his own commander.

'Get me a gun,' Hamilton snapped.

Ailette did not argue. Running back to the hatch he yelled an order down to the control room. Moments later he was back at Hamilton's side with a heavy calibre Schneider revolver.

'I hope you're not going to shoot him,' he grinned. Hamilton took the gun from him and smiled. Ailette's attempt at humour was a good omen. At least he was not going to panic in an emergency.

'It's a temptation,' he said laconically.

He looked over the side of the bridge. The launch was approaching from astern once again, but it was making barely one knot against the surge of the flood tide and it would take several minutes before the men on the fantail could throw a securing line. Well, sorry, Antoinette, he thought, but I cannot afford to wait that long. Resting his right arm on the bridge coaming, he sighted the revolver at the glaring white cone of light and squeezed the trigger. *Crack!*

The gun kicked viciously and the tongue of flame shooting back from the rear of the cylinder singed his eyebrows. He heard the shrill whine of a ricochet as the bullet glanced off the brass rim of the searchlight and screamed harmlessly away into the darkness.

'Stop firing! Have you gone raving mad!'

Hamilton ignored Bourdon's shrill protest, rested his forearm on the edge of the bridge screen again and gripped his right wrist with his left hand for extra steadiness. The glare of the searchlight made aiming difficult but, squinting down the barrel, he tried a second shot.

This time he missed completely and the splintering thud of the heavy calibre bullet burying itself in the wooden superstructure of the wheelhouse was followed by a string of Gallic curses from the unfortunate Phillipe. And, amidst the confusion, Hamilton's ear picked out a new voice – a woman's voice – screaming a torrent of abuse interspersed with obscene, if apt, oaths which seared the darkness with the ferocity of a flaming spear. Antoinette Bourdon might be the star of the Lido and the toast of Paris, but she was obviously a past-mistress in the unladylike art of swearing. Hamilton thought she sounded decidedly interesting.

The sinister drone of the aircraft was now plainly audible and Hamilton knew he had only seconds left to save the situation. Crouching behind the screen, he took careful aim.

This time he made no mistake. The searchlight snapped off like a snuffed candle and the sound of breaking glass tinkled across the black water. Bourdon vaulted down to the deck of the bridge with the agility of an angry monkey, pushed Hamilton back against the periscope standard, and snatched the revolver from his hand.

'You damned fool!' he shouted. 'Now we can't see the boat.' He raised the gun and pointed it at Hamilton's chest. 'If anything . . .'

But the threat was never finished. A sudden terrifying roar deafened his ears as the Ju-88 plummetted from the clouds and he stared in open-mouthed horror. Faced by this new dilemma he paused irresolutely. And in that split second of indecision Hamilton acted.

'Man the guns! Full ahead both engines!'

Ailette did not hesitate. The crisp authority of the command demanded instant obedience and he did not stop to question Hamilton's right to give orders. As the gun crews scrambled to their weapons he bent over the voice-pipe and translated the order to the men in the control room below. Black diesel smoke erupted from the exhaust trunks abaft the conning-tower and *Gladiateur* lurched off the sandbank like a slothful alligator moving to the attack.

'Stop engines!' Bourdon countermanded. 'Full astern both! Ailette, get a line over the fantail!'

Even as he shouted the orders, the enemy bomber swooped in from astern with its machine-guns blazing and, simultaneously, every man on the bridge threw himself flat on the deck to escape the hail of bullets. Only Bourdon remained on his feet – waving his revolver ineffectually at the departing Ju-88 as it circled upwards for its next attack. Despite everything, Hamilton could not help admiring the Frenchman's primitive courage, even though his defiance was more symbolic than practical.

The 20mm anti-aircraft gun came into action as the bomber climbed away and he ducked to one side to avoid the red-hot cartridge cases tumbling down from the breech chute. The French sailors might be badly led, but they certainly did not lack guts and the fierce defensive barrage would help to deter the enemy pilot from coming quite so close on his second run.

'Hard a'port!'

Ailette passed the order to the control room and the submarine's bows swung obediently in response to the English officer's command. Moving to the starboard side of the bridge, Hamilton stared into the darkness astern for a glimpse of the motor launch. A pin-prick of green light winked out of the gloom and he saw the boat was still within hailing distance and was closing on *Gladiateur*'s fantail. Phillipe, whoever he was, seemed to have intelligence despite his abysmal lack of seamanship.

'Ailette! Send a deck party to the fantail with lines and a life-belt,' he told the Executive Officer. 'Try to get a line to the launch and we'll take it in tow until we've got rid of that damned bomber.'

Ailette obeyed briskly. He could not help wondering

what would have happened if Hamilton had not taken over. The skipper seemed to have abdicated command of the submarine in his anxiety to rescue his sister.

'Look out, sir! Here comes the Boche again!'

Hamilton heeded the warning only just in time and, ducking behind the protection of the bridge screen, he heard the angry rattle of the Ju-88's machine-guns as the bomber made its second pass over the submarine.

The group of men caught on the fantail stood no chance and Hamilton saw them reel and stagger as a hail of bullets scythed across the after casing. Only Bourdon seemed to have emerged from the attack unscathed and he was already busy helping one of the wounded seamen.

'Ailette! Take over,' Hamilton swung himself on to the ladder leading to the stern. 'I'm going aft to give the skipper a hand.'

Jumping down on to the casing, he groped his way towards the fantail on his hands and knees. The narrow steel plating of the after deck was slippery with spray and freshly spilled blood and Hamilton shuddered with disgust as he felt his hands touch the yielding warmth of human flesh. Looking down at the grey-pink pulp, he retched violently. Then, after a pause to recover, he continued to crawl slowly along the exposed casing to where Bourdon was crouching over a seriously wounded sailor.

'This one's nearly gone,' the Frenchman told him unemotionally. 'I'll stay with him.' He nodded his head towards the stern. 'We managed to get a line to the launch. Try and haul it alongside.'

Hamilton glanced aft. The motor cruiser was in flames and it was drifting away from the submarine as the tide swept it into the darkness. Obviously dazed by the machine-gun attack, Bourdon had not grasped the realities of the situation. In the circumstances, however, Hamilton decided it might not be such a great disadvantage. At least the Frenchman would not be able to interfere. Crawling to the farthest tip of the fantail, he hauled himself on to his feet and clung to the jack-staff while he assessed the position.

It was not exactly encouraging. Whipped by an off-shore breeze, the flames were rapidly gaining control and in the red glare of the fire he could see the girl standing on the steel pulpit that overhung the bows. Unlike her brother, she seemed completely calm and self-possessed, but Hamilton could read the mute terror in her face. Shrugging off his jacket, he began to pull off his shoes.

'Jump for it!' he shouted. 'For God's sake, *jump*! She'll go up like a bomb in a few seconds.'

'I can't swim,' she yelled back.

'Don't worry – I'm on my way.' He tore off his remaining shoe and clambered carefully on to the propellor guard. 'You'll be okay – *jump*!'

He stared down at the white cauldron of water churned up by the starboard propellor and decided that, with a modicum of luck, he could probably escape the suction of the screw as he dived in, although getting back to the submarine would be a different matter. But this was no time to balance the odds. Taking a deep breath, he plunged into the ice-cold sea. As he hit the water he heard the motor launch explode into a thousand pieces of red-hot metal. If Antoinette had not carried out his instruction, it was too damned late now.

Kicking hard with both legs, he broke surface and looked around quickly to establish his bearings. What was left of the motor boat had already vanished beneath the water and now that the hungry sea had swallowed the flames the surface was suddenly black and empty. Striking out powerfully on the approximate bearing of the sunken cabin cruiser, he searched the darkness.

By some undeserved miracle the girl's head suddenly bobbed to the surface less than two yards ahead. Her eyes were wide open with fear and her arms were threshing at the water in blind, mad panic. Yet some primitive instinct gave her the sense to keep her mouth closed and, as she slid beneath the sea, Hamilton reached out, grasped her shoulders, and dragged her to the surface again.

Spitting the water from his mouth he gripped her firmly under the arms. 'Relax – you're quite safe,' he told her. 'Just let yourself go limp. And for Christ's sake don't struggle.'

Antoinette obeyed and as her body went slack Hamilton rolled over on to his back, hooked his forearm under her chin, and began the slow crawl back to the submarine. It seemed to take an eternity but, suddenly, a torch flashed out of the darkness to guide him and, as he approached the stern, a life-line snaked down over the side. Hamilton grabbed it thankfully and allowed himself to be towed gently towards the fantail. *Gladiateur* was lying stopped in the water and a dozen eager hands were waiting to drag him clear of the sea.

'Get them both below,' he heard Bourdon say. 'Take them to the wardroom and fetch plenty of hot towels and some dry clothing.'

Hamilton felt the hardness of the deck-plating under his feet and, helped by one of the men, he hauled himself upright. He swayed unsteadily as he walked across to the submarine's skipper.

'Return to base . . . your sister's alright but she might need medical attention. We can't afford to take chances.'

Bourdon put his arm around the Englishman's waist and helped him towards the conning-tower ladder. 'But the bombardment squadron,' he reminded Hamilton. 'You gave strict orders . . .'

'To hell with orders, Captain,' Hamilton said shortly. 'As Flotilla Commander, I am ordering you back to base. The girl must come first.'

Bourdon guided Hamilton gently on to the ladder. He made no comment, but he wondered why the Lieutenant had suddenly changed his mind. He shrugged. Antoinette seemed to have a habit of making men behave irrationally. And with a knowing grin he followed Hamilton up the companionway to the bridge.

'I'm okay now, thanks,' Hamilton told him, as he stuck his feet into the upper hatch. 'I just need a hot drink and some dry clothes.' He paused and the darkness hid the sudden gleam of eagerness in his eyes. 'You'd better stay on Watch. I'll look after Antoinette. I don't think we want the men involved.'

Bourdon nodded solemnly. It was a point he had not considered before. But of course the Englishman was right. The fact that Hamilton's motives may not have been entirely altruistic did not occur to him. But there were times when Bourdon could be incredibly naïve.

Hamilton paused outside the curtained entrance to *Gladiateur*'s wardroom and beckoned to one of the seamen loitering in the narrow passageway.

'Do you speak English?'

The man nodded.

'What is your name?' Hamilton asked.

'Grecy, sir.'

'Very good, Grecy. Now I want you to remain here on guard. No one, absolutely *no* one, is to be allowed into the wardroom. Is that understood?'

Grecy nodded. His expression remained stolidly blank, but his eyes betrayed what he was thinking. And he was thinking that the English officer was no fool. He chivvied the other members of the crew out of the passageway as Hamilton went through the curtained entrance to the wardroom and then, with a thoughtful look on his face, he took up his position guarding the corridor as ordered. At that precise moment he would have given a month's pay to have changed places with the Englishman.

Antoinette was lying on the lower starboard bunk. Her eyes were closed, but she seemed comfortable enough and, after briefly checking her pulse, Hamilton stripped off his wet clothes, quickly rubbed himself down with a warm towel, and began to consider what he should do next. Ducking into Bourdon's private cabin, he found a bottle of brandy and poured himself a generous measure. The spirit burned his throat, but as the warmth hit his stomach he felt the chill evaporating from his bones. Picking up the glass, he went back into the wardroom.

Despite her bedraggled appearance, Antoinette seemed none the worse for her ducking and as he looked down at her Hamilton was able to appreciate her beauty for the first time. She was in her late twenties, but her delicately smooth skin was unblemished and a subtle maturity in the set of her mouth added an exciting sophistication to her youthful appearance.

Hamilton knew what he had to do next and he swallowed another mouthful of brandy to bolster his nerves and quieten the tremor in his hands. The fact that she was unconscious made it easier, of course, but, even so, he felt slightly apprehensive as he reached down to unfasten the pearl buttons of her blouse. Lifting her gently, he slipped the garment over her shoulders, drew her arms from the sleeves, and dropped it down on the deck. The hook fastening of the skirt made his fingers fumble awkwardly, but he finally managed to undo it and, grasping the hem, he pulled it over her hips, lifted her feet clear, and let it join the sodden blouse on the floor beside the bunk. A small label inside the waistband proclaimed it to be a creation of Christian Dior. At that precise moment, however, it looked more like a dish-rag that had seen better days.

The Englishman stared down at her body and swallowed hard. Despite the chill still permeating his bones, he was sweating and he paused for another shot of brandy. Then, his courage suitably bolstered, he bent over the bunk to resume his self-imposed errand of mercy.

The delicate lace brassière presented several problems until he realized that it was front fastening, and, having discovered the vital secret, it took only a few moments to remove.

It was not difficult to see why Antoinette Bourdon was the star attraction of The Lido. Her breasts were small but exquisitely formed and, like so many Parisian showgirls, the nipples were large, prominently erect, and sensually inviting. Hamilton stared like a wide-eyed schoolboy savouring his first nude photograph in *Lilliput*. He had seen a woman naked before – several in fact – but there was a certain ambience about Antoinette's slim body that sent his pulse racing. In an attempt to cover his confusion he grabbed one of the warm towels and began drying her.

In the circumstances it was an unwise thing to do. And as he felt the firmness of her breasts yielding against his hands through the thin towelling he had to grit his teeth to fight off the distraction. He was just congratulating himself on his powers of self-control when she stirred softly under his hands and clasped her arms around his neck.

'That's nice,' she murmured. 'Do it some more.'

Hamilton started with surprise. And, suddenly realizing that his hands were still cupping her breasts through the thin towel, snatched them away like a scalded cat.

'How long have you been awake?' he demanded.

'All the time,' she told him with an impudent grin. 'I thought you might be shy if you knew I was watching you.'

'Satisfied now?'

'Not yet – but I'm sure I will be just as soon as I've got the rest of my things off.' She looked up at him and veiled her eyes demurely. 'After all, you should receive a reward for rescuing me.'

A loud commotion outside the wardroom curtains saved Hamilton from the embarrassment of finding a suitable reply. Outside, in the passage, Grecy was arguing with somebody.

'Good God! It's your brother. What the hell do we do?'

Antoinette seemed singularly unflustered and Hamilton suspected it was not the first time she'd been caught in a compromising situation. She pulled the towel up to cover her breasts and closed her eyes.

'He won't worry if he thinks I'm still unconscious.' She giggled suddenly. 'But I suggest you put your pants on or you'll give the game away.'

Hamilton flushed. He had forgotten he was completely

naked. Grabbing a pair of trousers he climbed into them. And with unnecessary modesty he turned his back on the girl as he fastened the flies.

Bourdon looked worried as he came into the wardroom. He glanced at his sister who was lying apparently unconscious on the bunk, ignored the story told by the dripping wet clothes lying on the deck, and turned to Hamilton who was busy sorting out some more hot towels.

'Is she alright?' he asked anxiously.

'She'll be fine. Luckily she didn't swallow any water and once she's dried off and into some warm clothes she won't be any the worse for her swim.'

Bourdon cocked an inquisitive eye at the bunk. Hamilton could guess what was in his mind, but he said nothing. Antoinette looked peacefully innocent.

'Do you need any help?' *Gladiateur*'s skipper asked.

Hamilton considered it was the last thing he needed. But somehow he doubted if that was what the Frenchman meant.

'No, I can manage. But thanks all the same.' He paused. 'I think she'll be coming to shortly. Can you get the steward to rustle up some hot coffee?' He grinned to himself. Antoinette would have heard the request. And with one of the crew likely to enter the wardroom within the next few minutes she would have to behave herself, like it or not.

Bourdon seemed reassured. He nodded and opened the wardroom curtains. 'Thanks again, M'sieur Hamilton. There are some sweaters of mine in my locker. They should fit her. I'll leave you to it.' He paused suddenly before finally leaving. 'By the way, we've had a signal ordering us to shift base to Sheerness. Apparently the flotilla's been moved from Harwich for some reason. The pilot says we'll be in the Medway inside three hours. And I've radioed ahead for a doctor and an ambulance, just in case.'

Antoinette waited until the curtain closed behind her

brother. Then she sat up on the bunk. The towel dropped down to her waist and her breasts heaved angrily.

'You're a pig!' she told Hamilton.

He sat down beside her on the bunk. She was obviously referring to his request for coffee. Taking the towel in his hands he started to rub her dry again. She shivered under his touch.

'But I'm a nice pig,' he reminded her.

Antoinette stretched like a cat. Then her arms went around his neck once more and she nuzzled him gently with her nose.

'When am I going to thank you?' she pouted.

Hamilton did not answer. Suddenly, he hoped the steward would take his time over making the coffee.

CHAPTER SIX

2330 hours. 4th June 1940

Hamilton leaned his elbows on the edge of the bridge screen and stared moodily ahead over *Rapier*'s bows. There were times, he concluded bitterly, when he seemed to be running a one-man lifeboat service instead of commanding a combat submarine.

He had saved his men from certain death during the depthcharge attack in the Skagerrak and he had rescued Bourdon's sister. Even his DSO, the blue and red ribbon of which glowed proudly on his left breast, had been won during a daring operation to save a group of captured English merchant seamen from the notorious prison ship, *Nordsee*.[1] And now he was setting out yet again, on *another* rescue mission.

Crockett-Jones had been unexpectedly understanding about the incident with Bourdon's sister and, to his surprise, Hamilton found the Captain all smiles and bonhommie when he made his report. The fact that he had allowed the Frenchman to disobey flotilla orders passed without comment and even the failure to join up with the inshore bombardment squadron failed to produce the anticipated reprimand. Crockett-Jones seemed far more interested in Bourdon's unguarded remarks on the war in general and in the possibility of a French capitulation, than the garbled details of the abortive patrol. And Hamilton noticed the Captain was scribbling hurried notes on a sheet of green paper – the colour code denoting a Top Secret report for the Director of Naval Intelligence. Hamilton had mentally shrugged and pushed the implications to the back of his mind. As a naval officer he had no wish to get involved in the politics of the war.

[1] See *Fighting Submarine*.

And now, as eight bells tolled the beginning of the Middle Watch, he could see Sosnkowski's *Bielik* and the Dutch *Swaardvis* following in *Rapier*'s wake. He wondered what the fiery little Polish skipper felt about their latest errand of mercy. Turning away from the rails he joined Collis by the binnacle.

'What's the situation on Dynamo?' he asked. Operation Dynamo was the code name for the evacuation at Dunkirk.

'It's more or less over, sir. The latest reports say we've managed to get over 300,000 men away.'

'After the way we've mishandled the war so far, we don't deserve miracles. Perhaps last week's national Day of Prayer did some good,' Hamilton observed cynically.

Collis glanced down at the gyro repeater and passed a helm correction to the steersman in the control room. 'Some people would believe anything,' he said. 'Mind you, the fog was providential. It kept the *Luftwaffe* away from the beaches. Not even the Navy could have pulled it off if Goering's dive bombers had got through.'

Hamilton glanced up at the myriad stars twinkling brightly in the clear vault of the night sky. 'One thing's for certain, Number One. There'll be no bloody fog to cover us when *we* go in. If the Stukas find us, we'll stand as much chance as a snowball in hell.'

Collis made no comment. Leaning over the side of *Rapier*'s bridge he checked to make sure their two flotilla mates were still following astern. Then he held his binoculars to his eyes and checked the horizon. He wondered what would happen when the dive bombers began attacking.

'Of course, Dunkirk is the Big Show,' Hamilton continued casually as if there had been no pause. 'They'll write books about it after the war – probably make films as well. The miracle of the beaches. That's what they'll call it. And no one will remember the dozens of minor operations that mugs like us had to carry out to bring off the rest of the army.'

'I suppose someone's got to do it,' Collis said simply.

'Too right *someone's* got to do it,' Hamilton agreed. 'But why does it always have to be us? And what bloody fool thought up the idea of sending three submarines to evacuate a bunch of bloody pongoes. If that's what they want us to do, they ought to strip out *Rapier's* torpedo tubes and fit her up as a damned troop transport. Then maybe I'd qualify for a job as skipper of the Woolwich Ferry after the war.'[1]

'Why don't they use destroyers?' Collis demanded bitterly. 'Why submarines?'

'Because of air attack, I suppose,' Hamilton told him – apparently forgetting he had asked the same question himself. 'It's a two hundred mile round trip. And no surface ship could make it in one piece. That's one thing we've learned about the limitations of sea power since Hitler invaded Norway. Surface ships can't operate in an area controlled by shore-based aircraft. A submarine stands a slightly better chance, because it can make its approach submerged and dive again once it has completed its mission. The only thing you and I have to worry about is the bit in the middle.'

Collis failed to see the humour in Hamilton's deliberate understatement. As far as he was concerned, they were heading on a suicide mission. And he did not find that in the least amusing. As Hamilton had remarked – it was the bit in the middle that worried him.

'We're not going to win this damned war, are we, sir?' he asked suddenly.

Hamilton did not seem surprised by the bluntness of the question, and as he turned to face the young Executive Officer his expression was deceptively bland.

'I think we will, Number One,' he said quietly. 'I know the French have practically thrown in the sponge and the rest of the world has written us off. But this isn't the first

---

[1] Hamilton's comments were prophetic. The Imperial Japanese Navy made considerable use of submarines to transport and evacuate troops during the Solomon Islands campaign. And later in the war the Japanese Army actually built and manned its own transport submarines.

time we've started a war badly. And I'm damned sure it won't be the last. So wash such ideas out of your head – I've had my bellyful from Bourdon already.'

Collis, for all his nervousness, was a determined young man and he did not intend to yield easily.

'Let's be frank, sir. You're the skipper. You *have* to say that. But we've served together for over a year now. Be honest.'

Hamilton was disappointed in the Lieutenant, although he did not despise him as he did Bourdon. Collis was young and highly intelligent – perhaps too intelligent. But he was soft. Born with the proverbial silver spoon in his mouth, he lacked the toughness his skipper had acquired in fighting his way from the Lower Deck to commissioned rank.

'Alright, Number One. I was being less than honest,' he admitted. 'When I said I thought we were going to win I was speaking as your commanding officer. If you want my honest personal opinion – I *know* we'll win.' He paused to let the statement sink home. 'It isn't a question of hard facts, or statistics, or lines and arrows on a map. It's an inner knowledge that Britain can never be beaten in a fair fight. And just think back to your history lessons at Dartmouth if you don't believe me. We've beaten damned nearly every country in the world at one time or another – the Germans, the Russians, the French, the Dutch, the Spaniards. I won't bore you with the complete list.'

Collis's knowledge of history was considerably deeper than the skipper's and he could think of various occasions when those self-same countries had also defeated England, but he diplomatically forbore to mention the fact. He could not, however, resist scoring one point.

'You're forgetting the Yanks, sir. They beat us in 1776 and 1812.'

'You can't count the Americans, Number One. They're the same as we are. If two Englishmen have a fight one of 'em has got to lose – unless it's a draw. So I'm not letting you get away with that argument. And,' he added petulantly like a child worsted by logic, 'we've certainly beaten everyone else.'

Collis had to admire Hamilton's confidence, even if he despised his chauvinism. But the skipper was only fooling himself with his jingoistic view of the world. His brother in the Foreign Service had warned him that Mussolini would soon be joining Hitler – in time to harvest the fruits of victory, without the inconvenience of fighting for it. And from what Collis had heard at his Club, the war clouds were gathering over the Far East as well. Unless the United States joined in, it would be impossible for the old European imperialist powers to hold on to their possessions with the limited resources at their disposal, if the Japanese decided to attack Malaya and the East Indies. He had served his last commission on the China Station and he had been suitably impressed by the efficiency and power of the Japanese Navy.

'Signal from *Bielik*, sir.'

The discussion ended abruptly as the Signal Yeoman spotted the shaded lamp flashing from the conning-tower of the Polish submarine and reported to Hamilton. Scribbling the morse letters of the signal onto his pad, he checked them quickly and sent back an acknowledgement.

'Let's have it, Yeoman.'

'Sir, signal reads: *Permission to torpedo hostile tanks when sighted*. End of message – sir!'

Hamilton grinned. Sosnkowski's signal, while humorous in style, nevertheless contained a subtle element of sarcasm that made it more than obvious what he thought of the operation. *Rapier*'s captain decided to maintain the humour and ignore the undertones.

'Yeoman, make back to *Bielik*: *Not until you see the whites of their eyes.*'

Drury nodded, raised the Aldis lamp to his shoulder, and began clacking the signal to the submarine astern. He always enjoyed the backchat between the skippers. It helped relieve the monotony.

Alistair Scott, *Rapier*'s navigation officer, stuck his head up through the hatch as Drury lowered the lamp and resumed his customary watchful stance.

'We're approaching the Wandelaar lightship, sir. We'll be into the south-west channel of the West Schelde in ten minutes.'

'Thank you, Pilot. All hands clear the bridge. Stand by diving stations. Yeoman – make to *Bielik*: *Alter course to line of bearing NE by E. Dive in two minutes, repeat two minutes, on execution of signal AB. Repeat to Swaardvis.*'

Drury passed the message across the dark waste of the sea and waited for the acknowledgement.

'Signal received and understood, sir.'

'Good. Now let me have the lamp and then get below. We'll be diving in ninety seconds.'

Hamilton glanced around the bridge to ensure it was empty and braced himself against the periscope standard so that he had a good view of the Polish boat. It was the first time he had had to handle a group of submarines at sea and, mindful of the disasters that had befallen the notorious steam driven K-class boats when they had operated in flotilla groups during the last war, he felt slightly apprehensive.

Provided the other two submarines moved onto lines of bearing, as ordered, there was little danger of collision during the simultaneous dive. But there had been no time to explain the dangers to the other two captains before they left the Medway and Hamilton was dependent upon their good sense and seamanship. He stared down at his watch as the final seconds ticked away.

Lifting the Aldis lamp he flashed the morse group AB three times. There was a pause before the long flash of acknowledgement flickered in the darkness from *Bielik*'s conning-tower and, as he saw the signal light, Hamilton pushed the diving klaxon.

Rapier responded immediately. The throb of the diesel engines suddenly faded and a series of hollow thuds echoed up as the vents swung open. Water bubbled and fountained along the side of the hull and the deck tilted sharply as the hydroplanes drove the bows under the surface. Hamilton had never stood on the deck of a diving submarine before and the tumultuous noise of rushing water was a breathtaking experience. It was several seconds before the spell was broken and he realized with a sudden start that he would find himself trapped on the bridge if he did not move quickly.

He waited to make sure the Polish submarine had changed course correctly and as he saw *Bielik*'s bows move away from *Rapier*'s port quarter he went down on his knees and pulled the upper hatch open. Even so, the momentary delay to check the other two boats was sufficient to court disaster. And as he pushed his legs down into the opened hatchway the sea burst over the lip of the conning-tower and crashed down on the empty bridge with the roar of a bomb blast. The weight of water swept him out of the hatch and threw him bodily against the steel bulwarks, knocking the breath from his body and scraping the skin from his hands as he tried to protect himself from the bruising impact. Dragging himself to his feet he staggered through the surging black water in search of the hatch.

Rapier was already half-submerged and the surface of the sea was lapping over the lip of the conning-tower screen as his feet thrust down into the narrow opening. Ice-cold water cascaded down through the hatchway, drenching him to the skin, and he felt as if he was standing underneath Niagara Falls. Blinded and spluttering under the onslaught he reached up, found the handle, and pulled the hatch lid shut. He clung to the conning-tower ladder for a few moments to regain his breath and then, shivering with sudden chill, he pushed home the dog-latches and secured the cover in position.

'Looks as if it's raining topsides, sir.' Collis grinned cheerfully as the skipper slid down into the warm brightness of the control room. 'You should have remembered to take your umbrella.'

Hamilton wondered whether the men realized how close

they had been to disaster. And all thanks to his own stupidity in hanging around to make sure that his orders had been obeyed.

'Permission to secure lower hatch, sir?'

He nodded his approval of the routine request and turned to check the depth-gauges.

'How much water do we have, Pilot?'

Scott glanced at the chart. 'Sixty feet, sir.'

'Level off at fifty, Number One. Trim to negative buoyancy and let her lie on the bottom.' He cocked an enquiring eye at Scott. 'I seem to remember the sea bed is okay in this area.'

'Yes, sir. Marked as shingle on the charts. The mud is further north, off the main estuary. I don't anticipate any difficulties.'

'Fifty feet, sir!'

'Stop motors. Planes amidships.' Collis checked the dials as *Rapier* hung suspended above the sea bed like a dragonfly hovering over a stagnant pool. 'Flood Number Eight and Number Ten main ballast . . . flood Nine and Eleven.'

Venables reached forward and turned the handwheels anti-clockwise. The numbered warning lights on the diving panel flickered from green to red and he listened for the sound of the sea entering the empty caverns of the ballast tanks and the shrill scream of high pressure air escaping from the valves.

'Eight and Ten flooded, sir.'

'Very good. Close vents.'

Venables's hands moved over the array of levers like a magician incanting a spell.

'Eight and Ten main vents shut, sir. Nine and Eleven flooded.'

'Close off Number Nine and Number Eleven vents.'

'Vents shut, sir.'

Collis saw the needle of the depth-gauge fall as the submarine sank gently under the gravitational pull of her flooded ballast tanks. The vessel lurched softly as her keel touched the shingle-covered bottom and a sound like scrunching feet on a gravel path echoed beneath the deck-plates as she settled into her nest.

'We're on the bottom, sir.'

'Thank you, Number One. Tell all hands to resume Watch Diving routine. We'll remain here until 4 am so I suggest we bed down for the night and get some sleep. There'll be plenty to do in the morning.' Hamilton walked over to the hydrophone cabinet and poked his head inside. 'Call up *Bielik* on the Fessendon, Baker.'

Leading Seaman Baker removed his head-phones and swung round in his seat. 'Sorry, sir. Can't be done. The other boats don't carry Fessendon equipment.'

Hamilton cursed himself silently but hid his annoyance behind a cheerful grin. He should have remembered that the Fessendon was a Royal Navy device. His sailing instructions to Sosnkowski and van Drebbel had been patchy and more than a little vague. Failing to think ahead, he had overlooked the fact that the other two boats were not equipped to receive underwater signals.

He had a habit of not crossing bridges until he reached them. And although planning was intended to cover – and find answers – to all likely or unlikely contingencies, he was reluctant to depart from his own way of doing things. He had never been an ideas man. And he had never been through the formal Naval College training that prepared officers to think and plan ahead. He was basically a pragmatist who relied on animal instinct to keep out of trouble. It had never failed him yet. And until it did he was quite happy to continue playing the game the only way he knew.

One of these days, lack of planning would land him in serious trouble, and he accepted the possibility. But again, this was crossing bridges before he reached them and he did not allow the prospect to worry him.

'In that case, we'll have to sort it out when we surface in the morning,' he said casually. Walking to the plotting table he stared down at the chart in silent contemplation.

A thin pencil line marked *Rapier*'s estimated track to the Belgian coast and a small circled cross showed their diving position.

'How accurate are your positions, Pilot?'

'They're by dead reckoning, sir, but they should be correct to within half a mile. I obtained a couple of radio bearings at ten o'clock and corrected the chart.' Scott pointed to the alteration of their DR position with its neat 2200 notation pencilled alongside.

Hamilton nodded. 'Time will be of the essence in the morning. And I don't want to waste a couple of valuable hours searching up and down the coast for the pick-up beach.' He was dying for a cigarette, but with *Rapier* shut down for diving it was impossible. Digging into his trouser pocket he pulled out a bag of boiled sweets and offered them to his companions. 'You've got a brother in the Army I believe, Scotty. How many men in a Company?'

'About two hundred, sir.'

Hamilton sucked at his boiled sweet in thoughtful silence for a few moments. 'In that case we're going to have problems,' he said finally. 'How the hell do we manage to squeeze two hundred bloody soldiers into three submarines? Flotilla orders say we're supposed to be lifting off B Company of the North Devons. Toffee never gave any indication of the numbers involved.'

'If they've been fighting their way back to the coast, I doubt if there'll be two hundred of 'em left alive by now,' Collis commented callously. 'Including walking wounded I reckon a hundred would be nearer the mark.'

'Even so, that means thirty men for each boat – it won't leave much room to breathe, let alone move.' Hamilton paused and looked at the chart again. 'I was only working on about thirty men, all told,' he said, voicing his thoughts aloud. 'And I'd decided to give Sosnkowski the job of evacuating them – *Bielik*'s by far the biggest boat of the three – while van Drebbel and ourselves gave covering support.'

'It's going to take time to get two hundred men off the

beaches, sir,' Collis pointed out. 'And how the devil do we bring them off to the submarine?'

Hamilton glanced at Scott.

'The rendezvous is at Etrincourt, about three miles south of Blankenberg,' he told the Navigator, pointing to the spot on the chart. 'What does the Flanders Pilotage Guide say?'

Scott pulled a small red-bound book down from the shelf over the plotting table and thumbed his way through the pages. He stopped, smoothed the book open and read in silence for a few moments.

'Here we are . . . Etrincourt. Popular watering place with shelving beaches and dunes to landward.' He read ahead and quickly paraphrased the facts. 'There's no jetty or pier, sir. Only bathing huts and a small wheeled platform for a speedboat. The three fathom line is two hundred and fifty yards from the Low Water mark – five hundred at High Water. Which means we'll have to stand off at least a quarter of a mile.'

'Nothing else?'

Scott consulted the book again and shook his head. 'Nothing important. There's a kids' paddling pool just in front of the dunes, with some pedal boats. And that's the sum total of the attractions.'

Hamilton rubbed his chin. *Rapier*'s small inflatable rubber dinghy stowed under the aft deck-plating only held six men at most and it would take far too long to paddle a relay service to and from the beach.

'What's the state of the tide at dawn, Pilot?'

Scott opened the Tide Tables and made a calculation on his scrap pad. 'High Water is at 3 am, so it will be on the ebb. Low Water is ten minutes before noon.'

'I suppose that's better than nothing,' Hamilton said shortly. 'I don't like the sound of that shelving beach. At least the ebb tide will keep us off the shore.'

'What's the drill, sir?' Collis asked. So far, Hamilton had given no indication of his intentions and the First

Officer felt happier with some sort of plan in mind before an operation started.

Hamilton shrugged. 'I don't know,' he said simply. 'We'll have to play it by ear. Have you lot got any ideas?'

Collis looked across at Scott and shook his head. It was all very well having a plan of campaign. But without suitable equipment and shore facilities it would be no better than building houses with straw. Perhaps Hamilton's open-minded approach was best.

'We'll simply have to improvise, sir,' he said brightly. 'That's the way the Navy does things best.'

Hamilton shrugged again. 'I suppose so, Number One. But if the worst comes to the worst,' he grinned, 'we could always make the buggers swim.'

Breakfast in the wardroom consisted of cold ham, potato salad, and hot toast with marmalade. Cooking was not permitted while the submarine was shut down for diving but nobody grumbled. Topsy-turvy eating habits were part of the routine of submarine life.

Zero hour had been set for 4 am – an hour after High Water – and fifteen minutes before sunrise. According to Hamilton's calculations, this would enable the three submarines to surface under cover of darkness and yet allow just sufficient time to weigh up the situation ashore before finally committing themselves to the operation. And it was the military situation that dominated the conversation as they worked through breakfast.

On the strength of his brother's army service Alistair Scott was regarded as the expert on land warfare and, as he pushed his empty plate away and reached for a slice of toast, Hamilton put the vital question to him.

'Are we likely to be under fire, Pilot?'

'It's difficult to say, sir,' Scott hedged. Unlike the skipper and the Executive Officer, who were fully absorbed every minute of the day and night with the responsibilities of command, the Navigator had time to listen to the radio news bulletins and follow the progress of the *blitzkrieg* on various maps he had culled from discarded magazines and newspapers. 'I'm no military expert, sir, but so far as I can see the Germans have directed their most powerful thrust towards the main Channel ports – Calais, Boulogne, and Ostend.'

'So what does that mean?' Collis asked, through a mouthful of hot buttered toast.

'The theory behind the offensive was, firstly, to drive a wedge between the French army and the BEF and, secondly, to seize the Channel ports and prevent evacuation. I suspect that Hitler put most of his efforts into securing the harbours and, for this reason, it is quite probable that the rest of the coast is not occupied by the Boche. Once they have cut off our escape routes to the sea they can take over the rest of the coast at their leisure. And always remember that their prime objective is the total annihilation of the BEF.'

'I wish to God you could answer a simple question, Alistair,' Collis chivvied him good humouredly. 'We don't want a bloody staff course lecture on strategy. All the skipper wants to know is – are we going to get shot at?'

'It *would* help to know,' Hamilton confirmed quietly.

'Sorry, sir. In my opinion, the Boche have been too busy mopping up Ostend to worry about the seaside resorts to the south. Especially as they have no harbour facilities.'

Collis poured himself another cup of coffee and stirred it thoughtfully. 'Well, that's a relief, I suppose. The problem, as I see it, is the fact that we're not carrying out the operation on our own. We don't know how the other two boats will perform. They could easily foul the whole show up.'

'That's a chance we'll have to take, Number One,' Hamilton told him. 'Personally, if I have to have anyone with me in a tight spot I'd choose Sosnkowski. The man's a bloody pirate. But he's as tough as they come and he won't let us down. The Dutchman seems a steady, reliable type. I don't think he'll do anything stupid. I'm just thankful they didn't land me with Bourdon.'

Collis glanced up at the brass-rimmed clock on the bulkhead behind the table. 'Only five minutes to go, sir,' he reminded Hamilton.

Hamilton nodded, swallowed a final mouthful of coffee, and stood up. He looked at the other officers in silence for a few moments.

'God knows what's likely to happen when we surface,' he said soberly. 'But I know I can rely on all of you. And you can be quite sure about one thing. I'm not risking my boat just to save a few bloody soldiers.'

He turned away from the table abruptly, pulled open the wardroom curtains, and made his way towards the control room.

'Do you think he means it?' Scott asked anxiously as soon as he was gone. It was only his second patrol with Hamilton and he found the skipper a difficult character to fathom.

'He always says the same sort of thing before we go into action,' Collis told him reassuringly. 'He seems to think it'll stop us worrying. I remember him saying exactly the same thing before we took those prisoners off the *Nordsee* – and he got the DSO that time.' He paused for a moment as he recalled the way Hamilton had fled from the enemy convoy in the Skagerrak. Perhaps, this time, he *did* mean what he said. Collis decided it unwise to confide his fears to the others. 'Come on, chaps,' he said breezily. 'Let's get on with it. The Old Man won't be too pleased if we're late at our stations.'

Hamilton was making a final check of the chart as Collis and Scott came through the watertight hatchway into the control room and he motioned the Navigator to join him at the plotting table.

'Let's suppose the Boche have already reached the coast,' he told Scott. 'What's the most likely direction they'll come from?'

Scott looked down at the chart. He scratched his ear and frowned over the symbols inscribed on the map. 'Probably from the north, sir,' he said finally. 'Along the coast road south from Zeebrugge.'

'How about the dunes?'

Rapier's navigator shook his head. 'The sand's too fine. I happen to know this bit of the coast. If they tried to take tanks across the dunes they'd be bogged down inside fifty yards.'

'Secured for surfacing, sir,' Collis reported.

Hamilton acknowledged with a nod and, still turning Scott's advice over in his mind, made his way to the periscope. The time was 4 am precisely.

'Thirty feet, Number One. Stand by to raise periscope.'

'Switches on – grouper up. Half ahead both. Close all vents; 'planes to rise. Start blowing.'

Rapier lifted from her shingle bed with a gentle lurch and rose slowly towards the surface. The lazy rotation of her propellors churned the sand like a desert dust storm and a shoal of frightened fish darted away as the iron-hulled monster stirred to life.

'Thirty feet, sir.'

'Trim level, Number One. Up periscope.'

'Stop blowing – 'midships 'planes.' Collis saw the bows lifting on the inclinometer. 'Flood Three . . . shut valves.' He glanced towards Hamilton. 'Trimmed and level, sir.'

'Very good, Number One. Stop motors.'

Hamilton guided the lens of the questing periscope to the north, located the low promontory marked on the map, and found the coast road. Satisfied that it was clear of traffic he swung the 'scope to port and checked the seaward horizon. A disturbance on the water some two hundred yards astern drew his attention. The sea frothed white, heaved like a saucepan of milk about to boil over, and then fell away to reveal *Bielik*'s black snout thrusting to the surface. As anticipated, Sosnkowski was dead on schedule and in exactly the right position.

Although it was still dark, the eastern horizon behind the dunes was beginning to lighten as dawn approached and Hamilton switched to the high-magnification lens for a closer inspection. Detecting a slight movement in the misty half-light he concentrated his attention and identified a group of figures moving cautiously across the sand. Then, suddenly, they were gone, as if the earth had opened and swallowed them up. Hamilton wiped the glass of the eye-piece with a piece of cloth before taking a second look. And several seconds passed before he realized that the men had dropped into a slit trench. Pushing the steering handles of the periscope upwards, he stepped back.

'Bridge party and gun crew close up. Take her up, Number One.'

Hamilton moved to the conning-tower ladder, climbed the lower rungs, and opened the lower hatch. Taffy Morgan, *Rapier*'s Gunner's Mate, followed close on his heels.

'Load with HE,' Hamilton instructed him over his shoulder, as he hauled himself up into the conning-tower compartment. 'And lay the gun on the coast road off the starboard bow as soon as we surface. But don't open fire unless I tell you.'

'Right, sir. Are we expecting trouble then?' Morgan asked in his lilting Welsh accent.

'You never know,' Hamilton said enigmatically.

The Gunner's Mate heard the clips of the upper hatch being unfastened and the blackness inside the conning-tower lightened fractionally as a blast of fresh salt air funnelled down from above. Hamilton's feet disappeared through the oval hatchway and Morgan followed him up to the bridge.

The first warmth of the rising sun had sucked a light mist from the sea, but it was fortunately not thick enough to reduce visibility and Hamilton could see a line of white surf breaking on the grey beach some five hundred yards off the submarine's starboard beam. It looked as quiet and desolate as a graveyard, but as the rosy fingers of dawn clawed over the rim of the dunes he could see the shadowy figures rising out of the ground and hurrying to the water's edge like ghosts. Lifting the lid of the voicepipe, he bent over the mouthpiece.

'Pass control to the bridge. Obey telegraphs.' He waited for the acknowledgement. 'Stop motors. Cox'n and Number One to the bridge.'

Looking over the edge of the conning-tower screen, he watched Morgan's men remove the tampion from the deck-gun and swing the barrel towards the coast road as it curved around a low bluff before swooping down towards the beach. Henniker had already broken open the ready-use ammunition locker and was passing a green-banded high-explosive shell to the loader. Riley opened the breech, pushed the shell into the chamber, slammed it shut, and pulled down the locking lever.

'Loaded and ready to fire, Chief!'

Morgan nodded. 'Smart work, boyo. But we don't fire nothing from this old pop-gun until the skipper gives the say-so, see. Now you just keeps your eyes skinned and watch that coast road. And if you see anything, you 'oller like 'ell.'

Hamilton smiled and turned as Collis and Ernie Blood emerged from the hatch to join him on the bridge. He dealt with the Coxwain's part in the scheme first.

'Take over the steering, Chief. And maintain position with the motors. We daren't put down an anchor and I don't want to waste time circling. Okay?'

'Aye, aye, sir.'

Hamilton turned his attention to Collis. 'And that brings us to our first problem, Number One,' he said casually. 'Communication. The army doesn't seem to have any signal equipment on shore.'

'They learn semaphore, sir. Have you tried wagging them?'

'Bunts! Get your flags and call them up.'

Drury unfastened the bridge flag locker and drew out his signalling flags. Climbing up on to the base of the periscope standard, so that he was clearly visible to the men on the beach, he began his weird and wonderful ritual. He persevered for several minutes and then gave up.

'They don't seem to understand,' he reported.

'Very good, Yeoman. You may stand down.' Hamilton swept the beach with his binoculars, but drew a blank. 'So much for your suggestion, Number One,' he grunted. 'But we've got to establish communication somehow. I must know how many men are to be lifted off.' He focused his glasses on the small wooden landing-stage that jutted out from the beach into the shallows. 'There's a motor boat tied up alongside that wheeled contraption. Haven't the bloody army got the gumph to use it?'

'What we really need, sir, is someone ashore with an Aldis lamp,' Collis said slowly. 'I reckon I could swim to the beach from here.'

Hamilton looked doubtful. 'It's all of five hundred yards, Number One. And you'd be swimming against the tide too.' He paused to consider the suggestion. 'If I take *Rapier* inshore, until her bows touch bottom, it could halve the distance. Do you still want to volunteer?'

Collis was already pulling off his sea boots. He looked up and grinned with enthusiasm.

'I'm ready whenever you are, sir.'

'Half ahead both, Cox'n. Steer eight points to starboard and make for the beach. Put the motors full astern the moment we touch the bottom.'

'Half ahead both, sir. Eight points starboard.'

Hamilton looked out over the port side as *Rapier* turned and glided towards the beach. *Bielik* was lying still in the water, some two hundred yards to seaward, and the Dutchman was rolling gently in the off-shore swell a further five hundred yards astern. Realizing that Sosnkowski must be wondering what was going on, he called Drury across.

'Yeoman – make to *Bielik* and *Swaardvis*: *Disregard my movements. Bielik to remain on station, Swaardvis to circle at half speed and maintain air watch. Fire red flares if hostiles sighted.*'

Having passed his orders, Hamilton returned to the landward side of the bridge to watch the soldiers crowding the water's edge in anticipation of rescue. A couple of enterprising privates, having pulled off their boots, had even begun paddling out into the surf with their khaki trousers rolled up to their knees, like Bank Holiday trippers at Margate. Sorry, lads, he said to himself, but I'm afraid you're in for a disappointment. And unless you're bloody lucky you're going to get more than your feet wet before this caper's over.

Turning away, he went forward to check the gun crew at their battle stations on the fore deck.

'Don't watch those bloody monkeys on the beach!' he roared. 'Keep that damned gun trained on the coast road. You won't have time to lay your sights if a couple of Panzers suddenly appear over the hill.'

Taffy Morgan translated the skipper's orders into picturesque Welsh obscenities and in disciplined silence the barrel of the 4-inch quick-firer trained back over the port beam to menace the Zeebrugge-Ostend road.

'Slow ahead both.'

The bridge telegraph tinkled and from deep down inside the hull came the echoing *ping-ping* of the repeater. The bow waves fell away to a whisper of spray as the submarine lost speed and the men on the bridge braced themselves in readiness for the jolting shock they knew was coming. Hamilton gripped the conning-tower rails and waited.

Thirty seconds later, *Rapier*'s sharp steel bows burrowed into the shingle and, misreading the significance of the situation, the soldiers watching from the shore gave a ragged cheer.

'Stop motors, Cox'n.'

Collis, naked save for his dark blue shorts and with the watertight rubber bag containing the Aldis lamp hanging around his neck, stood poised and ready on the edge of the bridge coaming. He looked calm and supremely confident; almost as if he was about to take part in a Fleet Regatta swimming contest.

'Away you go, Number One,' Hamilton told him. 'And good luck.'

He waited to make sure the Executive Officer was well clear of the ballast tanks before he gave Blood the go-ahead.

'Full astern both, Cox'n. Back her off.'

The reversed thrust of the propellors churned the sea into a white lather of bubbling foam and, with slow dignity, *Rapier* slid safely back into deeper water. The bows made a vulgar sucking noise as the submarine pulled clear of the shingle and Hamilton, who knew the wardroom's copy of *The Perfumed Garden* almost by heart, looked at Ernie Blood and grinned.

'Sounds just like the bleating calf,' he commented.

Blood said nothing. Having seen Antoinette Bourdon he had little doubt that Hamilton had had recent first-hand experience of such things.

CHAPTER SEVEN

0420 hours. 5th June 1940

In the course of the last fourteen days Major Clement Lloyd-Noble, adjutant and second-in-command of the 1st Battallion, the North Devon Regiment, had seen enough of war to last him a lifetime.

The son of an old military family, and the product of Wellington College and the Royal Military Academy, he had cut his teeth on exciting tales of glorious battles for the flag, colourful ceremonials, and the legacy of Imperial greatness. And now he knew it was all no more than patriotic crap.

So far he had seen only defeat and violent death walking hand-in-hand with chaos and corruption. It was an experience he could have cheerfully done without. Yet, against all the odds, he had succeeded in getting the pitiful remnants of B Company safely to the Channel coast and that, in itself, was a minor miracle. Now he could only put his trust in the mercy of God and the long arm of the Royal Navy. And, of the two, Lloyd-Noble had more faith in the capabilities of the Navy to get B Company out of trouble than in the intervention of his Maker. Wriggling deeper into his slit trench, he shielded the flame of the match as he lit his last but one cigarette and drew the smoke into his lungs.

His men had been fighting continuously for eighteen days. Not the heroic struggles described in the pages of the military history books, but battles for survival; with bayonets matched against armoured tanks, out-dated mortars against 88mm field-guns, and ancient Lee-Enfield rifles against those screaming banshees of modern warfare – the dive bombers. And always on the retreat. Inevitable, monotonous and soul-destroying retreat.

On the third day of the *blitzkrieg*, the Regiment had moved up into Belgium and four days later, Brigade had ordered a withdrawal to prepared positions. The message had arrived bare minutes after a dive bomber attack had virtually wiped out the Company transport and left twenty of B Company's men sprawled in the stark contortions of violent death, under the shade of the tall poplar trees lining the Belgian roadside.

The prepared positions had turned out to be hastily dug trenches already filled with terrified civilian refugees, fleeing from the invading hordes of Hitler's Third Reich. Lloyd-Noble could not find it in his heart to move them out. Instead he posted his troops under cover of the hedges, set up his own HQ in a dilapidated barn, and sent a runner back to Brigade for reinforcements.

The Major shivered at the memory of the bitter fight that followed and his hands trembled as he recalled the screams of the refugees crushed and buried in the shallow trenches as the Panzer tanks rolled over their ready-dug graves. He wondered whether Britain's enemies had suffered similar fates in the old days, when England was always the victor? The scrunch of heavy army boots on the pebbled beach disturbed his thoughts. They stopped beside the trench and someone coughed discreetly. Lifting the flap of the canvas cover he recognized the Regimental Sergeant-Major.

'Yes, Bonham?'

'Can you come outside, sir. Corporal Benson has reported some boats moving out at sea. Sorry to disturb you, sir, but I can't see so well myself at the moment.'

Lloyd-Noble appreciated the understatement. The RSM's left eye was covered with a blood-stained bandage and his right was swollen and bruised. How he could see anything at all was something of a miracle but, like most senior NCOs, Charlie Bonham never liked to admit defeat. The Major stubbed out his cigarette on the damp shingle and slipped the precious dog-end into his pocket. He glanced at his wristwatch. It was 4.21 am . . .

Lieutenant Goldsmith, B Company's only surviving officer, and the Corporal were standing at the water's edge staring out to sea when Lloyd-Noble and the RSM joined them. The Major peered through the early morning mist.

'Well I'm damned – submarines! What do they think we are – a bloody convoy!'

'They've been trying to signal us, sir,' Goldsmith explained. 'I could read the flashes alright but we had nothing to answer with. The Corporal's torch has run its batteries down.'

'What were they saying?'

'They kept asking us to acknowledge and report the number of troops to be taken off, sir.'

'And after that, sir,' Corporal Benson broke in, 'the same geezer stands up by the mast and starts waving flags about. And we couldn't make nothin' of that, neither.'

Lloyd-Noble watched the submarines carefully while he tried to think up some way of communicating with them. At the same time the other half of his mind grappled with the problem of how he could get his men off the beach to the waiting submarines. He dismissed both problems from his mind as he saw the nearest submarine turn towards the shore and glide slowly towards the beach.

'They're going to run their bows aground and take us off that way,' he explained to Goldsmith. He turned to the RSM. 'Fall the men in on the beach, Bonham. Walking wounded to embark first.'

'Very good, sir.'

'And leave the pickets in position, in case we need covering fire,' the Major added. 'Tell them to watch for my signal. When they see it, they're to run like hell for the shore.'

The RSM saluted and walked back up the beach, to rouse the sleeping soldiers huddled exhausted in their slit trenches. The parade-ground roar of his voice was quickly picked up and echoed by the other NCOs as they chivvied their sections awake and sent them scurrying towards the water's edge.

'You spoke too soon, sir,' Goldsmith said quietly as *Rapier* grounded her bows on the shingle and started going astern. 'I don't think he can make it.'

Lloyd-Noble tried to hide his disappointment as he watched the submarine back off from the shore. Every minute lost brought the danger of discovery by the Germans nearer. A passing Belgian villager had told him that a Panzer regiment was resting for the night two miles to the north and, according to rumour, was likely to move south towards Etrincourt after breakfast. And the Major had a suspicion that motorized infantry units were probably not far behind.

'Do you have any good swimmers in your Company, Goldsmith?' he asked the Lieutenant.

'I don't know, sir. I only joined the Regiment last month. I'll ask my sergeant if he knows of anyone . . .'

'Don't bother, sir!'

Lloyd-Noble looked up in astonishment as Corporal Benson suddenly plunged knee-deep into the shallow water. Stepping forward to investigate he found a half-naked man emerging from the sea with a rubber bag slung around his neck.

'Good God! Who the devil are you?'

Collis was shivering with cold as he walked up on to the sand. But he was grinning widely and looked none the worse for his swim.

'Lieutenant Collis, Royal Navy,' he announced by way of introduction. 'I take it you're in command, Major.' He glanced quickly at Benson. 'Be a good chap, Corporal. Get me a towel, before I die of pneumonia.'

Benson hesitated – uncertain whether he should obey the orders of a naval officer. But the RSM, who had loomed unexpectedly on the scene to find out what was going on, reinforced the request in his customary stentorian tones.

'Look lively, lad! You 'eard what the h'officer said. Get a towel – and be quick about it!'

The corporal had no idea where a towel was likely to be found on the desolate beach but he didn't believe in arguing with Regimental Sergeant-Majors. He hurried away obediently.

'How many men to be taken off, Major?' Collis asked briskly as he unshipped the bag from around his neck and took out the signalling lamp.

'Ninety-eight at the last count, Lieutenant.'

Collis whistled. 'Christ! We were expecting two hundred.'

'That's the number we set out with,' Lloyd-Noble said simply. 'Two hundred and seven, to be precise.' He played down the tragedy with a weary smile. 'We seem to have mislaid a few on the way.'

Collis raised the Aldis lamp, sighted it on *Rapier*'s bridge, and quickly informed Hamilton of the number involved. Almost immediately the submarine's lamp flashed back.

What boats or other means of getting them off?

Collis passed the question back to the Major who shrugged. He'd been too busy to check such matters and it was the RSM, Bonham, who came to the rescue. There was little that escaped the eagle eye of an RSM.

'There's a motor-boat tied up to the landing-stage, sir. But it seems to be almost out of fuel. I reckon those bloody Froggies drained it before they left. And there's a couple of small rowing boats up the beach, although only one of them has oars.'

Collis nodded and reported the uninspiring tally back to the submarine. He could picture the expression on Hamilton's face as he read the message. As an after-thought he added: *I will get something organized. Stand by to embark in thirty minutes.*

Having committed himself to the impossible, he handed the lamp to Goldsmith and showed him how to sight and operate the trigger.

'Pick up any messages the skipper sends and do your best to answer. I take it you know morse?' The army lieutenant nodded. 'Fine. I'm off on a tour of inspection. You can tell *Rapier* I'll report again in twenty minutes.'

Collis led the Major up the beach, with the RSM trailing

a respectful distance in the rear – near enough to hear what the two officers were saying but far enough away to make it seem he was not listening.

'Tell one of your MT drivers to check that motor-boat,' Collis instructed the Major decisively. 'Then get your lads to find some old planks they can use for paddles.' He stopped by the first of the rowing boats. It was an inshore fisherman's craft, stoutly built and capable of holding ten men at a squeeze. It looked sound enough. Moving on, he inspected the other boat – a small pram dinghy. 'Anything else up the beach?' he asked.

'I don't think so.' Lloyd-Noble glanced over his shoulder. Perhaps the RSM had seen something he'd missed.

'Not a thing, sir,' Bonham pronounced solemnly. 'There's a kids' boating pool behind those beach huts – and that's about all.'

There is nothing the Navy cannot do. For some inexplicable reason the boastful slogan painted over the doorway of Dartmouth Naval College flashed into Collis's mind. So be it, he decided. But there's always a first time – even for failure.

Even Hamilton's normal calm was beginning to crack as the hands of the clock jerked forward to complete the final minutes of the dead-line Collis had set himself. There seemed to be a great deal of activity on the beach but, for the life of him, he could make neither head nor tail of its purpose. Leaving Drury to watch the shore, he picked up his binoculars and searched the Zeebrugge road yet again. It was still empty of traffic – friendly or otherwise. Moving to the port side, he checked the other two submarines. *Bielik*, like *Rapier*, was rolling gently in the off-shore swell and he could see the Polish gunners at their battle stations. Sosnkowski was on the bridge and he waved cheerfully as he saw Hamilton.

Swaardvis was slowly circling, as ordered. Having completed the reverse leg to the south, van Drebbel was coming round at half-power ready to begin the long run-up past the beach. Every head on the Dutch submarine's bridge was staring skywards and Hamilton felt confident there was little likelihood of their being caught by a surprise air attack. Lowering his glasses, he glanced at the clock again before moving to the starboard side to join the Yeoman of Signals. Just one more minute to go . . .

'Christ Almighty!'

Unable to believe his eyes Hamilton raised his binoculars to confirm the extraordinary sight. About two dozen brightly coloured boxes had been launched from the shore and, shepherded by the motor boat, the bizarre flotilla was moving jerkily out towards the waiting submarines. Collis had certainly lived up to the Navy's reputation for improvisation. And Hamilton's mind boggled at the result.

The motor-boat, with the First Lieutenant at the wheel and loaded to the gunwhales with the more seriously wounded men, was towing the tiny over-crowded pram dinghy. Behind it came the fishing boat rowed by two soldiers whose experience in handling oars had apparently been limited to Sunday afternoon excursions on the Serpentine. Trailing manfully astern, it too, was crammed with over a dozen walking wounded. And finally, to wind up the unbelievable flotilla, came twenty luridly painted children's pedal boats, each with a two man complement of sweating but happy soldiers jerking their legs up and down with furious energy to keep the flimsy paddles turning.

'I reckon I've just about seen everything now, Yeoman,' Hamilton observed drily. 'Tell *Bielik* to move across our stern to take off the motor boat and its tender.'

The troops remaining behind on the beach were taunting their comrades with obscene jeers. And their unhelpful comments, coupled with strong overtones of coarse humour, only served to increase the confusion. Pedal boats veered to right and left and, in their haste to complete the course, two overturned without warning, spilling their cursing occupants into the water. Several members of *Rapier*'s crew leapt into the sea to help them and even Hamilton,

139

burdened though he was by the fear of a sudden surprise attack, joined in the laughter at the hilarious antics of the soldiery.

The first phase of the evacuation passed off without a hitch. Collis took the motor boat alongside *Bielik* where, with the eager help of the Polish sailors lining the deck casing, the wounded soldiers were lifted carefully aboard and taken below for medical attention. Then, towing the pram dinghy astern, he made towards *Rapier*.

'How many more?' Hamilton shouted down.

'Thirty-two, sir. If I tow the big rowing boat as well, I could probably lift them all off in two more trips.'

'What about fuel, Number One?'

'I'll have to take a chance, sir. The tank's empty, according to the gauge, but she's still running.'

Looking towards the beach Hamilton could see the remaining soldiers forming up hopefully, in a disciplined line at the water's edge. As Collis said – they would have to take a chance.

'Very well, Number One,' he agreed. 'Go ahead. But if you hear the klaxon, get back to *Rapier* as fast as you can. I'm not risking my boat to save a handful of soldiers.'

Collis nodded, pulled back the throttle lever, and eased the little pleasure launch away from the submarine in a sharp sweeping curve. The two empty boats bobbed unhappily in the wash but the tow lines held and Collis steered a careful course through the choppy waters inshore. As he stopped in the shallows the first rank of waiting men waded out into the sea.

The strident squawk of *Bielik*'s klaxon coincided with the ear-splitting bark of her for'ard quick-firer. Hamilton raised his binoculars and focused on the coast road.

A pair of field-grey tanks trundled leisurely into view. They were moving south from the direction of Zeebrugge and he could see the black crosses clearly painted on the slab sides of their turrets. Sosnkowski's sharp eyes must have spotted them while they were still hull-down behind the crest and he opened fire almost instantly. The enemy's speed of reaction was equally commendable. Although caught by surprise, they swung into action without hesitation as *Bielik*'s shell burst a bare twenty yards away from the first Panzer. The leading tank gathered speed and steered for the beach while the second vehicle stopped and swung its turret seawards.

'Permission to fire, sir?' Morgan shouted eagerly.

'Granted Mister Gunner – whenever you're ready.'

Rapier's deck gun recoiled, flame spurted from the muzzle, and the red-hot cartridge case bounced off the fore plating into the sea, as Riley opened the breech to reload. The exploding shell threw a fountain of fine sand high into the air alongside the stationary tank and Hamilton saw it rattle forward a few yards so that its turret gunsight was clear of the dusty murk.

A bright yellow flame spat from the Panzer's KwK L/24 cannon and the barrel recoiled smoothly into the turret, where the hydraulic recuperators absorbed the shock and allowed it to run out again for reloading. Otto Lange opened the breech, picked up another 75mm shell from the ammunition racks alongside his legs, and thrust it into the still smoking womb of the gun. It was the last conscious action he ever carried out. A well-placed shell from *Bielik*'s quick-firer exploded beneath the hull, ripped away the offside tracks, punched a hole through the unarmoured floor of the Panzer, and ignited the petrol tanks.

The Pz IV(A) went up like a torch and as the tank commander threw back the turret hatch, a pillar of flame seared past him and curled hungrily into the sky. Lange tried to shield his face from the roaring furnace that suddenly engulfed the interior of the tank and his screams echoed mockingly inside the iron confines of his wheeled coffin, as the flames devoured his flesh.

'Check fire, Mister Morgan,' Hamilton shouted. 'Change to target bearing Green-45. We must stop that other tank reaching the beach.'

But it was too late. The leading Panzer was already grinding on to the shingle and the heavy machine-gun in the nascelle alongside the driver chattered noisily as it scythed the soldiers down like ripe corn before a harvester.

Taffy Morgan's first shot was wild. It exploded harmlessly two hundred yards beyond the new target in the soft sand of the dunes but, even so, the tank changed direction smartly, in an effort to confuse the submarine's aim.

'There's two more bastards, sir!' Blood yelled above the noise of the gunfire. 'Off the starboard bow – coming over the crest of the coast road.'

The Coxswain was right. The tanks were only just visible through the pall of thick black smoke billowing from Otto Lange's funeral pyre but, with the help of his binoculars, Hamilton could make out two more Pz IV(A)s rolling over the top of the rise. Sosnkowski immediately sent a shot in their direction, but the Polish gunners had insufficient time to lay their sights accurately and the shell exploded a safe distance from the head of the approaching column.

It seemed madness to continue the fight. Only God knew how many more tanks would soon be joining in the battle and, once they settled down to make practice against the almost stationary submarines, it would only be a matter of time before they scored. And just one single hit could be enough to disable a submarine totally.

Leaving the gunners to deal with the tanks, Hamilton turned his attention back to the beach. Collis had safely embarked the next detail and the three overloaded boats wallowed through the surf as he cautiously steered his precious convoy away from the shore. The soldiers left behind on the beach had scattered when the first Panzers appeared and were frantically digging like moles, as they burrowed into the wet shingle to escape the devastating hail of machine-gun bullets. Hamilton had seen enough. He turned to Drury.

'Bunts – tell *Bielik* to maintain fire on the road. Then call up the Dutchman and tell him to close the beach and intercept Collis so that *Swaardvis* can embark the men in the boats. I'll try to cover the rest of the troops pinned down on the shore.' He made his way to Ernie Blood. 'Full ahead both, Coxswain. Steer for the beach!'

It seemed a suicidal decision, but Blood obeyed without question. *Rapier* gathered speed and, with the bow wave rising from her stem like a white moustache, the submarine swung to starboard.

Hamilton's target was the Pz IV(A) rumbling ominously across the bullet-torn beach. Sosnkowski, he assumed, would be able to keep the other Panzer units fully occupied, if he played his cards skilfully, but *Rapier* was now committed to single combat with the lone tank that had broken through onto the shingle and which was now advancing on the helpless soldiers crouched in their shallow, hastily dug holes. He wondered whether a tank and a submarine had ever staged such an unlikely duel before. And more importantly, if they had, which had won.

Rapier's gun-layer was settling down to the routine and this time the splintered fragments of pebbles thrown up by the near-miss rattled like hail stones on the armoured side of the tank. The Panzer stopped abruptly and its turret swung to the right, so that the barrel of its cannon was lined up on the submarine. Flame spat from the muzzle and Hamilton heard the sobbing whine of the 75mm shell scream over *Rapier*'s bridge. It hit the sea two hundred yards astern and a fountain of dirty water leapt into the air as it exploded.

Hamilton suddenly realized that, unlikely as it may have seemed originally, the submarine had more than an equal chance of winning the contest.

Rapier's gunners, like all naval gunners, had been trained to fire at moving targets from a moving platform that rolled and pitched with the motion of the sea. But tanks, in their present stage of development, could only fire when the machine was stationary. It was something he had never considered before and, of course, it was a matter they never covered in the lectures at *Excellent*.[1] And why

[1] *HMS Excellent* was the Royal Navy's gunnery school at Portsmouth.

should they? Who'd ever heard of a submarine fighting a tank?

'Keep it up, lads,' he encouraged the sweating men crouched over the gun. 'He's got to stop each time he fires. We've got the bastard licked!'

Rapier's next shot landed uncomfortably close to the Panzer. Its 250 hp Maybach engine snarled into reverse and it backed away ponderously, like a dog retreating from an unpleasant smell. Finding a new bearing, the turret gun retaliated with two shells that whistled low over the submarine's bows and burst harmlessly twenty yards beyond the stern port quarter. The movement of the turret prevented the tank commander from using the co-axial machine gun and the soldiers took advantage of the respite to drag their wounded comrades into the shelter of the hastily dug holes in the shifting shingle.

Lloyd-Noble crouched in this trench. The murderous hail of machine-gun bullets had already cost him nine men and he wondered how much longer the rest of them would survive. While the Navy had achieved the impossible by lifting off over half of the stranded troops, it would need a miracle to save the remainder and he knew that, even for the Navy, miracles took a little longer. Time was the one commodity in short supply. He glanced up as the RSM slithered across the wet shingle on his stomach and slid down into the fox-hole.

'They've got the second batch aboard, sir. Won't be long now, I reckon.' He peered cautiously over the rim of the trench. 'That submarine commander's taking a hell of a gamble coming so close inshore. He must be a bloody hero.'

Lloyd-Noble scrambled to the side of the hole and raised his head. The submarine was barely three hundred yards from the shore but, with more tanks moving up from the north, it was coming under increasingly heavy fire as its bows pushed closer to the beach. A vicious burst of machine-gun fire forced the Major to duck smartly back into the trench.

'I can't let him take any further risks,' he said suddenly. 'There's no justification for losing a submarine just to save a few dozen men.' The Major dug into his pocket, pulled out a handkerchief, and stared down at it thoughtfully. For a brief moment his determination wavered. Then, bracing himself to take the distasteful decision, he started to climb out of the trench . . .

'*Bielik*'s been hit, sir!'

Hamilton hurried to the port side of the bridge to confirm the lookout's report. A 75mm AP shell had torn a jagged hole in the Polish submarine's conning-tower but, undeterred, Sosnkowski's gunners continued to maintain a steady and accurate fire on the tanks lining the northern horizon. The shell had fortunately missed the vital pressure hull and the submarine's diving efficiency was unimpaired. But it had done a considerable amount of superficial damage and *Bielik* must have suffered a number of casualties.

Hamilton regarded the hit as an omen for the future. Despite his recent optimism, he had to admit that the tanks were quickly getting the measure of their unexpected challenge. And next time Sosnkowski might not be so lucky.

'Yeoman: Make to *Bielik*: *Withdraw and return to base.*'

Rapier lurched violently under his feet as he passed his instructions to Drury and he had to grab hold of the periscope standard to steady himself. A grinding screech echoed back from the bows as the submarine stopped with a sudden jolt and heeled slightly to starboard. For a brief moment Hamilton thought that *Rapier*, too, had been hit, but Blood's quiet reassurance quickly stilled his fears.

'We've grounded, sir. No damage.'

'Full astern both, Cox'n.' He peered over the side searching for a tell-tale patch of green water amongst the shallows. 'There's a channel to starboard. Half ahead both and full starboard helm!'

'We're still three hundred yards out, sir,' Blood pointed out doubtfully, as he rang down for half speed and steered for the channel of deeper water Hamilton's keen eyes had detected. 'We can't get much closer.'

'I'll be the judge of that, Cox'n,' Hamilton said sharply. 'Just keep steering for the shore.'

A near miss sent a deluge of dirty water crashing down over the exposed bridge and, seconds later, *Rapier* shuddered under its first direct hit. The shell landed for'ard and Hamilton hurried to the front of the bridge to inspect the damage.

It was bad – but it might have been worse. The explosion had blown a large hole in the outer casing and Riley, the loader, was lying on the deck with his left leg cut off just below the knee. He was barely conscious but, despite the agony of his terrible wounds, he was trying to crawl clear so that his body would not impede the efficiency of the remaining men serving the gun. Morgan, the Gunner's Mate, had blood trickling down his face from a splinter wound, but the rest of the gun crew seemed miraculously unharmed and, incredibly, the quick-firer was still in action. Hamilton opened the lid of the voicepipe.

'Stretcher party topsides at the double. And send up a reserve loader.'

Another shell exploded less than ten yards from the stern and Blood threw the submarine from port to starboard in a frantic zig-zag to confuse the enemy gunners.

'*Swaardvis* requests permission to withdraw, sir,' Drury reported calmly as he clambered down from his exposed signalling position abaft the periscope standards.

'Make to *Swaardvis*: *Affirmative. Return to base.*'

'And then there was one . . .' Blood murmured quietly to himself.

Hamilton ignored the *sotto voce* comment. He was quite conversant with the nursery rhyme. But in the circumstances it was better to risk one submarine rather than all three.

'Where the hell's Collis?' he snapped impatiently.

'Coming up from astern, sir.'

Having delivered its passengers to *Swaardvis*, the little

motor-boat was chugging steadily back towards the beach again. The pram dinghy had disappeared and the fishing boat, obviously holed, was dragging reluctantly behind in a waterlogged condition. Hamilton waited for Collis to come abeam of the submarine before picking up the hand microphone of the loud hailer. He ducked instinctively as another shell screamed over the top of the conning-tower and, as *Rapier* came within range of the co-axial machine-guns mounted on the tank's turrets, he heard the ugly *tak-tak-tak-tak* of the Schmeissers join the din of the battle. His thumb jabbed the button of the microphone.

'Come in, Number One. Your time is up!'

Coxswain Blood exchanged a grin with Drury as they shared the joke. But Collis, if he had heard the raucous bellow of the loud-hailer above the noise of the gunfire, chose to ignore the request and continued chugging slowly towards the shore. Hamilton swore. Although he was not above disobeying orders himself when the situation demanded, he expected instant obedience from everyone else. No doubt Collis would excuse his disobedience by claiming not to have heard the recall order. And he certainly was not the first naval officer to try to wriggle out of trouble with the help of Nelson's notorious blind eye, or more appropriately, in this instance, deaf ear.

The enemy tanks, however, had also spotted the motor-boat and Hamilton could see two of them trundling towards the water's edge. A quick burst of machine-gun fire raked the sea in front of his bows but Collis showed a similar disregard for the enemy's bullets as he had for his skipper's orders. Ignoring the danger he plunged through the surf towards the beach.

'The damned fool's going to get himself killed,' Hamilton said sourly, as a salvo of shells bracketed the tiny boat.

'And all for nothing, sir,' Blood broke in. 'Those bloody pongoes are waving a white flag!'

The Coxswain was right. The hastily dug slit trenches were now completely encircled by the Panzers and, through his binoculars, Hamilton could see an officer walking slowly across the shingle, holding a small white cloth knotted to an empty bayonet scabbard.

'Useless bloody bastards,' Blood spat disgustedly.

Hamilton made no comment. He intuitively sensed the true reason for the Major's decision to surrender. And it certainly was not lack of guts. Lloyd-Noble must have known that while one single British soldier remained alive on the beach the Royal Navy would continue its rescue attempt, regardless of cost. And realizing the hopelessness of the situation he had taken the responsibility for deciding on the withdrawal of the submarines away from Hamilton and placed it upon his own shoulders.

'Full astern both, Cox'n.'

Rapier backed away from the beach in a flurry of foam as the engines roared to maximum power. A salvo of 75mm shells exploded under the bows but the sudden burst of speed had upset the gunner's aim and they fell providentially short. Hamilton pressed the button of the diving alarm.

Collis turned his head as he heard the raucous squawk of the submarine's klaxon. The southerly breeze was blowing the black smoke from the knocked-out tanks across his bows and, blinded, he was unaware that the soldiers had surrendered. So far as he was concerned, *Rapier* was pulling out and the skipper was running away, again.

The acrid fumes of the smoke made his eyes water as he peered over the shattered windscreen of the motor boat but, gritting his teeth, he plunged on into the black, swirling darkness. With bitter memories of Hamilton's refusal to engage the enemy convoy in the Skagerrak, Collis was determined that he, at least, would not let the reputation of the Navy down.

As he emerged from the rolling clouds of smoke, the glare of the sun suddenly dazzled his eyes. But not before he had caught his first horrifying glimpse of the enemy tanks lined up along the water's edge, waiting for him.

Twisting the steering wheel hard over, he opened the

throttle, and made a mad dash for the cover of the smoke-screen astern. But the Goddess of Fortune had deserted him. Finally drained of fuel, the outboard motor spluttered fitfully, coughed and died. Drifting at the mercy of the tide the little motor-boat was swept broadside and slithered on to a bank of shingle, where it came to an abrupt stop. And with their victim lying stranded and helpless the guns of the tanks opened fire at point-blank range.

The water was barely waist deep and floundering to his feet as the boat sank under him Collis hauled himself upright and began to wade ashore. And as the machine-guns opened up again he reluctantly raised his hands in surrender.

Leutnant Heinrich Krebs pushed open the lid of the hatch, hoisted himself on to the armoured top of the tank's turret, and watched in silence as the British officer walked unsteadily up the beach with his arms high above his head. Reaching down into the turret he lifted out his personal Spandau and cradled it tenderly in his arms, like a mother nursing her baby.

He waited until Collis was ten yards from the tank before leisurely releasing the safety catch and pulling back the bolt.

The life of one naval officer seemed poor recompense for the sixty English soldiers the submarines had successfully evacuated to safety. He looked down at Collis and shrugged as his finger tightened on the trigger. It was, however, better than nothing.

CHAPTER EIGHT

1200 hours. 12th July 1940

The flower blossom, the heady scent of the roses, and the lazy drone of bees made the war seem very far away. And as Hamilton strolled slowly through St James' Park it was difficult to recollect the horrors he had witnessed the previous month on the blood-stained beaches of Etrincourt.

There were, however, numerous reminders that London was now a city under siege. Discreet signs pointed the way to the nearest air raid shelter. And the park-keepers in their brass buttoned waistcoats and black leggings were busy turning the soft green turf into bare-earthed vegetable plots, in response to Home Secretary Herbert Morrison's urgent exhortations to *Dig for Victory*. Even the little hooped iron boundary railings edging the meandering paths had vanished – torn up for scrap many months before.

High above the trees lining The Mall, the silver barrage balloons glinted like bloated fish in the July sunshine while, higher still in the deep blue of the summer sky, the Spitfires of No 11 Group weaved a white tracery of vapour trails as they patrolled the roof of the capital in search of the *Luftwaffe*'s marauding bombers.

The air raid warning sirens were sounding as Hamilton left the underground Operations Room at the Admiralty and his first instinctive reaction was to take cover. But realizing that the Londoners were ignoring the battle raging above their heads and were continuing their work with stoic indifference, he decided against taking shelter and turned through the gates into the sunlit park.

After the stuffy confines of *Rapier*, the park was spaciously refreshing and the scent of the flowers was like nectar particularly by comparison with the dank stink of diesel oil mixed with sour vegetables and human sweat that made up the turgid atmosphere of an operational submarine. And as Hamilton strolled slowly under the trees he turned his mind back to the conference he had just left at the Citadel – the underground war-room beneath the Admiralty in Whitehall.

A great deal had happened since *Rapier* had returned from her partially successful mission to the Belgian coast in June. From a personal point of view, things had changed very little. And apart from breaking in a new Executive Officer to replace Collis, the two short patrols that had followed – the first in the vicinity of the 'Broad Fourteens' to guard against a possible German attack towards the Dover Straits and the other back into the inhospitable waters of the Skagerrak – had proved both uneventful and irritatingly unproductive. Hamilton felt that the fates were against him. Ten months of continuous combat patrol and, with the exception of the U-boat off Norway,[1] not a single sinking to his credit – although, admittedly, very few submarines could boast a battle flag celebrating the destruction of three Panzer tanks. Perhaps he should consider asking for a transfer back to surface patrols.

Internationally, and in the Grand Strategy of the war, the situation had completely and irrevocably altered. Following the total collapse of its Army and Air Force the French Government had signed armistice terms with their Nazi conquerors at Compiègne on the 21st of June. In the same month, fascist Italy, prodded unwillingly by the Duce, Benito Mussolini, had entered the war on the side of her Axis partner and the last Allied troops had been evacuated from Norway. Finally, just two days ago, Goering's *Luftwaffe* had launched itself against Britain in overwhelming numbers in a deliberate campaign to gain air superiority over England in readiness for Hitler's invasion – the infamous *Operation Sealion*.

As he brooded over the sudden unexpected change in Britain's fortunes, Hamilton recalled Crockett-Jones's

[1] See *Fighting Submarine*.

doleful prophecy a few months earlier. It had all seemed so impossible at the time. And yet now it had become a reality. Britain was standing defiantly alone against the might of the Nazi war machine and the worst had come true. It was a frightening prospect.

Finding a bench facing the lake, he sat down to reflect on the current naval situation and, more immediately, the difficulties besetting his own flotilla – in particular the pressing problem of *Capitaine de Corvette* Gaston Bourdon. Certainly Vice-Admiral Warden had summed up the Navy's dilemma very aptly when he wound up the conference just before lunch:

'Under the terms of the Armistice signed on the 21st of June, Hitler has given France solemn guarantees as to the control of her fleet. Well, gentlemen, we all know what Adolf's promises are worth. The Prime Minister and the War Cabinet consider the continued existence of the French Navy as an unacceptable threat to Britain's interests. And, accordingly, the British Government delivered ultimatums to all French units giving them the choice of joining with us in the continuance of the war under the French flag, demilitarization at suitable neutral ports outside the German sphere of influence, or scuttling. The alternative to acceptance of these terms was made quite clear - destruction by the Royal Navy.

'You all know what happened. Cunningham has managed to persuade the French flag-officer at Alexandria to demilitarize his ships peacefully but, unfortunately, we were less successful in North Africa. The French admiral, Gensoul, defied us and Somerville's forces had to open fire – an action that destroyed half of the ships in Oran harbour. Some units managed to escape and return to Toulon but, militarily speaking, our attacks were a success. I will say nothing about the morals of firing upon men who had, only a few days earlier, been our allies. I will only say that, in my opinion, a day may come when we will live to regret our action. But the Royal Navy was acting in obedience to orders from the highest authority of the Government and when orders are given, no matter what we may think privately, they must be carried out.'

Like many other naval officers, Hamilton entertained mixed feelings over Churchill's ruthless decision to destroy the French fleet at Oran. And while appreciating that Britain could not allow the French Navy to pass into Hitler's control, he felt certain that a slightly less belligerent attitude might have achieved better results. Many of the French sailors killed at Mers-el-Kebir were decent, honest patriots, obeying the lawful orders of their Government. And, as Admiral Warden had pointed out, only days earlier they had been staunchly fighting side-by-side with their British comrades. But as Lord Fisher had been so fond of saying: *the essence of war is violence – moderation in war is imbecility.* And Hitler had proved the stark, unpalatable truth of the former First Sea Lord's dictum, many times over.

All of which brought Hamilton reluctantly back to his own dilemma. What the hell was going to happen about Bourdon?

Gladiateur had left for a patrol along the Norwegian coast only two days before the French surrender. And while Bourdon had no doubt heard of the British attack on Oran from the BBC's news bulletins, he had given no indication of his own reaction to it. Fortunately he was safely beyond the range of the French Navy's radio transmitters at Toulon and all his operational orders came via the Admiralty long-range wireless station at Rugby.

Yet, to Hamilton's surprise, Bourdon had apparently made no move to return to France. He had remained on station off the Norwegian coast in accordance with flotilla orders and the few brief signals he had sent back were uninformative and laconic. The skipper of *Unwieldy*, returning through *Gladiateur*'s billet a few nights ago, had reported the French submarine still in position. And, according to Hamilton's calculations, Bourdon now had insufficient fuel left to make for unoccupied France – a trip that would entail passing down the Portuguese coast and through the Straits of Gibraltar, if he was to reach Toulon.

But the question remained – what did Bourdon intend to do when he finally returned to England at the end of his patrol? Was he going to join up with the Free French forces under this new chap, de Gaulle? Or would he defy the British ultimatum like his comrades in Oran?

Hamilton sat watching the ducks circling the edge of the lake, in their eternal quest for titbits. Characteristically, he was averse to making plans. He preferred to dismiss the problem from his mind and just wait to see what happened. Flexibility seemed the only possible way to cope with the situation. And there was always a chance that the French-man had a weak spot which could be exploited when the time came.

The ducks squawked angrily as Hamilton got up from the bench without feeding them. If he played his cards right, there was one place where he might discover a clue to Bourdon's loyalties and he dug into his pocket for the small white envelope containing Antoinette's letter. He looked at the address, memorized it, and made his way out of the park into the Mall in search of a cab.

At that precise moment, unbeknown to Hamilton, Anglo-French relations seemed in equal danger of breaking down in a small office in a Soho backstreet less than a mile away.

The office belonged to Augustus Quinn, who, amongst other things, owned the Adam Club in Beak Street and who regarded the war as a heaven-sent opportunity for making money.

The Club was famous throughout London's West End for its cabaret, its girls, and its cellar. And it was a popular Mecca of relaxation for officers of all three services enjoying a brief forty-eight hour pass in the capital. In the circumstances, it was only to be expected that, having arrived in London alone and penniless, Antoinette Bourdon should put the Adam Club at the top of her list when she began searching for a job.

Augustus Quinn had been delighted. The mushroom growth of small drinking clubs created by the demands of the thousands of servicemen flocking to the capital in search of entertainment had left him short of girls. And the chance of signing-up one of the most famous cabaret stars in Europe was not to be missed – even though the salary Antoinette demanded caused him considerable misgivings. However, everything had proceeded smoothly. The contracts were signed, the dance routines approved, and rehearsals were going ahead without a hitch.

Sitting back in his chair and lighting a large cigar, Quinn viewed the future with complacent optimism. A consignment of black market whisky delivered at the back door of the Club by a Maltese gentleman driving an anonymous plain van was now nestling snugly in the cellar and, at a rough calculation, Quinn anticipated making at least ten pounds profit from every illicit bottle. And now Harry the Needle had brought round a portfolio of the new costume designs. Augustus turned the coloured drawings over one by one and nodded approvingly. They looked good and, even to his untrained eye, they seemed brief enough to keep them cheap. Quinn was very cost conscious.

Picking up the telephone, he asked for Mac's Rehearsal Rooms in Wardour Street and invited Antoinette to his office with Kevin, the show's artistic director and choreographer, to see the sketches and to try on a few of the sample costumes Harry had thoughtfully brought along with him.

Fifteen minutes later, Augustus Quinn was beginning to discover why Churchill had had so much trouble coming to an amicable agreement with his erstwhile allies across the Channel.

'I will not wear them!' Antoinette told him decisively, having glanced at the sketches and thrown them on to the floor with an imperious gesture. 'They are an insult to me!'

'Well, perhaps the material is a little on the – er – cheap side,' Quinn agreed placatingly. 'I'll tell Harry to buy some real top quality stuff.'

Antoinette wrinkled her delicately shaped nose. 'I do

not care if you make them from eighteen carat gold thread. I refuse to wear them.'

Augustus examined the sketches again. They seemed perfectly alright to him. He called Kevin over for a second opinion.

'I suppose you could say they were a little brief, dearie,' Kevin observed dispassionately. He was not really interested in girls.

'*Brief*!' exploded Antoinette. She got up from her chair angrily, seized one of the offending costumes from the top of the desk, and waved it in front of Quinn's mesmerized eyes. 'They are an insult!' she repeated.

Augustus did not like the way Antoinette was waving the costume around. He had paid Harry the Needle fifteen quid apiece for the dresses and they were not insured. He held up his hand, in an effort to stem her anger.

'Alright, darling. Relax. If they're too brief I'll get Harry to add some net or something.' He looked down at the sketches again and rubbed his chin. 'Perhaps they are just a little too revealing,' he admitted.

Antoinette did not deign to answer. Snatching the costume out of Quinn's nerveless fingers she vanished behind the changing screen by the fireplace.

Quinn shrugged and exchanged glances with Kevin. The producer made a gesture to indicate that Antoinette was apparently changing into the costume – presumably in order to have further evidence to support the torrent of abuse she was hurling at the two men from behind the screen. They waited uncomfortably for her to appear again. And both mentally girded themselves for another argument.

Her appearance, however, provoked a surprising reaction. And even Antoinette seemed momentarily disconcerted by the horrified silence that greeted her flourishing entrance. Quinn took one look, gulped unhappily, and closed his eyes with a strangled groan. Kevin's normally pallid face went two shades whiter.

It was the choreographer who recovered the powers of

speech first. 'Good God, darling! You can't go on stage like *that*!'

Antoinette looked down at her naked breasts. She was wearing only the flimsy skirt of the costume and the ornately decorated head-dress. The discarded brassière was still lying over the back of a chair behind the screen.

'Why not? This is how I appear on stage in Paris.'

Quinn could not bring himself to speak. He appeared to be fighting off an imminent attack of apoplexy. And it was Kevin who came to the rescue again.

'Because this is London, darling. Not Paris.'

'I don't see what difference that makes,' Antoinette pouted. 'I have the most beautiful figure in Paris. I want to prove I have the most beautiful figure in London as well.'

'Well, we've got someone in London called the Lord Chamberlain. And he certainly won't allow it. Augustus would lose his licence if you walked out on stage dressed like that.'

Antoinette shrugged. 'Very well, then I will go and see this Mister Chamberlain.' She paused for a moment. 'Is this the same man who was your Prime Minister?' she asked brightly.

Augustus Quinn took out his handkerchief and mopped his brow. Most of the problems in the past had involved persuading reluctant girls to appear in public wearing the flimsy costumes for which the Adam Club was justly famous. It was the first time he had encountered a girl who thought the costumes were not brief enough.

'Alright, love,' Kevin said soothingly, as he rummaged in the costume box beside the desk. He found what he was looking for and passed them across to Antoinette in the upturned palm of his hand. 'We'll forget the bra. But you'll have to wear these . . .'

Antoinette looked down at the two gold sequinned cones on his palm. She seemed to be genuinely puzzled.

'Where?' she asked innocently.

Kevin sighed. Taking a cone, he placed it carefully on one of her pert brown nipples.

'Right there,' he told her.

Antoinette looked down at the golden cup surmounting the tip of her right breast and took a deep breath. The cone immediately fell off.

'They'll be stuck on,' Kevin pointed out hurriedly.

'No they won't!' she snapped back.

The internal phone on Quinn's desk buzzed suddenly and Augustus jabbed the switch with obvious relief. The interruption might give Kevin time to persuade the silly bitch that she would have to do things the English way.

'Yes?'

'There's a Lieutenant Hamilton for Mam'selle Bourdon,' the secretary in the outer office told him primly. 'Will you be long?'

Antoinette's frown of annoyance suddenly vanished. The smile that followed was as dazzling as the afternoon sun after a shower of summer rain.

'Tell him to come in,' she instructed Quinn.

Augustus was a broken man. He complied with a meekness that would have surprised his many enemies.

'Please send him in, Miss Brown.'

Hamilton showed no sign of surprise when he saw Antoinette's costume. He had seen it all before – several times.

'Sorry to butt in, sir,' he said to Quinn. 'But I'm only in London for a few hours and I must have a word with Miss Bourdon. It's a matter of some importance.'

Quinn nodded. He was glad of a face-saving excuse to bring the argument to a close. 'Of course, Lieutenant. Perhaps you might be able to convince Miss Bourdon that, in England, there are such matters as laws to protect public decency.'

Antoinette's dark eyes blazed again. 'Nicky! Why do you let him insult me? Why don't you hit him?'

'Because I've got better things to do,' Hamilton told her

158

curtly. 'Now get some clothes on – you and I have got to have a quiet little chat somewhere.'

She flounced back to the screen, pausing dramatically before disappearing behind its privacy, and seized the opportunity of the last word.

'You Englishmen are all the same. Always it is – put your clothes on. Cover yourself up.' Her breasts wobbled as she gestured her arms at the ceiling. 'Don't any of you know what a woman is *for*?'

Quinn mopped his brow again as Antoinette went behind the screen. 'Is she always like this?' he asked the Lieutenant.

'Sometimes,' Hamilton grinned, 'she's worse.'

The restaurant in Mount Street was discreetly understanding. A young naval officer escorting a beautiful woman would obviously want a suitably shaded corner where they could not be seen or overheard and Guido guided them across the room to an appropriately secluded table. Hamilton ordered a bottle of wine and wondered whether he should charge it up to the Admiralty as official expenses. Much as he wanted to see Antoinette again, it was strictly business on this occasion. And with typical bluntness he wasted no time on polite preliminaries.

'We killed over a thousand French sailors when we attacked Oran,' he told her with brutal frankness. 'What do you think Gaston's reaction will be when he hears about it?'

'He'll probably want to kill a thousand Englishmen in return.'

'Try to be serious, Antoinette,' he said sharply.

'I do not know,' she shrugged. 'I am not interested in politics.'

'This isn't politics,' Hamilton pointed out. 'It's a matter of life and death, as far as your brother is concerned.'

'You mean the British would kill him too, if he doesn't do what you want?'

Hamilton was beginning to understand Quinn's exasperation. Antoinette could be extremely difficult when it suited her.

'Don't be silly.' The irritable rasp in his voice was impossible to hide. 'I don't mean I'm going to kill him personally. But if he refuses to accept the British proposals the Navy might be forced to open fire on his submarine. And if it does, anything might happen.'

Antoinette's sultry indolence instantly vanished as she realized that Hamilton meant the warning to be taken seriously. 'Are you telling me that your Government would have my brother killed, simply because he refused to do what they wanted?'

'Not in so many words. But there are already a thousand Frenchmen lying dead in North Africa to show that Churchill means what he says. With luck it won't come to that. Admiral Cunningham persuaded the French units at Alexandria to carry out our wishes without bloodshed. And no doubt a little more patience would have resolved the Oran affair in the same way. That's why I must know how Gaston will react. If we have some idea in advance, I might be able to do something to avoid a confrontation.'

Antoinette stared down at the wine in her glass for several minutes without speaking and Hamilton made no attempt to break into her thoughts. Leaning forward with his elbows resting on the table, he waited patiently for her reply.

'I am sure my brother will do what the French Government orders him to do. He is not a man to disobey an order,' she said very quietly.

'In that case we'll have to separate him from his boat as quickly as we can,' Hamilton told her. 'Churchill is only concerned with the ships themselves – not the crews. In fact he has offered to repatriate every single man if necessary. But isn't there just a chance he'll want to continue the fight? General de Gaulle is apparently setting up a Free French force. Gaston would still be sailing under the tricolour.'

'I have never heard of this man, de Gaulle,' Antoinette

said dismissively. 'The only legitimate Government of the Republic is at Vichy. The allegiance of every Frenchman must rest with Pétain.'

For someone who professed to know nothing about politics, Bourdon's sister seemed remarkably well-versed in the current political situation. And she had made her own loyalties abundantly clear. Hamilton decided to change tactics.

'I suppose you've got a valid point,' he agreed, with apparent sincerity. 'But surely Gaston wouldn't return to France and leave you behind in England. He took a great deal of trouble getting you here in the first place, if I remember correctly.'

'But you forget, he did not get me out of France for political reasons,' Antoinette countered. 'I am quite safe in England. So safe,' she added with a wicked smile, 'that they won't even let me show off my breasts in public. And now that Gaston knows I am not in danger, he will do his duty and return to France. After all,' she concluded with a grin, 'he knows *you* will be here to look after me.'

Hamilton flushed as he remembered the brief interlude in the Rochester hotel the night after Antoinette's arrival in England. He wondered whether Bourdon meant the burden of responsibility to be quite so intimate. Lighting a cigarette, he tried to focus his mind on the more immediate problem.

'So you think Gaston will want to return to France?'

'Undoubtedly.'

Hamilton reflected for a moment. 'Would it do any good if I took you down to Sheerness to speak to him?' he asked tentatively.

Antoinette shook her head. 'No, Nicky. I would have to tell him to obey the orders of the French Government. What else *could* I say?'

Thanks very much, Hamilton thought to himself. We provide you with a haven from the Nazis and all we get in return is a kick in the teeth. He could not help wondering what he would do in a similar situation – if the British

Government had ordered him to haul down his flag and throw in the towel. Despite his long years of discipline and obedience to orders, Hamilton felt confident about what his answer, and that of thousands of Britons like him, would be.

Pushing back the chair, he called the waiter and paid the bill. Much as he liked Antoinette, he felt he would never be able to understand the attitude of the French towards Hitler. And he was still seething with repressed anger as he called a taxi, helped her into it, and instructed the driver to take her to Beak Street.

Antoinette wound the window open as the driver put the cab into gear and banged down the flag of the meter. 'I know what you're thinking, Nicky,' she said quietly. 'But please try to forgive us. France has had enough of war. All we want is peace. And please do what you can for Gaston. Apart from you, he's all I have left. Look after him . . .'

The taxi pulled away from the kerb, wriggled out into the traffic stream, and quickly vanished into the dusk, leaving Hamilton standing on the edge of the pavement with the fragrance of her perfume still lingering in his nostrils.

He wondered if she realized that, when the crunch finally came, her precious Lieutenant Nicky Hamilton was likely to find himself cast in the role of her brother's executioner . . .

Sitting in the corner seat of an empty first-class compartment, Hamilton stared moodily out of the window lost in his private thoughts as the Chatham train rattled noisily over the last few miles of track to Sheerness. Due to an air-raid alert they were running over an hour late and he had already regretfully said goodbye to any chance of lunch.

It had, he reflected, been something of a wasted thirty-six hours. The Admiralty conference had, like all such affairs, been uninformative in content, evasive in guidance, and utterly dull in delivery. And Antoinette Bourdon had proved to be almost as irritatingly intractable as her brother. Despite Crockett-Jones's optimism, she was obviously not prepared to help. She had been in such a foul temper when she returned to her hotel after the show that she had slammed the door in his face and told him to go away.

With his lower-deck background, Hamilton was, rather naturally, not a member of a London club and, unable to obtain a room, he had tramped the blacked-out streets for several hours before finally spending the night on a hard, companionless bed at the YMCA in the Strand – a memory he was anxious to forget at the earliest opportunity. The double frustration had done little to improve his temper.

The train wheezed to a clanking halt alongside Number Two Platform and Hamilton reached for his briefcase. For some unaccountable reason he sensed an atmosphere of urgency and fear that he did not normally associate with railway stations. But putting it down to an uneasy conscience and a sleepless night he dismissed the feeling from his mind, pulled open the door catch, and jumped down on to the platform.

He could hear the dying cadences of the 'All Clear' fading away soulfully as he emerged from the station entrance and he looked anxiously for a taxi to take him to the dockyard. But the normally busy cab rank was deserted and, as he started to walk down the hill, he noticed a convoy of civilian and naval ambulances hurrying along the High Street. Glancing in the direction of the river he could see a dense column of black smoke billowing skywards. Obviously something had been hit and, on an impulse, Hamilton grabbed at a likely-looking passer-by.

'What's going on?' he demanded in his best quarter-deck manner.

The man stopped and shook his head. 'Dunno, mate. I reckon Jerry must have attacked a convoy in the estuary. I'd take cover if I was you.'

He pulled away from Hamilton's grasp and scuttled towards the public air raid shelter in the station forecourt.

Other people rushed past too quickly to stop and they, too, were obviously making for cover. Hamilton wondered why the devil everyone was running for shelter when the 'All Clear' had sounded. And as the busy street miraculously cleared of people he spotted a War Reserve policeman standing in the centre of the road holding up the traffic so that the ambulances had an unimpeded passage. In the midst of the panic he looked like an immovable rock in the middle of a raging river.

'Can I help you, sir?' He put the question in the same stolid tone he would have used to ask an old lady if she wanted to cross the road.

'Yes. What the hell's going on, Constable?'

'There's been an air raid, sir.' The policeman contrived to make it sound like a routine occurrence, of little importance. 'I don't have too many details. But some damned fool has started a rumour that an ammunition ship has been hit and everyone thinks the town's going to get blown sky-high.'

So that was why people were dashing for shelter, Hamilton thought. But if the bombers had hit a convoy out in the river – why all the ambulances?

'What's been hit?' he asked.

'I can't say for certain, sir. But I heard they shot up the aerodrome on the Isle of Grain . . .' He paused while he held up a small private car and allowed one of the ambulances into the High Street. 'An ARP warden told me they'd copped a packet at the submarine base as well.' He beckoned the driver of the car to continue with an imperious gesture. 'But I don't rightly know if that's true.'

Hamilton's heart sank. That was all he needed. And to judge by the direction of the tall column of smoke the policeman could well be right.

'I've got to get down there as quickly as possible,' he said curtly. 'Where can I get a taxi?'

'Not a chance, sir. We've only got three left, what with all this petrol rationing. And they're out at the cemetery for old Joe Higgins's funeral.' He paused to think for a moment. 'I'll tell you what, sir. You can borrow my bike, if it's any help.'

As far as Hamilton was concerned, any means of transport, no matter how humble, was better than his own two feet and he accepted the offer without hesitation. If the base *had* been hit, Crockett-Jones would need every officer he could lay his hands on. Taking hold of the handlebars of the heavy police bicycle he lifted it away from the wall, swung his leg over the saddle, and pushed his feet on to the pedals.

'I'll get one of my lads to bring it back to the station as soon as I can,' he shouted back to the policeman as he wobbled unsteadily down the High Street towards the river.

'What name is it, sir?'

'Hamilton – Lieutenant Hamilton. 24th Flotilla.'

Constable Neale watched the Lieutenant pedal furiously down the hill and, unbuttoning the top pocket of his tunic, he pulled out a small blue notebook. Licking the stub of his pencil thoughtfully he opened the book, found a fresh virgin page, and wrote in his best script:

Bicycle loaned to Lieutenant Hamilton of 24th Flotilla. He paused to look up at the Town Hall clock and added: *Time: 11.47 am.* Constable Neale had a tidy mind and not even Hitler's bombers could upset his methodical routine. And, in any event, the Station Sergeant would want chapter and verse about the missing machine when he came off duty. Perhaps, he thought regretfully, he should have obtained a receipt.

A pall of fine grey dust hung in the air like a morning mist as Hamilton pedalled through the dockyard gates and took a short cut between the store sheds. Buildings and huts were blazing furiously on all sides and the ground was strewn with debris and broken glass that crunched and crackled under the tyres. Water hoses snaked wildly across the road as the fire pickets struggled to subdue the flames and, every now and again, he had to wrench the handlebars to avoid running into a lifeless body sprawled in the contorted agony of violent death.

Reaching the quayside of the submarine basin he found Crockett-Jones directing operations. The Captain, wearing a steel helmet with his rank insignia painted on the front and stripped down to his shirtsleeves, was struggling to put out the fire in one of the flotilla's tenders with the aid of a small hand extinguisher snatched from the cab of a nearby truck. Grimed with smoke and covered from head to toe in the fine chalk dust that was still drifting down from the sky, he looked like a third-rate slapstick comedian who had just had a bag of soot and flour emptied over his head. And, if his language was any guide, he was fighting a losing battle with the flames.

At that precise moment, however, Hamilton was not interested in him or his problems. The fate of his own flotilla was his only concern. And, standing on the edge of the quay, he peered through the rolling clouds of dense black smoke, straining for a glimpse of the submarines. It was impossible to identify them individually in the murk and he could only pray that *Rapier*, at least, had survived the attack.

One of the submarines had an ambulance tender alongside and Hamilton had little doubt that the boat, whoever she was, had suffered casualties. A second was lying in the centre of the harbour basin with her bows sticking up clear of the water and its stern resting on the muddy bottom of the dock while a third, seemingly undamaged, was moving slowly out into the river beyond the narrow entrance to the basin on its motors.

'Thank God you've arrived, Hamilton,' Crockett-Jones shouted up. 'Come down and give me a hand with this damned tinder-box.' Hamilton started to descend the stone steps when the Captain changed his mind. 'No. Stay where you are. I'll come up.' He threw the extinguisher to one of the Petty Officers who had been using a battered slop bucket to scoop water from the dock to throw on the flames. 'Use this, Chief! And I hope you have better luck than me.'

Jumping over the gunwhales of the smouldering launch, Crockett-Jones hurried up the steps to join Hamilton on the quay. He stared out across the base and mentally assessed the extent of the disaster.

'Nasty business,' he observed without apparent emotion. 'The Boche really caught us with our pants down this time. There'll be hell to pay when Max[1] hears about it.' He paused as a naval ambulance accelerated past with its bell clanging.

'Is *Rapier* okay, sir?' Hamilton asked anxiously.

Crockett-Jones ignored the question. He had other and more important problems on his mind. 'Come along, Hamilton,' he said testily. 'I want to see you in my office. This damned air raid is only the least of our troubles.'

Hamilton followed him across the railway track. They detoured to avoid a blazing store hut and then plunged through a blizzard of red hot sparks as the wind whipped the flames from a burning truck into an angry fury. Crockett-Jones stopped every few yards to give instructions or to encourage the sweating men struggling to bring the fires under control but he confided nothing to his companion and Hamilton trudged along in his wake wondering what the hell was going on.

Reaching the sand-bagged entrance to the flotilla's underground command post he followed the Captain down the steps into the cool candle-lit gloom. The atmosphere of unhurried calm stood in sharp contrast to the chaos and confusion above ground and it was difficult to appreciate that only two feet of reinforced concrete separated the two different worlds above and below the surface. Telephones jangled incessantly in obscure corners as information filtered down from various parts of the dockyard and signal ratings carried messages quietly from one desk to another. Two officers were noting the casualties on a large board in the centre of the room while a Lieutenant-Commander,

[1] Admiral Max Horton, Flag Officer, Submarines.

assisted by an attractive Wren, was checking off the damage reports and passing the priority incidents to the Senior Control Officer directing the fire and rescue parties above ground by means of an emergency field telephone.

Crockett-Jones pushed open a wooden door and invited Hamilton inside. The office was barely eight feet square and its bare concrete walls were damp to the touch. The roof was made up from lengths of steel piling – originally intended to reinforce the crumbling harbour walls – and rusty droplets of water trembled precariously on the ceiling.

The Captain picked up an enamel jug of cold water, poured it into a chipped china basin, and began washing off the worst of the grime from his face and hands. Then, having dried himself with a towel, he reached for his favourite whisky bottle and poured two generous measures into the waiting tumblers.

'You haven't told me about *Rapier* yet, sir,' Hamilton reminded him as he took his glass.

'She's undamaged, as far as I know,' Crockett-Jones said wearily. 'I only wish I could say the same for the rest of your flotilla. Mind you, if your new Number One hadn't taken *Rapier* out of the basin and headed for the river when the attack started I daresay she'd be on the bottom as well by now.'

'What about the others?'

'Van Drebbell and his Executive Officer are both dead. A bloody Messerschmitt sneaked through and machine-gunned the conning-tower. Fortunately the Dutch boat has only sustained superficial damage.' In Crockett-Jones's view, men were expendable and submarines were not. '*Bielik* went down after a direct hit on the stern and I doubt if she'll be worth salvaging.'

'Is Sosnkowski alright, sir?'

The Captain sipped his whisky and grinned. 'It would take more than a German bomb to stop that damned Polish pirate. The old devil actually seemed to be enjoying it. Last I saw of him he had taken command of a Bofors battery on the seaward end of the quay and was telling the Master Gunner what to do. The only trouble was that, in the excitement, he was giving his orders in Polish. It was the biggest bloody balls up you've ever seen.'

'How about Bourdon?' Hamilton asked. 'He should be back by now, surely?'

'Not yet. We managed to get a radio signal to him when the raid started and he's stooging around in the vicinity of the Tongue lightship until we give him the all clear to proceed.' Crockett-Jones looked down at his empty glass, thoughtfully. 'So that means *you'll* have to do the dirty work, Lieutenant.'

'I don't quite follow, sir.'

The Captain stood up, stretched, and reached for his jacket. Although he was loath to admit it, he still had a nagging uncertainty in his mind about Hamilton. Admittedly, he had done some good work in the past but, equally, there was always *something* which left him open to criticism. Crockett-Jones had not forgotten the convoy which Hamilton had failed to attack in the Skagerrak – or the loss of his First Officer during the Etrincourt affair. And bearing in mind Hamilton's lower-deck beginnings and lack of family background, he could not help wondering whether the young Lieutenant had enough steel in his make-up to handle the delicate task now being thrust upon him.

'I've been called to an important meeting at Northways,[1] so you'll have to run your own show while I'm away,' he said brusquely. 'I had intended to deal with our friend Bourdon myself before I left, but this blasted air raid has completely messed up my plans. *Gladiateur* won't arrive before 5 o'clock and I'll be on my way to London by then.' Leaning over his desk the Captain pulled open the left hand drawer and took out a large buff envelope. 'Here are the Admiralty's instructions regarding Bourdon. As far as

[1] The operational headquarters of the Royal Navy's submarine service was in temporary residence at a block of flats at Swiss Cottage in the north-western suburbs of London.

I can see, they're exactly the same terms Somerville had to offer Gensoul at Oran. I only hope you have more success than he did.'

Hamilton took the envelope. He made no attempt to look at the papers inside. 'I take it you want me to deliver the terms to him, sir?'

'Yes. And do it as soon as he gets in. Don't give him time to make contact with Toulon. And make sure he can't get away. Put an armed guard on board *Gladiateur* if necessary.'

'Anything else, sir?'

'Not at the moment, Lieutenant. I should be back by breakfast tomorrow – but I will expect you to have the matter under control by then.' Crockett-Jones took his cap off the hook by the door. 'Get all the remaining boats refuelled and tell them to tie up to the mooring buoys in the river until they receive their sailing orders. I don't want a repetition of today's bloody holocaust. If there's another air raid alert all submarines are to submerge to periscope depth until the attack is over.'

'What about Bourdon's boat, sir?'

The Captain put on his gold-peaked cap and opened the door. 'If I were you, Lieutenant,' he said slowly, 'I'd paint a bloody great Red Cross on it. If our friends in the *Luftwaffe* think it's a hospital ship, they're 100% certain to make a bee-line for it. And if they'd be considerate enough to drop a couple of bombs on him, it might save *us* the trouble of sinking the bastard ourselves.'

CHAPTER NINE

2100 hours. 13th July 1940

Bourdon was sitting alone in *Gladiateur*'s wardroom, quietly reading a book, when Knievet, the submarine's Master-at-Arms, reported the approach of a small harbour launch flying the White Ensign. From the first moment of his belated arrival at Sheerness, the *Capitaine de Corvette* knew that a formal official visit was inevitable. And he had no doubts in his mind what the approaching boat portended. The fact that he had been ordered to moor to one of the quarantine buoys outside the entrance to the main basin was significant in itself. And his isolation from the other submarines in the flotilla made it clear that the British intended to keep him at a safe distance.

'You are to permit only one officer to come aboard,' he warned Knievet. 'If he has been foolish enough to bring a boarding-party with him they are to remain in their boat. You have my authority to use force if necessary.'

'Very good, sir. How is the officer to be received?'

'He is to be shown every courtesy. Have him piped over the side in the customary manner. After all,' he added with an expressive shrug, 'we do not, as yet, know the reason for his visit.'

Bourdon poured himself a cognac as the Master-at-Arms saluted and went back on deck to receive the visitor. Despite his public display of ignorance, *Gladiateur*'s skipper had few private doubts as to the reason for the visit. And although his knowledge of the events that had taken place during the past few weeks was scrappy and incomplete, he had gleaned sufficient information from the radio news bulletins to hazard an intelligent guess. He drained his glass and put it down on the table. The British were certainly wasting no time. But perhaps they were right. Perhaps it would be better to get it over with quickly.

Remarkably similar thoughts were also passing through Hamilton's mind as the harbour launch reversed engines and came neatly alongside *Gladiateur*'s port beam, abreast of the conning-tower.

The submarine, rolling gently on the flood tide, looked strangely sinister in the gathering dusk and its shaded lights glowed like ghostly phantoms at the bow and stern. The launch nudged its starboard rubbing strake against the pregnant bulge of the ballast tanks and, as Coxswain Druce shut off the engines, a silent figure on the deck above threw down a line which the bow number, Blenkinsop, caught expertly and hauled tight. A flexible ladder followed and, bracing himself for the task that lay ahead, Hamilton put his foot on the bottom rung and started climbing up to the deck of the darkened submarine.

For once in his life he felt genuinely frightened. As he neared the top of the ladder his guts tightened in a spasm of nervous anticipation. Denis Sprague, the skipper of *HMS Thames*, had been shot down in cold blood by a French sentry in identical circumstances when the Royal Navy had tried to take over the submarine-monitor *Surcouf* in Devonport dockyard, a few weeks earlier. Hamilton was beginning to regret his over-hasty decision to leave his service revolver behind.

The sudden shrill of the bosun's pipe made him jump, but, recovering his composure, he hoisted himself on to the foredeck casing and saluted the *Tricolour* trailing limply from the conning-tower jackstaff as the wail of the pipe died away. He noticed that the Officer of the Deck was not present to welcome him over the side, but *Gladiateur*'s Master-at-Arms received him with the full honours appropriate to his rank and there seemed no significance in the absence of the submarine's officers. Perhaps, he concluded charitably, they were busy.

Returning Knievet's salute, and maintaining the formal courtesies of the occasion, he asked to be taken to the

Commanding Officer. The Master-at-Arms stepped politely to one side and indicated the for'ard torpedo loading-hatch.

'*Bien, M'sieur. Suivez-moi.*'

So far, so good, Hamilton congratulated himself as he followed Knievet down the vertical steel ladder into the fore-ends torpedo storage space and through the door in the watertight bulkhead into the for'ard mess space. The off-duty *matelots* watched him with silent curiosity and Hamilton could read the undisguised hostility in their eyes. Knievet, however, seemed unconscious of the atmosphere and he made no effort to reprimand a senior rating who spat ostentatiously into a slop bucket as the British officer passed him.

He received an equally hostile reception on entering the control room and, although the submarine's officers refrained from a similar display of bad manners, they made no attempt to conceal their contempt. Even Ailette, *Gladiateur*'s Executive Officer, looked uncomfortably ill at ease and Hamilton noticed that the young Frenchman studiously avoided meeting his eyes. Returning the coldly formal salutes of the four officers, he trailed dutifully behind Knievet, ducked through the hatchway, and passed into the narrow passageway leading to the wardroom.

Bourdon was still sitting at the table. He made no effort to stand up and greet his visitor and, aside from an almost imperceptible nod of the head, scarcely even acknowledged his presence.

Hamilton chose to ignore the Frenchman's rudeness. He felt neither surprised nor annoyed by his frigid reception. Indifference – or even undisguised hate – was preferable to the bullet in the guts that had greeted the unfortunate Sprague when he boarded *Surcouf*.

'I'm glad to see you back safely, Gaston,' he said easily. Despite the gauntlet of hostility he had run in the course of his passage through the submarine, Hamilton gave the impression of being totally relaxed and self-confident. But Bourdon was not so easily deceived.

173

'Is this an official visit, Lieutenant?' he enquired coldly.

'I suppose you could call it that,' Hamilton agreed pleasantly. 'But I always prefer to keep these things informal – don't you?'

Bourdon offered no reply. The British officer's friendly approach had rather spiked his guns. He picked up another glass, poured some cognac into it, and passed it across the table. Hamilton accepted the olive branch with a smile, raised his glass in salute and savoured the smooth bouquet before taking the first sip.

'I saw Antoinette yesterday,' he said conversationally. 'She sent you her love.' The lie flowed from his tongue with deceptive sincerity. Hamilton personally doubted whether Antoinette's temper would have allowed her to love anyone last night, but it seemed a good way to break the ice. Bourdon's reserve melted a few degrees.

'How is she?'

'Fine. I've fixed her up with a cabaret spot at one of the best clubs in London.' Another lie, thought Hamilton, but what the hell. By the time Bourdon discovered the truth it would be too late. 'She's hoping you'll come up to see her in the show when you're on leave.'

Bourdon sipped his brandy. He said nothing. He had no intention of even *being* in England when his next leave fell due, but he saw no reason for acquainting Hamilton with his plans.

'I expect you've heard all about our air raid this morning?'

Bourdon shrugged. 'Not very much. As we are not allowed to enter the dockyard basin,' he added pointedly, 'it is difficult to acquire information.'

Hamilton mentally noted the fact that Bourdon apparently had no secret links with the shore. It would help to make things easier if the balloon went up.

'You're a suspicious old devil, Gaston,' he laughed. 'None of the flotilla boats are being allowed into the basin. The Captain wants all submarines to moor or anchor in at least thirty feet of water, so that they can submerge immediately the warning alert sounds. It seems a sensible idea to me – so what are you griping about?'

'What happened this morning?' Bourdon asked, his curiosity getting the better of him.

Hamilton made no attempt to conceal the seriousness of the disaster. '*Bielik* was sunk,' he said flatly, 'and *Swaardvis* damaged. Van Drebbel was killed and we suffered over a hundred casualties, all told. Now perhaps you can understand the reason for the new mooring orders.'

Bourdon shrugged. 'Perhaps. But it is convenient for your plans.' He fell silent for a few moments. 'I have looked upon you as a friend, M'sieur Hamilton,' he said finally. 'Can I trust you to tell me the truth?'

'I'll do my best.'

'*Bien*! You will understand I have only heard odd scraps of news over the radio. Is it correct that the British Navy opened fire on our ships at Oran?'

Hamilton wondered what Bourdon had heard. *Gladiateur*'s wireless could probably pick up German propaganda transmissions from Berlin just as easily as the BBC's overseas broadcasts. He might even have listened to the highly coloured and emotive newscasts from Radio Paris as well. So there was little point in evading the question or telling lies. And yet . . .

'You probably know as much about the affair as I do,' he said slowly. 'You ought to have realized by now that the British Government is not in the habit of confiding in mere Lieutenants like myself. But, speaking personally, I doubt if it was as bad as the Germans have pretended.'

The expression on Bourdon's face indicated what he thought of Hamilton's answer. 'I suppose I was optimistic to imagine you would tell me the truth. You English are all the same – murdering hypocrites who prefer to kill their friends rather than their enemies. Especially when their victims don't fight back!'

'Your facts are incorrect, Captain Bourdon,' Hamilton retorted with equal bitterness. 'Your ships *did* return fire at Oran and we suffered a number of casualties from French shell-fire.'

'A thousand dead?'

'I'm sure that figure is an exaggeration,'[1] Hamilton assured him quickly.

Bourdon drew himself upright. 'If only one single French sailor was killed by the deliberate action of the Royal Navy, *that* would be sufficient,' he said frigidly. 'I assume you have only made this visit in order to deliver your Government's despicable ultimatum to me as well. I suggest, therefore, that we observe the formalities. You have my permission to proceed.'

Bourdon's hostility had created the precise situation Hamilton had tried to avoid. The terms of the British Note were brutally frank. And he knew full well that no Frenchman conscious of his national honour could possibly find them acceptable. He had hoped to soften the severity of the ultimatum by engaging Bourdon on a friendly basis so that, instead of reading the terms, he could paraphrase them and make them sound a little more acceptable. It was clear, however, that *Gladiateur*'s Captain had other ideas.

Delving into his pocket, Hamilton brought out the envelope which Crockett-Jones had handed him earlier in the day, withdrew the typed sheet or paper inside, and unfolded it.

'*Paragraph One*,' he began to read. '*His Majesty's Government have sent me to inform you as follows:*

Two. They agreed to the French Government approaching the German Government only on condition that if an armistice were concluded, the French Fleet should be sent to British ports to prevent it falling into the hands of the enemy. The Council of Ministers delcared, on the 18th of June, that before capitulating on land, the French Fleet would join up with the British Force or sink itself.'

Bourdon shook his head fiercely. 'I dispute the correctness of your statements. The French Navy knew nothing

---

[1] In fact, Bourdon's figure was conservative. Post-war records reveal that the French suffered 1,297 killed and 351 wounded.

of such an arrangement. Do you imagine for one moment that if my Government had made such an undertaking, they would have failed to carry it out? France may have been defeated, but she has not abdicated her honour.'[1]

Hamilton made no comment. He was in no position to argue the point with the Frenchman. He was there to carry out an unpleasant task and, having embarked upon it, he intended to see it through. He continued reading:

'*Three. Whilst the present French Government may consider that the terms of their armistice with Germany and Italy are reconcilable with these undertakings, His Majesty's Government finds it impossible, from their previous experience, to believe Germany and Italy will not at any moment which suits them seize the French warships and use them against Britain and her allies. Italian armistice prescribes that French ships should return to metropolitan ports and, under the armistice, France is required to yield up units for coastal defence and minesweeping.*'

Bourdon indicated his impatience with a heavy, theatrical sigh. He was not interested in the British Government's excuses. He wanted to know what terms were being offered. Hamilton, too, found himself bewildered by the tortuous and badly constructed sentences. But, ignoring the interruption, he continued with the dreary, uninspiring recital:

'*Four. It is impossible for us, your comrades up till now, to allow your fine ships to fall into the power of the German or Italian enemy. We are determined to fight on until the end, and, if we win, as we think we shall, we shall never forget that France was our ally . . .*'

'Hypocrites!' Bourdon snapped angrily.

Hamilton felt a certain sympathy for the Frenchman. The turgid prose and high-flown sentiment of the statement had an irritating abrasiveness. But, pushing his personal feeling aside, he read on:

'*. . . that our interests are the same as yours and that our*

[1] Bourdon's protest was justified. It was established at a later date that the facts quoted in the British Note were incorrect.

common enemy is Germany. Should we conquer, we solemnly declare that we shall restore the greatness and territory of France. For this purpose, we must be sure that the best ships of the French Navy will also not be used against us by the common foe.

'Five. In these circumstances, His Majesty's Government have instructed me to demand that, as the officer commanding this boat, you shall act in accordance with one of the following alternatives:' Hamilton paused for a moment and Bourdon made an impatient gesture for him to continue.

'(a) Sail with us and continue the fight for victory against the Germans and Italians.

'(b) Remain here under British control. Your crew will be repatriated at the earliest moment.

'(c) Alternatively, if you feel bound to stipulate that your ship should not be used against the Germans or Italians, since this would break the armistice, then sail with us, with a reduced crew, to some French port in the West Indies where your submarine can be demilitarized to our satisfaction, or perhaps entrusted to the United States of America and remain safely there until the end of the war, the crew being repatriated.'

Bourdon acknowledged the terms with a curt nod. 'And what,' he asked, 'if I refuse to do any of these things?'

It was a rhetorical question. Bourdon knew quite well what the alternative was. The action at Oran had proved beyond doubt that the British Government was not bluffing. But he wanted to savour Hamilton's obvious embarrassment as he had to read out the threat. Unable to meet the Frenchman's eyes, *Rapier*'s skipper looked down at the paper clasped in his hands. He spoke quietly as he read out the final paragraph, as if the gentle tone of his voice would soften the harshness of the ultimate threat.

'I am instructed by the Admiralty to inform you that if you refuse these fair offers I must with profound regret require you to sink your ship within six hours. Finally, failing the above, I have the orders of His Majesty's Government to use whatever force may be necessary to prevent your submarine from falling into the hands of the Germans or Italians.'

'In other words, Lieutenant, you have been ordered to open fire on my boat and murder my crew – as your comrades have done already to my countrymen at Oran.'

'I am sure it will not come to that, Captain,' Hamilton said quietly. 'You have six hours in which to make your decision. And, as a friend, I urge you to think about the alternatives with the greatest care. Don't come to any hasty conclusions. And, for heaven's sake, don't allow your decision to be influenced by what happened in North Africa. I can tell you, in confidence of course, that the British Admiral did everything in his power to persuade the Government not to make him open fire upon his friends and allies. The Royal Navy was not to blame for what happened. In the final analysis, an officer must carry out the orders given to him by his superiors.'

'I am glad you have pointed that fact out, Lieutenant. I, too, must carry out orders given to me by *my* Government.' Bourdon reached down, opened the drawer of the table and pulled out a sheet of paper. 'I received the full text of the armistice agreement on the radio. With your permission, I would like to read you Article Eight – the section relevant to the French Navy.'

'Read it by all means, Captain. We might well find some small detail, some loophole, which could be used as a basis for negotiation.'

Judging by Bourdon's expression, he did not share Hamilton's optimism. He read slowly and paused every now and again as he translated the text: '*Article Eight. The French Fleet, with the exception of that part left free to the French Government for the protection of French interests in its colonial empire, is to be assembled in ports to be specified and demobilized and disarmed under German and Italian control. The choice of ports will be determined by the peacetime stations of the ships.*' Bourdon looked up. '*Gladiateur*'s peacetime station is Toulon,' he added, by way of explanation.

Hamilton nodded. He was thinking fast. There *had* to be a solution to this dangerous farce.

'As I see it, Gaston,' he said slowly, 'both the British

and German Governments want your ship demobilized and disarmed – so, on that point, at least, we have *some* common ground. It appears to be merely a question of where the demilitarization should take place and who supervises it. And, to my mind, provided *Gladiateur* is demilitarized it doesn't matter a damn where it takes place.'

'That, of course, is a matter of opinion,' Bourdon retorted sharply. 'Permit me to read you the other relevant sections of the Article. You will then see that I am under specific orders. *"The German Government solemnly declares to the French Government that it does not intend to use for its own purposes in the war the French Fleet which is in ports under German control. All war vessels which are outside French territorial waters are to be recalled, to France."* '

Hamilton nodded sympathetically. 'I appreciate your problem. But the terms of the armistice are hardly direct orders to individual ships. Such orders could only come from your own senior officers. Surely, if you follow the *spirit* of the terms, that will be sufficient. And if *Gladiateur* is demilitarized, you would seem to have complied with the main requirements of the German Government.'

'Unfortunately not, Lieutenant,' Bourdon said, shaking his head. 'You see, I *have* received a direct order from my superiors – from Admiral Darlan himself.' He felt in his pocket and produced a slip of pink paper. 'These are my instructions: *"Cease military operations. Do not obey orders from England. Make for a French port. Long live France. Darlan."* '

'Did you cease military operations?'

'We made no attacks,' Bourdon replied, evasively.

'But, if you regard the order as mandatory, why return to England at all?' Hamilton asked. 'Surely you had enough fuel to reach Cherbourg or Brest?'

'Those two harbours are now in enemy occupied territory. I take the phrase "French port" to mean a naval base in unoccupied France. And we had insufficient bunker reserves to reach such a port.'

Hamilton searched for a straw and found one. 'I don't think you should pay much heed to the signal. It was probably put out by the *Kriegsmarine*.'

'The message came from Admiral Darlan,' Bourdon insisted. 'It was signed with his name.[1]

'But can you trust Darlan?' Hamilton asked. 'I understood he was a Nazi sympathizer.'

Bourdon did not answer. His mind was too busy to worry about the loyalties of his Commander-in-Chief.

'Does Antoinette know about this?' he asked suddenly.

'I told her nothing about the British terms, if that's what you mean. But she's an intelligent girl. And she seems very knowledgeable about politics. She must have guessed this would happen as soon as you returned to England.'

Bourdon poured himself another brandy and drank it quickly. He could feel his hands trembling and he needed some Dutch courage. 'Am I permitted to phone her?' he asked.

Hamilton shook his head regretfully. 'Sorry, but my orders are quite specific. I cannot allow you to go ashore. But,' he suggested suddenly, 'there's nothing to stop me getting in touch with her. And I know her telephone number.'

'No – I must speak to her personally. Can you get her down to Sheerness and bring her out by boat?'

'I don't know about that,' Hamilton said doubtfully. 'Even if I could get permission, it would probably take more than the six hours allowed under the time limit.'

Bourdon could see the British officer weakening and he quickly exploited his advantage. 'Admiral Gensoul was given several extensions of the time limit by your Admiral Somerville. Am I to be denied my request because I am only a *Capitaine de Corvette*?'

[1] In fact, the signal which *Gladiateur* had picked up *was* false and almost certainly came from a German source. On 17th June 1940, in anticipation of such a situation, Admiral Darlan had issued instructions to all commanding officers to act only upon signals bearing the code name *Xavier 337*. Bourdon was apparently unaware of this secret instruction.

Rapier was scheduled to leave on patrol at dawn the next morning. If an extension of time was granted, Hamilton realized he would be safely at sea and out of trouble when the ultimatum expired. He had no wish to open fire on *Gladiateur* – after all, she was one of the boats in his own flotilla – and Bourdon's unexpected and rather puzzling request to see his sister could be a heaven-sent opportunity to escape the consequences of the Frenchman's intransigence and the British Government's impatience.

'I have no authority to extend the time limit,' he told Bourdon. 'But I will contact the Admiralty as soon as I get ashore. If permission is granted, I will send an official car to London to collect your sister and bring her down to speak to you.'

'And may I ask my Commander-in-Chief for instructions?'

Hamilton shrugged. 'Short of smashing your radio equipment, I can't stop you. But don't blame me if our wireless boys try to jam your signals.' He stood up and picked up his cap. 'I reckon that just about winds it up. There's nothing more I have to say.'

'I appreciate your courtesy, Lieutenant. You have done your best in a very difficult situation. Allow me to escort you to your boat.'

Hamilton paused as he reached the curtained entrance to the wardroom. 'Look, Gaston, just between ourselves – have you any idea what your ultimate decision will be?' he asked. 'I'm sure we are agreed that a repetition of the tragedy at Oran must be avoided at all costs. You know you can rely on me to do all I can to help.'

'I shall carry out my orders, Lieutenant,' Bourdon said enigmatically.

'Whatever they may be?'

'*Mais oui*, Lieutenant. Whatever they may be.'

Bourdon personally accompanied his visitor back to the picket boat and there was no repetition of the ill-mannered scenes that had greeted Hamilton on his arrival. Bourdon ruled his men with a rod of iron and they sat in impassive silence as the British officer walked through the fore-end's mess space and climbed the companionway to the for'ard deck.

The harbour launch was still alongside the submarine and as the side party came to attention Hamilton turned to salute *Gladiateur*'s captain.

'Until we meet again, Captain Bourdon.'

The Frenchman bowed slightly and returned the salute with punctilious politeness. 'And let us hope, Lieutenant,' he said softly, 'it will be in more pleasant circumstances.'

Hamilton's return to the shore, however, was delayed by the untimely arrival of two armed boarding vessels and a coastal tanker which was being brought in for examination by Contraband Control officials. It was a routine occurrence and the special anchorage set aside for the purpose was in the deep-water channel just to the north of Sheerness.

All three vessels were steaming with screened lights and the difficulties of navigating in black-out conditions were compounded by the lack of shore beacons and a thickening sea mist. Having narrowly avoided running down *Gladiateur* in the darkness, the tanker swung its bows across the entrance to the main basin, stopped engines, and let go its starboard anchor.

It took nearly an hour of argument to persuade the skipper of the tanker to shift his anchorage. The commander of the leading ABV had the advantage of a loud-hailer to make his wishes known. The French tanker skipper, however, having at first denied all knowledge of the English language, maintained a steady flow of Gallic invective from the bridge, interspersed with angry and deafening blasts from the ship's siren when he felt he was getting the worst of the argument.

Hamilton soon gave up the unequal task of making himself heard from the picket boat and he finally came alongside the first boarding-vessel to sort matters out. And by the time the tanker had been shunted into a safe berth, close to *Gladiateur*'s mooring position, he was hoarse, short-tempered, and utterly exhausted. But, with *Rapier* due to leave on the morning tide, there was little likelihood of any sleep that night and, as soon as he arrived at the flotilla office, he sent for Sosnkowski.

The Polish skipper apparently thrived without sleep and after a frantic series of telephone calls he was finally located in the wardroom bar consoling himself with a glass of Russian vodka. He entered the office like a large black bear and grinned good-humouredly as he saluted his flotilla commander.

'I'm in a spot,' Hamilton admitted, as the Pole perched himself unceremoniously on the edge of the desk. 'Your boat will be out of commission for several weeks, both the Norwegian boats are out on patrol, and *Swaardvis* has no skipper.'

'I can take out the Dutchman,' Sosnkowski volunteered.

Hamilton shook his head. 'I wish you could – but you don't speak the language and you'd never be able to run things. In any case, *Swaardvis* will have to go down to Chatham for repairs before I can send her to sea again. And that means *Rapier* will have to carry out the standing patrols on her own until the 9th Flotilla can send down a couple of relief boats.'

Sosnkowski nodded. The standing patrol to which Hamilton referred involved a continuous submerged watch on the French coast, so that Hitler's growing invasion fleet of flat-bottomed barges could be monitored and reported upon.

'I've been on the go non-stop for nearly seventy-two hours,' Hamilton continued. 'And I haven't finished yet. If I don't get some sleep soon, I'll collapse on my feet.' He looked up at the Pole. 'Will you come along as my First Officer?'

Sosnkowski beamed. 'But of course, my friend. *Rapier* is the finest boat in the flotilla. You sleep all you want. I will do the work.' He held up his hands to grasp an imaginary periscope, tracked an equally imaginary target, and fired his torpedoes with a satisfying *Bang! Bang!*

Bang! He stopped suddenly. 'But what about your new First Officer? He won't like it.'

'I don't suppose he will,' Hamilton admitted. 'But young Clive's too inexperienced to command the boat, except in an emergency. He's only had two patrols as a Number One. And it's no picnic crawling down the French coast now that the Boche has laid those new anti-submarine minefields. I need an experienced skipper to back me up.'

Sosnkowski nodded. He slid his buttocks off the desk and stood up. 'In that case, I'll get my gear together. What time do we leave?'

'Meet me at the steps at four. High tide is at four-thirty and I want plenty of water under my keel, in case we have to dive before we're out of the river.'

'I'll be there,' Sosnkowski promised. He walked to the door, put his hand on the knob, and paused. 'By the way,' he said casually. 'What's happening with the Frenchman?'

Hamilton shrugged. 'I'm trying to arrange an extension of the time limit. Bourdon wants to see his sister.'

'Having seen her photograph – don't we all?' Sosnkowski grinned. 'But if we are leaving at four-thirty, we'll miss all the fun. I was hoping to be in at the kill.'

'You're a bloodthirsty bastard, Stanislaus,' Hamilton said with a laugh. If the Polish captain were around when the Navy tried to board *Gladiateur*, bloodshed would be inevitable. Sosnkowski hated Bourdon's guts and it would be a perfect opportunity to settle old scores. 'I'm sorry to disappoint you, but I expect Bourdon will accept the British terms without putting up a fight. And I'm sure Antoinette will be able to persuade him to be sensible.'

In his heart of hearts, Hamilton feared it was a pious hope. From what he had seen of Antoinette, he felt certain she would egg her brother to defy the British ultimatum. She seemed to be one of those people who was only happy when they were quarrelling with everyone in sight.

'I think you made a mistake mooring the Frenchman outside the basin,' Sosnkowski pointed out.

'I don't see why,' Hamilton objected. 'All operational

boats are being moored in the river as a measure of protection against air attack. And the further Bourdon is from the shore, the less chance he has of causing trouble.'

'I agree, my friend. But you have no way of stopping him from escaping down river at any time he chooses. If he were inside the dock, he couldn't even start his motors without attracting attention. And the entrance is so narrow you could drop a couple of hand grenades down his conning-tower hatch as he passed through. He'd be caught like a rat in a trap.'

Sosnkowski obviously did not understand the psychological basis of Crockett-Jones's decision. Bourdon had a chip on his shoulder. By being left reasonably free, he was more likely to see reason. But to lock him up like a prisoner inside the tiny harbour would only make him more obdurate than ever. Hamilton made no attempt to explain the subtleties of the British plan. Sosnkowski, as a man of action, would not understand.

'Bourdon hasn't enough fuel to get across the Channel, let alone reach Toulon,' he said, voicing the obvious objection. 'So it would be pointless to try and escape.'

The Polish skipper shrugged. 'Let's hope you are right, my friend. But don't say I didn't warn you.'

Hamilton picked up the telephone and gave Antoinette's number to the operator. Putting his hand over the mouthpiece while he waited to be connected, he looked across at Sosnkowski.

'Alright, you old pirate. I've got the message. Now get along and leave me to get things organized. And if you've got any ideas about rowing out to *Gladiateur* with a time-bomb tucked inside your beard, forget it!'

The Polish skipper grinned, made a vulgar gesture at his flotilla commander, and closed the door.

CHAPTER TEN

0955 hours. 14th July 1940

Antoinette Bourdon was completely naked. And she was dancing on *Gladiateur*'s foredeck in the silvered beam of a shore searchlight, against a swirling background of sea mist. Hamilton looked again and realized she was not dancing but semaphoring with the aid of two large flags – a Union Jack and the French *Tricolour*. The nature of the message was not very clear and she was getting progressively bad-tempered.

It was all a trifle odd, to say the least. Especially as Augustus Quinn was sitting perched on top of the bow jackstaff waving a sequin spangled brassière at Crockett-Jones who, in turn, was deeply engrossed in a game of chess with Antoinette's brother – a task rendered infinitely more difficult by the fact that Bourdon had turned his back on the board. The pieces the Captain was moving so laboriously were warships of the French Navy.

Antoinette suddenly turned into a very large and ferocious dog which leapt at Hamilton without warning, sank its teeth into his shoulder, and began shaking him like a rat . . .

'You're wanted in the control room, sir.'

Hamilton opened his eyes to find Scully, the new wardroom steward, shaking him by the shoulder to wake him up. Still half asleep, he swung his legs over the edge of the bunk, pushed his feet into the waiting sea-boots, and reached for his sweater. The clock on the bulkhead facing the bunk indicated the time was 9.55 am and Scully put a helping arm around the skipper's waist, as his legs buckled with exhaustion.

'Steady, sir.'

Hamilton took a deep breath and straightened up. He

felt strangely weak. His legs were like rubber, every muscle in his body ached, and his head was muzzy.

'Thanks, Scully. Don't worry – I'm okay. Just rustle me up some hot black coffee. I'll be in the control room.'

Pulling the wardroom curtains aside, Hamilton stepped into the companionway and made his way to the control room, feeling like death warmed up. He had spent most of the night telephoning various Admiralty officials for authority to extend Bourdon's time limit, while simultaneously trying to locate Antoinette. Yet, despite his physical exhaustion, he had insisted on taking *Rapier* down the Thames on the first leg of her patrol and it was only when they reached the open sea in the vicinity of the Tongue lightship that he had yielded to the demands of sleep and handed over the Watch to Sosnkowski. And now, barely two hours later, he was on his feet again.

'We've received an urgent signal from Flotilla, sir,' Sosnkowski told him as he entered the control room. 'Best read it for yourself.'

Hamilton took the signal slip, rubbed the sleep from his eyes, and digested the message in silence.

SECRET

MOST IMMEDIATE

From: FO(S/M)
To: RAPIER. Repeated Admiralty, ACIC, AIG-21.[1]
Gladiateur refuelled and left moorings at approx 0530 hours.
Proceeding south-east from Tongue light destination unknown.
Find and report. TOD: 0935

'Where the hell did Bourdon get his fuel from?' Hamilton demanded. 'I left specific instructions he was not to be allowed to replenish his bunkers.' He crumpled the signal into an angry ball and threw it into a convenient slop

---

[1] AIG-21 was a code group that included, amongst others, the C-in-Cs of the Portsmouth, Plymouth and Nore Commands and the Flag Officer Dover.

bucket. 'Someone's head is going to be on the block for this.'

'Most likely yours.'

'What do you mean?' Hamilton snapped tartly at Sosnkowski.

'Well, *you* allowed that French tanker to anchor alongside Bourdon's submarine. It was asking for trouble. And don't say I didn't warn you!'

The significance of the tanker's berth had not struck Hamilton before. The unexpected arrival of the oiler had been no more than another pin-prick irritation on an already difficult night and his only concern at the time was to have it secured clear of the harbour entrance. The fact that the tanker's skipper was French had not registered in his mind and Hamilton mentally kicked himself for his stupidity. He turned to Scott, *Rapier*'s Navigation Officer.

'What's our present position, Pilot?'

Scott leaned over his chart, scribbled some figures on a scrap of paper and opened his dividers to measure the distance against the scale. He drew a small cross two miles to the south-west of the dotted outline of Thornton Ridge. Hamilton nodded.

'Stand by to surface, Number One,' he warned Sosnkowski.

'Hands to diving stations – stand by to blow. Grouper up. Full ahead both.' The Polish captain took his place at the periscope and waited.

'When you're ready, Number One.'

'Up periscope!'

Stanislaus caught the guide handles of the 'scope as the column slid upwards under the telemotor power. Circling quickly through 360°, he thumbed the lens into the sky search position.

'All clear topsides! Down periscope. Hydroplanes to rise. Start blowing!'

Sosnkowski stepped back to watch the depth-gauges. *Rapier* was holding trim nicely and he could feel the deck tilting beneath his feet as the submarine rose towards the surface.

'Fifteen feet, sir.'

'Release lower hatch!'

Harrison unclipped the bottom lid, pushed it open, and stepped away as Sosnkowski and the lookouts clambered up the vertical ladder into the gloomy cavern of the conning-tower compartment. Confident in the Polish skipper's ability to handle the submarine, Hamilton turned back to the chart to continue his conference with Scott.

'Judging by what Bourdon said last night, I'm certain he'll make for the Spanish coast and then go down through Gib and make for Toulon. I got the impression that neither Brest nor Cherbourg were suitable for his purpose. Given that he left the Medway at five-thirty, Scotty, and bearing in mind his ultimate destination, where do you reckon he is now?'

The Navigator rubbed his chin thoughtfully. Hamilton was demanding instant miracles as usual. A crystal ball would be a damned sight more accurate than a chart.

'It depends whether he's running surfaced or submerged, sir.'

Hamilton nodded his agreement. 'Okay – work it on this basis. I reckon he went down river on the surface at maximum speed. He'd want to get clear of the Thames as fast as he could and he'd probably rely on the mist to hide him. If I was in his shoes I'd dive when I came abeam of the Tongue – that way I'd have plenty of sea room, and a bigger choice of options. I think I'd run south-east until I was clear of the Straits. Then I'd surface and go like hell for the French coast.'

'Would that be wise, sir?' Scott asked dubiously. 'He'd soon get spotted by the Boche coast watchers.'

'You're forgetting that France is neutral now. If one of their warships tried to make a run for it, the Germans would do all they can to help it escape.'

Scott grunted doubtfully. He measured off various distances, worked out some intricate calculations on his note pad, and then carefully drew a circle with a pair of compasses.

'He'll be anywhere within that area, sir,' he said confidently.

Hamilton looked at the chart. 'God Almighty, Pilot! That circle covers over a thousand square miles. Why not put a ring all the way around the British Isles and have done with it. I can't possibly cover that area of water with a single submarine.' He glanced at the chart again and turned to *Rapier*'s helmsman.

'Steer 1-9-5.'

'Steering 1-9-5, sir.'

Hamilton looked across at Hall. 'I'm going up top, Number Two. Keep an eye on things down here. And transfer control to the bridge.'

'Very good, sir. And good hunting. I hope you find the bastard.'

Hamilton started up the conning-tower ladder into the fresh sea air. 'Well, *I* don't,' he said sourly.

Sosnkowski was busy scanning the horizon with his powerful binoculars as the skipper came through the upper hatch.

'What the hell do we do if we find Bourdon?' he asked.

'God knows! According to orders we only have to send a sighting report.' Hamilton raised his own glasses and swept quickly across the north-west rim of the sea. 'It's like looking for a needle in a haystack. There must be dozens of other boats and aircraft in the search by now. I suppose that, with luck, it might turn out to be someone else's problem rather than mine.'

'If I had my way,' Sosnkowski said with a bloodthirsty grin, 'I'd put a torpedo into the bastard as soon as I saw him.'

'And just suppose he has his sister on board with him,' Hamilton pointed out gently.

The Polish captain looked up sharply. 'Good God!' he said. 'I hadn't thought of that.'

Hamilton made no comment. But he felt better for

sharing his previously unspoken fear. Picking up his glasses, he scanned the French coast in silence as it fell astern and vanished into the morning mist.

'There's something funny going on,' Sosnkowski said doubtfully, as he lowered his glasses and leaned back against the periscope standard. 'We're running on the surface in full view of the Boche and no one seems to do anything about it. Why the hell don't they send some dive bombers in after us?'

Hamilton shrugged. 'I rather suspect the Boche know what Bourdon is up to. And they're hoping we'll shoot him up and create another diplomatic incident. Sinking a lone British submarine would have little propaganda value by comparison.'

'What good would that do?'

'Quite a lot, as far as Hitler is concerned. The French have never forgiven us for the attack on Oran – and other less well publicized incidents. It would need very little further provocation to persuade the Vichy Government to declare war on us and join forces with Germany. Don't forget, they've already bombed Gibraltar. And Adolf would get the French fleet without having to break his so-called solemn promise.'

'Are you serious?' Sosnkowski asked.

'I've never been *more* serious. Bourdon, whether he realizes it or not, is the bait in the trap. And our damn fool Government has fallen for it. If we attack and sink *Gladiateur*, it's my considered opinion that France will be at war with us within forty-eight hours.'

Sosnkowski made no reply. He was a simple seaman. The moves in the diplomatic chess game held no interest for him. His own country had vanished from the map of Europe – torn asunder and swallowed by the German wolf and the Russian bear. He had no future to which he could look forward. All that remained now was to fight to the bitter end. And after Poland's valiant struggle to retain her independence he felt only contempt for the French.

'Object six miles off port bow, sir! Bearing Red-zero-five!'

As his companion raised his binoculars to check the lookout's report Hamilton prayed that it would not be *Gladiateur*. He had no wish to emulate Somerville's butchery.[1] Picking up his glasses to examine the object, he twisted the knurled focusing ring of the binoculars to bring it up into sharp relief. It was a submarine. And it was heading down the Channel at maximum speed!

'It's Bourdon,' Sosnkowski snapped decisively and Hamilton felt his stomach turn over as the Pole confirmed his worst suspicions. 'I can see the *Tricoleur* flying from the conning-tower jack. I don't know why the bastard doesn't wear a swastika instead.'

Now that the million-to-one chance encounter had happened, Hamilton pushed his own personal reservations and doubts from his mind and moved swiftly to the voicepipe.

'Number Two? This is the Captain. Send report to Admiralty: Gladiateur *sighted. Bearing 2-8-0 at range six miles. Surfaced and running at maximum speed. Am moving to intercept. Please instruct.* Got that? Good! Ask the Pilot for our DR position and add it to the signal. And let me know the reply as soon as it is received.'

'Do you want it coded, sir?' Hall enquired.

'No – transmit in plain language. We've no time for messing about. And as Bourdon has a copy of our general cypher it won't make much difference any way.' He paused to check the magnetic compass. 'Steer 2-5-0 and tell Mister O'Brien I want more speed.'

Sosnkowski, hunched over the rails on the starboard side of the bridge, was still keeping watch on the French boat through his glasses. 'Have we got enough speed to cut him off?' he asked anxiously, as he overheard the skipper's orders.

'*Rapier* has a one knot advantage for what it's worth,'

[1] In a letter to his wife Admiral Somerville had described himself as 'the unskilled butcher of Oran'.

Hamilton told him. 'I'm counting on that damned Irishman to screw a few more revolutions out of the engines to increase the margin.'

'But that means we're only making up just over a mile in an hour,' Sosnkowski pointed out dubiously. 'Allowing for, say, another 25% advantage, if we can maintain our present angled approach, it will be at least four hours before we're in torpedo range. And that's always supposing Bourdon doesn't pull something out of the bag himself.'

'Well, that's the way it's going to be,' Hamilton snapped. 'You've been in the submarine game long enough to know there's no alternative. It's probably academic anyway. Now we've located the target, we're bound to get some support.'

Sosnkowski did not share the skipper's optimism. In his experience, it was always when you wanted support that you were least likely to get it. Shrugging his shoulders he focused his glasses on the quarry again. It was apparent that Bourdon had sighted his pursuer at last and *Gladiateur* was now steering to the south-west. But the Frenchman had not increased speed, despite the approaching danger, so the submarine was presumably going as fast as she could.

'Target has altered course two points to port, sir,' he reported to Hamilton. 'It looks as though he's trying to slip across our bows while he's still ahead.'

'I reckon we can head him off, provided we steer inside his turning circle and keep him to starboard,' Hamilton said with easy confidence. A shrill whistle from the voicepipe brought the discussion to an abrupt close and, leaving Sosnkowski to keep the French submarine under observation, he opened the watertight cock.

'Reply from Admiralty, sir,' Hall reported.

'Send it up with a runner – at the double!'

Hamilton snatched the paper impatiently from Widdowson's hand as he appeared through the upper hatch. The brevity of the signal underlined the brutal starkness of its message:

SECRET

MOST IMMEDIATE

From: Admiralty.
To: RAPIER. Repeated FO(S/M), ACIC, AIG-21.
Re my 0935 and your 1157. extended time limit expired 1000.
Destroy repeat destroy.

TOD: 1205

He passed the slip to Sosnkowski without comment and he saw the corners of the Polish captain's mouth curl with satisfaction.

'Well?' Sosnkowski asked as he read it.

Hamilton moved to the front of the bridge and stared at the fleeing submarine on the horizon. He could picture the tension on *Gladiateur*'s conning-tower as *Rapier* inexorably closed the range. And he could almost sense Bourdon's growing desperation. His knuckles whitened as he gripped the rail.

'I can't shoot him down like a dog,' he said finally. 'He must have intercepted that last signal, so he knows the score. I don't care what the Admiralty says – I'm going to give Bourdon one last chance to negotiate terms.'

'But you have your orders,' Sosnkowski protested. He waved the signal slip in front of Hamilton's face as a reminder. 'You must do as you are instructed.'

Hamilton allowed himself the barest vestige of a smile. 'You forget that *Rapier* is a ghost ship, Captain. And I am, officially at least, a dead man. *No* one can give me orders. And if I choose to offer Bourdon another opportunity to consider his position, the Admiralty can only blame itself for being stupid enough to tell lies about the Skagerrak incident.' He leaned forward over the bridge parapet. 'Fire a warning shot across the target's bows!' he shouted down to Morgan.

'Deck gun, aye aye, sir.'

He turned to Drury. 'Call up *Gladiateur*, Yeoman. I'll give you the message as soon as they acknowledge.'

'Aye aye, sir!'

'Load with HE! Bearing 0-3-5 Green. Elevation zero –
ten. Stand by.' Taffy Morgan stood back from the gun and
looked up at the bridge. 'Permission to fire, sir?'

'Granted, Mister Morgan.'

The deck gun recoiled smoothly and a wisp of smoke
curled from its mouth as Kells opened the breech to eject
the red-hot cartridge case. There was a brief pause and
then, with a vivid flash, a column of dirty water erupted
some fifty yards ahead of *Gladiateur*'s bows. The dull
crump of the exploding lyddite drifted back across the
empty sea a few seconds later and Sosnkowski waited
expectantly for Bourdon's reaction.

'Any reply, Yeoman?'

Hamilton knew full well that the French signallers had
not acknowledged *Rapier*'s flashing light but, as a matter
of routine, he wanted Drury's confirmation.

'You're not likely to get one, by the looks of it,'
Sosnkowski broke in. 'Bourdon's diving!'

Hamilton raised his binoculars. Tall geysers of water
shot upwards as the French submarine opened her vents
and he saw the bows dip sharply into the white, lathering
foam.

'All hands below! Stand by to dive!'

Even though *Gladiateur* was too far away to pose an
immediate threat, Hamilton knew he had been outsmarted.
Morgan's gun team on the foredeck would have to climb
back to the gun tower hatch before they could get below and the additional bodies crowding down the narrow
ladder could increase *Rapier*'s diving time by a vital thirty
seconds. By submerging, the Frenchman had put an
effective end to any further chance of negotiation. The die
was now irrevocably cast. Bourdon had left him with no
alternative.

'Gun crew below, sir. Duty Watch below. All clear for
diving.'

Hamilton pushed the diving alarm as Sosnkowski made
his report and he followed the Pole into the hatchway in

double-quick time. Finding a foothold on the steel rungs of the ladder he reached up to close the conning-tower hatch.

'Upper hatch shut and clipped!'

'Diving stations! Open main vents. Clutches out; switches on. Grouper up; half ahead both; 'planes to dive!'

Hamilton slid safely down the ladder into the control room, as *Rapier* dug her bows into the sea. He glanced at his watch. Fifty-five seconds. Slow by normal standards, but commendable in the circumstances. Standing directly behind Coxswain Blood, he watched the needle of the depth-gauge.

'Level at thirty feet, Number Two,' he told Hall. 'Take over the Watch from Number One. I'm going to need Sosnkowski with me – two heads will be better than one in the present situation.'

'Permission to shut lower hatch, sir?'

'Secure lower hatch. Close up attack team.' Hamilton picked up the telephone to the fore-ends torpedo compartment. 'Blow up one, two, three and four tubes, TGM. Stand by for launching.'

'Fore-ends, aye aye, sir.'

'Attack team ready, sir,' Hall reported, from his station behind the blowing and venting panel.

'Up periscope!'

The big search 'scope whined from the well in front of his feet. Sosnkowski walked across the control room, so that he was standing beside the skipper as Hamilton grasped the guide handles and swung the lens on to the last known bearing of the French submarine. His experienced eye quickly located the patch of disturbed white water marking *Gladiateur*'s diving position and he searched ahead for the tell-tale wisp of spray from Bourdon's questing 'scope.

'Down periscope!'

Hamilton turned to the Polish officer. 'Not a damned thing,' he said quietly. 'Bourdon's obviously going to make a dash for it. He's running deep and steering blind.'

'That's where he's got the advantage,' Sosnkowski nodded. 'He only needs to steer a compass bearing for the French coast. He couldn't possibly miss. But we've got to pin-point *him* exactly.' For once in his life, *Bielik*'s Captain was glad it was not his responsibility. Tracking another submerged submarine was probably the most difficult task any skipper could be called upon to carry out.

Hamilton, however, seemed undismayed at the prospect. He walked over to the hydrophone cabinet and pushed his head inside.

'Any HE?' he asked Baker.

'Yes, sir. Picking up high-powered electric motors. Range three miles – bearing north-east and approaching.'

'It *must* be Bourdon,' Sosnkowski whispered. 'There's nobody else in the area.'

Glover, *Rapier*'s Asdic operator, lined his equipment onto the bearing given by the hydrophones and the steady *ping* of the sonic pulse echoed around the cramped and overcrowded compartment. Hamilton watched the wave pattern on the oscilloscope screen and waited. There was nothing he could do until he had some hard facts to work on. The oscilloscope suddenly changed its monotonous single pulse pattern.

Ping-ping . . . ping-ping . . . ping-ping . . .

'Positive contact, sir,' Glover reported calmly. He watched the instruments carefully as he plotted distance and speed. Unlike the primitive mechanical ears of the hydrophones, Asdic sensors were scientific instruments based on the known speed of sound travelling in a fluid medium and the data they yielded was a hundred times more accurate. 'Range, two point eight miles, sir. Speed, eight knots.'

'He's going flat out,' Sosnkowski whistled. 'The batteries won't last more than two hours, at that speed.'

'I don't suppose he cares,' Hamilton observed quietly. 'He will have covered a distance of sixteen miles in those two hours – and that will bring him safely inside French territorial waters.' He banged a balled fist into the palm of his left hand. 'We've *got* to intercept him as he crosses our track.'

Sosnkowski could think of a thousand reasons why Hamilton could fail, as he followed him back into the control room. It was like giving a man a .303 rifle and telling him to hit a six inch target at a thousand yards. If the man could see he stood an outside chance of hitting it. But if he was blind you might just as well give him a pea-shooter. And, with Bourdon running deep, Hamilton was blind.

Walking to the chart table and picking up Scott's pencil, Hamilton drew a line bearing south-west from *Gladiateur*'s observed diving position. Then, extending the line representing *Rapier*'s track, he marked the point of interception and measured off the distance with a pair of dividers.

'If we both maintain course and speed, I estimate that Bourdon will pass three hundred yards across our bows in exactly eleven minutes.' He glanced up at the brass chronometer. 'At 12.37, to be precise.'

'Okay,' Sosnkowski agreed, 'so that narrows our chances. But he could still be running anywhere between thirty and two hundred feet. And unless you're at exactly the same depth, you'll be aiming at the empty sea.'

Hamilton nodded. 'Quite right. But at 12.35 I will arrange for Bourdon to come to the depth I require.'

'How the hell do you do that? Throw some bread crumbs on the water and see if he comes up to feed?'

'Work it out for yourself,' Hamilton told the Polish skipper. 'Remember Bourdon has the same sound location equipment that we have. *He* can detect us just as easily as *we* can detect him. And that's precisely what I'm gambling on.'

Gaston Bourdon glanced anxiously at the flickering dials as he lifted the telephone to the motor room.

'How many amp hours left, Mouton?'

'Sixty-eight minutes, if we maintain full power, sir. All ammeters are showing maximum discharge.'

'And the motors?'

'They're holding up at the moment – but the rear bearing of Starboard Two is running hot. I'd like to ease the load as soon as possible, sir. The motors haven't had a proper overhaul since we left Toulon in December.'

Bourdon made no comment. He cradled the telephone on its hook and turned to Ailette.

'Are we still picking up HE, Number One?'

'Yes, sir. De Verte reports a submerged submarine moving at high speed on an interception bearing. Probably doing around seven or eight knots.'

Bourdon nodded. 'A pity we are not equipped with Asdic apparatus – it puts us at a disadvantage.'

'But even Asdic echoes can't provide depth data,' Ailette pointed out. 'And that's the crucial thing in these circumstances.' He paused. 'Do you think we can get across *Rapier*'s track and run clear?'

'Provided the enemy is forced to rely on listening and sound ranging devices and is unable to make visual contact, I would say we have a better than even chance. And if I have judged our Mister Hamilton's character correctly, I doubt whether he will even try to attack.'

'If that's the case, sir, why refer to *Rapier* as the enemy?'

'For convenience,' Bourdon shrugged. It scarcely seemed an appropriate time for a discussion on semantics. 'We can hardly regard any British warship as friendly after what has happened in the course of the last few weeks.' He turned to Moirreau, *Gladiateur*'s helmsman. 'Steer one point to starboard. And hold her level at ninety feet,' he reminded the two coxswains at the hydroplanes.

'We're still picking up HE,' Ailette reported. 'Range decreasing. De Verte says the other boat will be directly abeam in about five minutes.'

Bourdon seemed unconcerned by the prospect. Unless *Rapier* was operating at exactly the same depth as *Gladiateur* and unless her bows were pointing directly at the French submarine's broadside, there was no chance of a successful submerged torpedo attack. And it did not require a mathematical genius to calculate the fantastic odds against such a coincidence. He walked across to his favourite chair and sat down. It was difficult not to feel pleased. The gamble had come off and in less than five minutes' time *Gladiateur* would be safe from her pursuer. Now there was nothing left to do, except maintain depth and avoid visual contact with the enemy. And by running ninety feet below the surface, the possibility of being sighted was out of the question.

The sudden thunderous rumble of the underwater explosion was sufficiently close to roll the submarine several degrees to starboard and Bourdon saw the inclinometer tilt violently as the bows were lifted by the pressure wave. A depthcharge attack! He dismissed the idea almost as quickly as it flashed into his brain. There was no evidence of surface ships in the area. He considered the alternative.

'Are there any mines in the area, Number One?'

'Not according to the charts, sir. But there could be a few drifting with the tide after that storm on Tuesday night.'

'*HE has stopped, sir!*'

'When?' Bourdon asked de Verte sharply.

'Immediately after the explosion, sir.'

'Are you quite sure our hydrophones were not damaged?'

'Yes, sir. I am still picking up normal water noises.'

Ailette checked the dials of the diving panel and then turned his attention to the warning lights glowing on the bulkhead display above his head. Everything seemed to be functioning correctly. He automatically glanced up at the clock. It was 12.34.

'What the hell's happened?' he asked Bourdon. 'Do you think *Rapier* has struck a mine?'

Bourdon did not reply. A vivid memory of the Englishman diving into the cold black sea off Nieuport suddenly came into his mind as he recalled Hamilton's efforts to rescue Antoinette from the burning motor boat. And he shivered as he pictured the hideous end of the sinking submarine – the nightmare terror of escaping from the rat-trap of torn and mangled steel. The dazed bewilderment of the half-conscious men struggling in the water. It was a fate he had always feared and dreaded. Perhaps at this very moment, blinded by clogging oil sludge and choking for breath as the diesel fumes clawed his throat, Hamilton was amongst the survivors fighting for their lives on the surface.

'Take her up to thirty feet, Number One!'

'Up-helm 'planes. Half ahead both. Blow Six . . . blow Eight . . . blow Four and Two. Level at thirty feet, Cox'n.'

Bourdon moved to the periscope and waited. *Gladiateur* rose slowly up through the water. Exactly one minute of time had passed since Ailette's question had triggered his doubts. It was 12.35.

'Thirty feet, sir!'

'Stop blowing! Fore and aft 'planes amidships! Trim level.'

'Up periscope!'

Bourdon clicked his fingers impatiently as the heavy column hissed upwards and, bending his knees slightly, he caught the guide handles and pressed his face to the rubber eye-cap. On the bulkhead directly behind his back, the minute hand of the brass chronometer jerked forward to 12.36.

Gladiateur's Captain peered through the prisms. The horizon was clear and the sea seemed disappointingly empty. There were no bobbing heads of survivors on the surface and no oil-slick to mark the grave of the sunken submarine. He wiped the eye-pieces with a silk cloth and looked through the 'scope again.

This time his vigilance was rewarded. Barely eight hundred yards away, and directly on *Gladiateur*'s beam, a thin black stick jutted from the shimmering sun-dappled waves. *It was Rapier's periscope!*

Bourdon stared through the eye-piece in shocked disbelief, like a man caught looking through a bedroom key-hole by the eye of a stranger on the other side.

'Torpedo noises, sir!' de Verde reported from the hydrophones.

The Frenchman tilted the upper lens of the periscope just in time to see the bubbling tracks of the approaching torpedoes racing towards the helpless submarine at forty knots. On the bulkhead behind his back, the minute hand of the clock jerked forward into the next segment of the dial and then shattered into a thousand pieces as the two RNTF Mk IX torpedoes slammed into *Gladiateur*'s hull and exploded.

The time was 12.37. And for *Capitaine de Corvette* Gaston Bourdon it marked the beginning of eternity.

Captain Crockett-Jones looked understandably pleased as Hamilton concluded his de-briefing report. The War Cabinet had screamed blue murder when news of the French submarine's escape reached Whitehall and the PM's terse message to 'annihilate the Vichy traitor' had a typically Churchillian ring to it. To avoid the possibility of signal errors, Crockett-Jones had simplified the instruction to 'destroy' and he was already basking in the reflected glory of Hamilton's achievement.

'A nasty little job,' he told the Lieutenant, with transparent insincerity. 'But these things have to be done in wartime.' He paused to light his pipe. 'I thought I knew all the tricks, Hamilton,' he observed between puffs, 'but tell me – how the devil did you bluff Bourdon up to periscope depth?'

Hamilton felt no pride in his success. In fact all he wanted to do now was to wipe the entire episode from his memory. Unlike the Captain, or the PM for that matter, he found no pleasure or satisfaction in killing a former ally and flotilla mate.

'Well, sir,' he said slowly. 'I knew the only way I could hit *Gladiateur* with a torpedo was to be in visual contact with her and at the same depth. So I tried the same trick I used on the Germans in the Skagerrak. I pretended to be dead.'

Crockett-Jones nodded. Perhaps this man Hamilton *did* have something, despite his lack of family background and lower-deck beginnings. He certainly seemed blessed with an abundance of low cunning in an emergency.

'The coastguards reported an underwater explosion about three minutes before you torpedoed Bourdon's boat,' he said. 'What happened?'

'I worked it out with my TGM, sir. We removed the pistol from the torpedo in Number Six tube and inserted a couple of nine-ounce discs of guncotton up against the detonator charge. Then Newton rigged up a simple electrical detonator, working off torch batteries, and sealed off the aperture with a soluble plug – a piece of soap, as it happens. All we had to do then was re-set the controlling gear so that the torpedo dived to the bottom on firing. Of course, it was a gamble whether the plug would dissolve in time, but we were lucky. As soon as it exploded, I stopped engines and went into silent routine. After that I had to rely on Bourdon's loyalty.'

Crockett-Jones frowned. 'Loyalty?' he asked raising his eyebrows. 'What the deuce to you mean, Lieutenant?'

'Well, sir, I knew that, on a personal level, Bourdon regarded me as a friend. I calculated that the sudden disappearance of engine noises immediately after the explosion would make him think *Rapier* had struck a mine. And if he thought *Rapier* had been sunk, I knew he would surface to look for survivors. I just sat and waited at periscope depth and I fired two tubes as soon as I saw him.'

The Captain sucked at his cold pipe. Despite the overpowering heat in the tiny airless office, he suddenly shivered. He could not help feeling glad that Hamilton was fighting on the same side that he was.

'May I ask a question, sir?'

Crockett-Jones nodded.

'Was Bourdon's sister on board the submarine?'

The Captain paused. He had come to the conclusion that he did not really like Lieutenant Nicholas Hamilton DSO. Searching for a match, he lit his pipe again with slow deliberation, while he savoured Hamilton's anxiety.

'You mean Antoinette – the girl who dances around naked in some scruffy little club in London.'

Hamilton kept his patience with difficulty. 'Yes, sir. Bourdon wanted to see her – that's why he was granted the extended time limit.'

'You needn't worry, Lieutenant. She wasn't aboard *Gladiateur*. In fact, if we'd got her down to Sheerness earlier, we could have saved ourselves a good deal of trouble.'

'How was that, sir?'

'Bit of a mystery, that girl,' Crockett-Jones grumbled. 'Seems to know a damn sight more than she ought. She recognized that blasted tanker as soon as she saw it. Said it was a French naval auxilliary. But of course, by that time, Bourdon had replenished his bunkers and gone.' The Captain paused and stared up at the ceiling. 'I wonder how she came to know a thing like that?' he asked reflectively.

Hamilton said nothing. He had brushed up against British Intelligence in the past,[1] and very little surprised him. Perhaps Bourdon had not been told the truth about his sister's reason for wanting to leave France so hurriedly. A girl like that could be very useful. His thoughts were interrupted as Crockett-Jones pushed a file across the desk.

'You'll see that we've already received an official complaint from the Vichy Government. Perhaps you'd like to read the Foreign Office's reply.'

Hamilton picked up the sheet of paper on top of the file and looked down at the carbon copy:

HM Government regrets the loss of the submarine Gladiateur but wishes to make clear to the French Government that no ship currently borne in the Navy List was involved in the incident. HM Government also desires to confirm that no serving officer of the Royal Navy was responsible for the attack. It is suggested, with respect, that a German U-boat may have mistaken the identity of the submarine.

'I thought we had a reputation for integrity and honesty,

[1] See 'Fighting Submarine'.

sir,' Hamilton commented drily, as he handed the file back to the Captain.

Crockett-Jones leaned back in his chair. 'So we have, Lieutenant, so we have. You seem to forget that *Rapier* was sunk in the Skagerrak two months ago. She has therefore been deleted from the Navy List. Similarly, you're dead, so you cannot be a serving officer of His Majesty's Navy. We haven't got around to commissioning corpses yet, although, looking around the Admiralty, I sometimes wonder. So, you see, our reply to Vichy was truthful and accurate in every detail.'

Hamilton said nothing. It was, perhaps, reassuring to know that he was not the only two-timing bastard fighting Hitler. And it was presumably this kind of thing that ultimately won wars. It was a pity that it never got recorded in the history books. Crockett-Jones watched him silently for a few moments. Then he stood up.

'I am to inform you that the Admiralty considers the report of your death to be a little premature, Lieutenant. As from 0900 hours tomorrow, you will be reinstated and *Rapier* will be recommissioned.' He paused, raised his bushy eyebrows, and looked Hamilton straight in the eye. 'So if you wish to disobey any further orders, Lieutenant, I suggest you do so between now and 9 o'clock tomorrow morning. Because after that you're not even going to be able to wipe your nose without my permission!'

APPENDIX

HMS RAPIER

(Improved 'S' Class)

Builders:	Fairchild & Chandler Ltd, Clydebank.
Launched:	15th October 1938.
Cost:	£243,750. (Emergency War Programme.)
Displacement:	765 tons – full load. (Surface)
	935 tons. (Submerged)
Dimensions:	187 (pp) 202½ (oa) × 24 × 10½ feet.
Machinery:	Two shaft 8-cylinder Admiralty diesel engines.
	Electric motors 1550 BHP/1300 SHP.
Speed:	13.75 knots (Surface) 10 knots (Submerged)
Bunkers etc:	45 tons oil fuel. 3,690 miles @ 10 knots.
Complement:	4 officers. 32 ratings.
Armament:	One 4-in quick-firer, one .303 Vickers machine-gun.
	Six 21-inch torpedo tubes. (All bows) 12 torpedoes.
Diving limit:	300 feet.
Equipment:	Type 129A Asdic.
	Type 109 hydrophone receiver.
	Type 46 wireless-telegraphy apparatus.
Motto:	*Invisibilis Quaero*. (Unseen I seek.)